JAMIE JACKSON loves fiction, poetry, house music, a juicy porterhouse steak, and pens all his stuff in a mansion filled with the skulls of his ancestors xxx.

His novels *Adventures in LovE* and *Lifetimes of FamE* are being published 2025 and 2026 respectively by Northodox Press.

Follow Jamie on X/Twitter @JamieJackson___

Substack: jamiejackson.substack.com

CW01551300

Adventures in LovE

Jamie Jackson

NORTHODOX PRESS

Northodox Press Ltd
Maiden Greve, Malton,
North Yorkshire, YO17 7BE

This edition 2025

1
First published in Great Britain by
Northodox Press Ltd 2025

ISBN: 978-1-917005-45-6

This book is set in Caslon Pro Std

Printed and bound by CPI Group (UK) Ltd,
Croydon, CR0 4YY

For my 3 angels, Gaynor, Martha and Sonny – always XXX

what they felt – this:
they would always be young
would always be kids in their hearts
the girls and boys of the Blackburn warehouse parties

Part One

1,000 Es

1,000 Kisses

Sunday, 22nd July, 1990

The lights going off over Gildersome; the scene lit fantastical.

A star-spangled sky of violets and crimsons and oranges and dream hues.

An explosion through us. Through warm air and sweet summer fragrance; through the never-ending sound of night. The sound of the young and the beat going on.

And the vocal: 'Alright, alright, alright.' The drive from Lancaster to Shadsworth Road, Blackburn. Dancing in Sett End until lights at 1am.

Remembering this now; remembering this as history in twenty, thirty, fifty years. Forever. Ephemeral, shimmering sense of what is occurring. The experience of it all.

Leaving Sett End and hitting a thousand-motor convoy and the time of our lives. In the convoy and driving over the moors for Gildersome and arriving and jumping out and entering the warehouse. Diggers and dumper trucks and speakers and the DJ and the first tune and starting to dance and hoping this will go on forever.

At the warehouse party in Nelson, near Blackburn, 10,000 revellers got inside. 10,000 lives sparked. You danced and wondered at life rushing at you. Then Nelson was raided; at 7am the police stormed the warehouse in riot gear. They packed batons and yapping dogs and fear. The kids were scared and the police were scared - of what we were, what they were not.

That was Nelson, Blackburn. This is Gildersome, Leeds. They cannot stop us. We will not be denied. Except: the police did it again, pulled the same stunt. Raided the party, closed the fun down and tried to close us down too. Arrested everyone inside the warehouse.

Everyone.

They lined up cameras on tripods and filmed all the kids as they filed out.

As they walked into the dawn; walked dreamy-eyed into-WOW.

Endless police officers and cars and vans. The police lined the kids up. Lined them all up and put them in cars and vans and drove them to stations across West Yorkshire.

Processed them; locked all the kids up in cells.

But.

Can't escape the image; the strobe lights.

Warm Yorkshire air; the music still playing in the head, down the years, into old age, into personal history. The music: everything starts with the music and ends with the music. Tunes and tunes to move you. Make you recall these days. Relive these times.

Those times.

Nancy and Joey stood hand-in-hand on a hill overlooking the warehouse and watched the last police van take away the last kid - reveller No 836. The 836 kids arrested at Gildersome by West Yorkshire Police on the morning after the night before of Saturday, 21st July. The biggest mass arrest in British history.

836 kids.

It should have been 838.

But Nancy and Joey escaped; they escaped the police and escaped with £20K-plus in hot cash.

Except, it wasn't over yet; they still hadn't made it. They packed their passports and romance and had to make it from Gildersome to Manchester Airport and flee on escape-to-adventure airways before they were caught.

Caught by those Nancy and Joey ripped off.

Smile-a-minute, meanman Romany - Gerard 'Frenchy' Toces.

And, the man. Mr Numero Uno who wholesaled Gerard T the 1,000 Es they stole from the Romany.

Have to make it.

They have to.

That sound–

Going around our heads.

Those words.

Always.

For us – Nancy and Joey.

ALWAYS.

'Just as long as we've got the other – we've got enough.'

Chapter One

Nancy

A few days before

Nancy Kools in the Merchants public house waiting for the writer. Listening to one of her DJ mixes on a Sony Walkman - bright yellow, 1988 issue, sponge-covered headphones clamped to ears. She wore dungarees decorated with daisies, a white Chipie grandad shirt, sandals by Kickers. Hair black and pigtailed, face freckled.

She sipped a pint of Red Stripe and listened to the mix; listened and dreamed of spinning piano tunes on Saturday at the warehouse party.

She was booked to DJ so got told where it was - Gildersome. On an 'industrial estate' the organisers said. 'Keep it to yourself. After Nelson, the police raid, how they got us all - we have to be careful. Everyone has to be.' Nancy was au fait with that. She was from well-to-do Haverbreaks, Lancaster affluent-central; she was seventeen and recently left Lancaster Girls Grammar School and didn't take E or speed or smoke dope or do anything. She DJed the local circuit. Harvey's Nightclub, Crystal T's, The Carleton, Brooks International, Gems, The Grange, Sugarhouse. Lancaster and Morecambe's nighttime palaces. She played the dancing dens of Blackburn and Burnley: Sett End, Monroes, Manhattan Heights, Angels, et al.

Nancy with an Italian dad, a Lancaster-born mum; she showed her dad's dark looks and packed her mum's mind. She's seventeen and mixes house music like a dream, rivalling DJ Ducky as the best around.

Nancy pressed fast-forward on the Walkman and heard a soaring sound. Like everyone danced on the skies. She'd spin tunes to move them at the warehouse on Saturday: ones that gave the rush of release. She could name them all. It's Magic, Let Me Love You For The Night, Pacific State, Airport '89, 2 Hype, Hardcore Uproar, Hold Me Back, Dream 17-

Dream 17. End the set with this; watch the lights flash across the heads of partiers as they dance in their groups making one big group, a throng that gets inside themselves like the music gets inside them.

But: the Margaret Thatcher Government engineered moral panic. Newspapers were fed scare stories, alarmist bull. They wanted to be fed. Headlines screamed. Tabloids made serious hay.

The Sun - SPACED OUT! And: SHOOT THESE EVIL ACID BARONS.

Maggie T created the mood; it's populist, a vote winner. Classic divide and rule shtick. The youth didn't care; the kids were kids partying until the break of yawn. And yawn never broke.

Nancy fast-forwarded to Dream 17 by Annette and hit play. Bum-bum-bum, bum-bum: the bassline a strut, swagger. Tickle-tickle-tick: the snare a brag and promise. 'Can you feel my love/can you feel it, hold on to me boy/stay close to me boy': the vocal haunting.

The sound of Blackburn. The sound of the night.

Nancy pondered again the records that kept coming out of nowhere; where were they made/who made them? House Music a rush of youth that kept rushing. Like the past two years - the drive to Blackburn to Shadsworth Road and partying at Sett End before the convoy to the party.

The warehouse.

A thousand cars on the hills of Blackburn.

Lights as far as you could see.

Then, eerie, poetic vision - the warehouse building looming and the kids arriving and parking up and rushing to be inside and hear the first song. Orchestral, glorious, uplifting, fun-fun-fun.

Everyone young.

Never being so young again.

This summer - never coming around again.

Chapter Two

Harry

Williamson Park

Harry Blue watched the vista where Morecambe Bay went past Lancaster to the Lake District to the mountains. He sat in his cream-coloured Bentley '87 and dialled the volume up - to Mozart, a requiem of his. Harry was a writer; he did hackwork for the Lancaster Guardian, was a stringer for the local rag. He wrote slimmed down memoirs of small-town figures and disc-jockeyed a late-night radio show on Primrose FM, the local station. He was Mr Local who nipped Johnnie Walker Red and nurtured an ever-growing frustration. He began recently to compute, clarify what stymied, upset him.

Something like this: boredom and how to escape boredom. He worked on it. He was Lancaster University educated, an approaching-brilliant student who got a 1st in Russian Studies, who pushed thirty-five, had a wife, a little girl, a nice place on South Road. And a ball-busting urge to escape boredom; to live a life. Whatever this was.

He kept on gazing at the vista, past the castle and across the water; the view of the mountains where the Lake District lay spectacular. In winter, the peaks were snow-covered - went alpine; in summer they were purple-brown and shimmered sun haze. He eyed the Bentley temperature dial - it read twenty-four degrees. There was a bona fide, buttock-drenching heatwave incoming - the radio blared incessant about it; early next month mercury would hit mid-thirties and beyond, August 1990 was going to be a roaster. July was already warm and getting warmer.

Harry B swigged Johnnie Red and thought about the girl and what an easy sell it was. Nancy Kools, the name had to be made up - no-one got called that, did they? He looked into her - yes, the electoral roll showed her family name as Altobelli, Italian, her dad owned the eatery of the same name in town - Altobelli's.

When they met, Harry told Nancy: 'I'm writing a book on the Second Summer of Love.' He blushed and said, 'Guess what it's called? Yes, that's right - Second Summer of Love. It's about the Blackburn warehouse parties and the kids drawn to it. The social fabric, how youth coalesces around a cultural once-in-a-generation happening.'

He was elevating his language, hoping to hint sophistication.

Nancy Kools, demure and impressed. Like his wife never was; Amber had his number. Harry Blue was an ideas-machine and nothing else. He was thwarted and nothing else. But not this time. What he cooked up this time would show Amber. The book plus the clandestine act that became more and more comfortable. This was showing Amber, this showed him - what he was truly capable of.

The Mozart went epic - Wolfgang M was born and died that way. Harry had ideas but not the talent, that's what Amber kept telling him. 'Be happy,' she repeated. 'You've got a niche. You're established - in Lancaster and Morecambe. Stop having pretensions.'

The choir on Mozart took the vista places; the Johnnie Red jolted. Harold Blue flew over mountain-tops and saw himself fizzing and pulsing and alive.

He had to laugh - at himself. He laughed at this, too: the same play about the book that snared Nancy worked on the lad as well. He lapped up Harry's Second Summer of Love routine.

The lad - Joey Miller, who was nicknamed 'Two-brain' because his reputation said he was clever, too clever. 'Preternaturally', apparently - the word Joey used to explain his smartness. Two-brain eyed Harry like he didn't expect Harry to understand. Harry told him, 'Give me an example of this 'beyond normal' brain of yours.' And Joey laughed and said, 'I've got two, remember, and be patient, you'll see.'

It sealed the deal; Joey Miller was in the book, would fill the 'acid house raver role' in Second Summer of Love, compliment Nancy's DJ act. Harry switched from Mozart to Haydn, read 'Symphony No 45' on the CD player, the Bentley tricked out in ivory-leather seats, maple-wood trim.

Harry 'got the car off his folks'. That's what he told Amber, how he sold driving up to the house one day in the brand-new motor. It was a slick cover story. Truth as lie. He got the move from the Russians he studied, those Kremlin operators knew how to dissemble, masquerade. His folks were rich, remained filthily so. They owned acres of Bentham farmland. In fights with Amber, Harry claimed she married him solely for the family money. It was untrue - Harry knew it; knew he sounded pathetic as always when they argued.

The one other Bentley Turbo around town had been the velvet-red number driven by the Romany who lived on the Lancaster/Morecambe border: Gerard 'Frenchy' Toces. Then Gerard got rid of the Bentley for a white-coloured Sierra Cosworth that had fins on the back because it was far less showy. Apparently.

Harold Blue knew all about Gerard, but the Romany didn't know all about Harold Blue.

He dialled up Hadyn, a sombre note hit the '87 Turbo; like the whole world was sorry for itself. He liked the line, wrote it down in his pad - and added a note: 'Maybe weave this into the intro of Second Summer of Love - why Acid House is needed for the youth - because "the whole world is sorry for itself."'

He fired the ignition and pointed the Bentley down Quernmore Road towards town, the Merchants pub. Yes, Two-brain Joey Miller was the acid house raver, and Nancy

Kools the DJ who would give him chapter-and-verse about the warehouse from the inside.

The party was happening on Saturday night, at Gildersome, was top-secret because of what happened at Nelson - the warehouse raided a few months ago. Nancy told Harry all about it; the party on an industrial estate near Leeds where the ravers from Blackburn would drive in convoy across the Pennines and converge.

With what Harry cooked up; it was ideal. All was nice and ideal.

Chapter Three

He parked the Bentley by the castle and had a good taste of Johnnie R and walked down the hill to the juicer.

The Merchants packed out. Town faces, students, workers, older folks downed lunchtime pints. Harry clocked her in an instant; Nancy K hanging over the jukebox by the end of the bar, drinking at a bottle of Red Stripe. The Merchants an exposed stonework joint; three tunnels for seating plus steps to a first floor and another bar.

Nancy turned and saw him and pointed outside; the track she selected on the jukebox started, flooded the sound system. He bought a pint of Red Stripe and joined her.

Nancy smiled. 'Not offering me a drink?'

Harry indicated her bottle and smiled. 'When you finish.'

They sat at a table and watched traffic chug along Meeting House Lane. Lancaster where everyone knew everyone or knew someone who did. Harry eyed her flower-power/dungarees get-up and felt squaresville in his suit. It was expensive, off-the-peg, from Joseph's in town, and he still vibed total stiff.

Nancy indicated the music coming from speakers mounted above the door. 'You know this one?'

Harry shrugged and tuned to the lyrics. 'I've got the power?'

'Power by Snap.' Nancy tossed her dark hair and grinned. 'Come on, Mr Writer, this book is going nowhere if you are not authentic.'

Harry got a wooze from the lager mixed with Johnnie Red. 'That's where you come in - you're the DJ, the acid house expert.'

'I prefer house.'

'Why?'

She shrugged. 'Because that's where acid house comes from, Harry - house music - and that comes from Chicago, Detroit, New York.'

Harry did a faux-snort. 'You want to play this game, you could go prototype house, disco, blues, African. These antecedents.'

Nancy laughed. 'Impressive. You have done some research.'

Harry nodded. 'And for the purposes of the Second Summer of Love, it will be acid house.'

Nancy nodded, drained her Red Stripe. 'Come on, Mr Meany - a drink. The least you can do.'

Harry felt a surge of well-being as he made the bar. She was smart and near half his age and made him feel great. He got a look of himself in the bar mirror: straight-haired, this side of ugly; how he'd describe himself as a character in the novel he'd never write. This side of ugly.

He ordered a pint of Red Stripe for himself and a bottle for Nancy and went back outside, walking into glinting sunshine and Nancy's dark eyes.

Heard what Amber implored: 'Be happy.'

Try, at least.

He sat down and slid Nancy's beer to her. 'About Saturday - my plan is, as I told you, get to the place early, for colour, atmosphere. Make sure I don't miss anything.'

She nodded.

'It's on the Treefield Estate, right?'

Nancy smiled. 'That's what I've been told. Harold - are you really going to be able to write a whole book about Saturday night? Come on, Nancy K needs to know.'

He shrugged and eyed her. Clever, cool Nancy Kools. 'This weekend - more or less, sure. That's the skill of the writer.' Harry threw his best smile and she met his eyes and he looked away. 'Sure. Plus, you and other contributors telling me stuff - about the warehouse parties before this one, the thrill and excitement of them. What Nelson was like, too. I was there as an observer. I wasn't there like you were. In it all when the police raided, Strawberry Fields by Candyflip playing as they rushed in at 7am with dogs, riot gear, batons, scaring you all. That's prime colour, novel-like material. I can do a chapter or more, too, about the first summer of love - the sixties, all that stuff. Backstory to enable the front-story.'

Nancy nodded - he told her before, the last time they met. 'You ready to say who the other people you're speaking to are yet? There's three of us in total, right? Three main people in the book?'

He was prepared for the question. 'I can tell you one of them. A lad called Joey Miller - lives in Scotforth, was at Nelson, has been at many other warehouse parties, he tells me. He's going to Gildersome. Do you know him? Everyone calls him-'

'Two-brain.'

'You know him.'

Nancy got a look. 'I know who he is.'

'Okay.'

'His reputation.'

'Which is?' Harry knowing what Nancy was going to say; wanting to hear it from her.

She shrugged. 'A bit full of himself. Vain. Forget two-brain, he's too-vain - what I like to call him.' Nancy giggled and gave Harry the same look. Like she understood the world on her terms despite being seventeen. 'But sure, he is smart –'The look became a smile. 'So, now, come on.'

'What?'

'Who else is in the book? You said three main people, there's me, Joey. And? Come on, shoot, who's the third?'

Harry grinned, enjoying this. 'Can't tell you - or they'll kill me.'

'Haha.'

It was true. Gerard Toces agreed to talk, be in the book on an anonymous basis only. He and cousin, Temmy, would be selling Es at Gildersome the same way they sold pills at previous warehouses, and the same way they dished them out around Lancaster and Morecambe. Via their No 1 foot-soldier. Joey Miller. The lad worked for them since ecstasy hit the area circa six months before and Gerard procured a large slice of the local market. Doing so in his quiet way. The Romany only two-years-older than Nancy and Joey - nineteen, yet was deferred to by Temmy, the rest of his Traveller circle and the coterie of street dealers who grafted for him.

So: if Harry revealed who Gerard or Temmy were - gave any clue to their identity, then Gerard would be out of the book, and he and Temmy would be sure to come and see Harry, and Gerard 'Frenchy' Toces would have his cousin administer a lesson in why it was prescient to keep your mouth shut when told to do so by Frenchy.

Harry heard all about what happened to Joey's predecessor as Gerard's prime pill seller and-

He closed off the thought, killed his drink, watched Nancy do the same and remembered why he came here to see her.

'The reason for this meeting is for you to give me a sense of how you're feeling a few days out from the warehouse party. You know, I can build a nice chapter out of this - your hopes, fears, how you-'

'Come on, Harry, you can do better.' Nancy laughed, '"Hopes and fears"? You sound corny, I hope your writing is better than this kind of chat.'

Nancy laughed more; Harry felt his blood prick. 'Actually, how people speak is never an indicator of how they will wri-' He laughed, caught himself. 'I do sound pompous.'

Nancy, toning surprise: 'I was only joking. Or maybe… half-joking, half-teasing.'

'My wife and daughter say the same. I bang on about ideas for books and they tease me and I rise to it, and Lottie, my little girl, says, "Daddy, calm down, we're only joking."'

Nancy's eyes lit. 'How old is she?'

'Five.'

'Bright, by the sound of it - like my sister. Here.' She brought a photograph from her dungarees pocket. 'There's Esmerelda.'

Harry looked at a picture of a mini-Nancy, dark hair, dark-eyed, maybe five or six. 'She looks the same age as Lottie.'

'Six. You have a photo I can see?'

'Of?'

'Lottie - your daughter.'

'Oh. No.'

'You should - it's a nice thing to have with you all the time.'

Harry nodded.

'Esmerelda's standard line at the moment to me is, 'Nancy, can we play that song again?''

Harry pulled his notepad, pen. 'This is the kind of stuff I mean. Your sister - Esmerelda - wants you to play acid house music - which song?'

'Call it a record or tune, and it's not acid house - I told you, it's house. And no it's not house either. It's, I am the Resurrection.'

Harry blanked; Nancy read him instant. 'The Stone Roses - indie, baggy, not house or acid house or rave.' She laughed, Harry still blanked. 'Jesus,' said Nancy. 'You're writing a book and you've got the Second Summer of Love title right and that's about it.'

More laughs, Harry joined in now - had to. 'The Stone Roses. I've heard of them, don't worry about that.'

'But you don't know the song?'

He shook his head.

'A classic, believe me.'

'I do.'

'Spike Island?'

'Eh?'

She smiled. 'Never mind. Here.' She palmed him the Walkman, placed the headphones to his ears. Hit play and Harry heard a bang-bang of drums, a bassline that crept in and kept creeping, now taking over, taking control of the way Harry began to feel.

The sound went on, Nancy kept smiling. And now at the end of the song: another part, as if the first song was followed by this, an outro. The first song was supposed to stop. It did, dead, but then came back to life. The lyrics and bass and drums a warm-up for this; which was an assault on sensation. Guitars, a crashing beat becoming noise and melody and a strange tenderness, like everything - this hot July, his book, the kids partying, the sunshine burnishing Lancaster got raised up and he felt a fleeting sense of the town glistening, golden, and Blackburn and Nelson and Gildersome never so beautiful as when hearing what he heard. Epic, sweeping, like Mozart, Beethoven, Haydn, Brahms, the best of all of them.

Nancy watched him. 'You get it don't you, Harold? Feel it.'

'Not my usual thing. But certainly, yes.'

The song tapered off, finally ended.

'As I said, that wasn't even house. And house is better.' A blush now from Nancy. 'What's your usual thing?'

'Classical music.'

Nancy nodded - like that was cool.

Harry said. 'I'm not sure why.'

'Is it like the posh car you drive?'

'Eh?'

'For effect.'

'Haha. No.' Harry waved his notepad. 'Come on, more drinks and then start giving me a flavour of what you feel like, days away from a warehouse party that will be illegal and could be raided.' Harry smiled and brandished his pen. 'Come on, tell me.'

Nancy Kools did. She started riffing on Thatcher and the media hysteria over house music and parties. She spoke quick, with passion. About the music, the summer going on right now. She was in her element and Harry got that. And he got this, too. There was an exuberance about her that was different, special. And it made him feel - what?

Just that.

It made him feel.

Chapter Four

Joey

Lancaster–Morecambe border

Joey pointed his Fiat 127 Extra at Gerard Toces' trailer and motored forward.

Joey Miller in lilac Marc O'Polo t-shirt, Classic Nouveau jeans, desert-coloured Clarks. The look pronounced; the number of flying ones he gave numbering zero. He schooled up on Paninaro style - the Italian girls and boys who wore Stone Island, C.P. Company, deck shoes and suck-on-this shades. Joey had his own take, as with everything. He wore his hair long, admired himself in the mirror. Why not? He knew what the lovely Nancy Kools called him on the sly. So what? Everyone was vain - too much or not enough. Vanity was the ultimate driving force. He understood this a long time ago. People needed to, too.

He finished the look off with a pair of suck-these-all-the-way-up Ray-Ban aviators. He was a Lancaster Tom Cruise. Risky Business, not Cocktail. The Paninaro kids would approve. He never took the glasses off, in winter when it froze and in summer when it was hot, hitting the north 20s as it did on this sun-drenched day

He was here on business. The Romany site sprawled every direction you looked. Asda lay a mile one-way, White Lund Industrial Estate the other. The mobile homes were buffed, sheened, the Romany chalets well established. The land decades old Traveller turf. Tots and horses ambled about. Teenage lasses and lads sat around and drank booze and fired barbecues. Radios were tuned to the charts. And other stuff. Joey recognised the sound instantly. House music. It sounded like a mix by her.

Nancy Kools, with her smile and lit up eyes, DJing to a packed warehouse or club like she DJed in her bedroom. Cooler than cool could be cool.

Joey cruised forward, his Fiat familiar on the site; a rust-bucket, first set of wheels that was tri-tone coloured and clashed with his threads and sunglasses. The bumper, yellow. The body, a hue of tan. Boot, orange. Joey couldn't drive yet. Not officially. He had a provisional licence and prayed he wouldn't be stopped by the police, especially with what he packed in the car, what he punted for Gerard Toces.

Toces the big man in a big family, community centred around Lancaster and Morecambe. Gerard was auburn haired and smiley, not yet twenty and rolled with most occurrences until it was time not to. He fancied himself a honey-piped crooner on the quiet. Loved old-time balladeers from across the pond. Frank Sinatra, Dean Martin his faves.

When Joey realised, he came close to guffawing in Gerard's face. Sinatra, Dean Martin? Could he not do better? How about Sammy Davis Jnr? He killed laughs at birth, seeing the look on Gerard's face. Like he knew Joey mocked him and waited for clear proof so he could administer a punishment.

Gerard had an interesting effect on Joey. The Romany excited and scared hell out of him. This, the thrill of knowing Gerard 'Frenchy' Toces. The thrill of punting pills for him. Frenchy had an edge. Was his essence. And he offered, too, a sense of fascination, adventure. Frenchy befriended Joey, was good to him, trusted Two-brain to street-deal his twenty-bags of white New Yorkers. He knew Joey was ex-Lancaster Royal Grammar School dayboy and didn't care and he allowed Joey to pilot his

Sierra Cosworth to Blackburn and Sett End on Shadsworth Road. And, then, afterwards in convoys to warehouse parties. The white Sierra's engine souped up, making the baby torque like a beast and making it difficult to control and fun to try and control. Joey leaped at the chance to motor Gerard's wheels to the parties and drove Frenchy and his sixteen-year-old wife, Tina, and his cousin Temmy to copious warehouses at Haslingden, Boom Town. The one that went off inside an old abattoir. One by a canal with windows in the rafters that let in the sunrise on an ingot-tinctured morn. The one last new year's eve by Ewood Park; the one at Nelson when the police raided early in the AM and the kids panicked and the mood changed forever.

Saturday night was about Gildersome and defiance. Post-Nelson, the parties tapered off and near-died. This was about to change on Saturday, 21st July, 1990. Joey got a preternatural sense that this shindig would go down in history.

Joey parked the Fiat and pulled his Head bag from the boot, made Gerard's chalet and knocked on the door. Tina answered. Gerard's wife sent a shot through him each time he saw her. She was a festoon of gold. Of gold bangles, gold earrings and a gold necklace, and on her fingers, gold sovereign rings that studded her digits on most of her fingers right to where her nails were heavily red and pink and sometimes orange painted.

She flashed a front tooth and smiled like she looked into his thoughts and approved of what she saw. Waved Joey in.

Joey hit the front room. A slew of kids from nappy wearing age onwards. In their usual near-to-chaos state. Not all of them belonging to Gerard and Tina.

He saw Frenchy in the kitchen at the back of the chalet, at the table he always sat at. Marvelled again at the Romany's physique. Five-feet-five or six inch packed into a light heavyweight's frame, wavy blonde hair grown to a mullet, chip-blue eyes, their vividness somehow reminding Joey of the dark eyes of Nancy.

Gerard wore shell suits permanently; today's number a purple

Flash Gordon-type affair. Silky material with gold piping at the arms and ankles, a gold bolt of lightning across the front. A pair of white Reebok Classics rounding off the regulation Frenchy look.

Temmy sat next to him at the table. He sported a pale-green shell suit. Sharp eyes in a face that showed a scarred chin. His perma-thinly worn grin.

A molehill of white powder before them. Charlie. Cocaine a rarity in Lancaster and Morecambe, which for an age was speed, dope smoking turf. Until ecstasy started flooding the area, getting trafficked in from London. With these new dancing tablets of love came a new white king of the world - marching powder. Coke, posh, showbiz, nosebag, or sixty-five, the price of a gram. Gerard and Temmy did sixty-five near constant. Like they did near constant barbiturates, speed, acid, dope and E. Anything to make the world whirl.

Joey got a surge. He was seventeen and he was raw and he knew it; sensed that being a sucker for the glamour of Gerard, dazzled by how the Romany moved and operated, was a greenhorn look and he gave precisely more zero ones.

Gerard tossed his wavy locks. 'Mr Joseph Miller, let's have you.' He spoke with a Romany accent. Near Irish, near not. Temmy thin-smiled a row of silver teeth, chin scar flexing.

Joey took the seat Frenchy offered, placed the Head bag at his feet, pointed. Next to the pile of powder, a large array of pills that were unfamiliar.

'They're pink, Frenchy.'

He smiled and snorted coke off the key to the Cosworth up first his left nostril, then the right. When finished, white powder coated each of them. The Romany brushed this away in a nonchalant move and put an arm around Joey. 'No wonder they call Mr Joseph Miller Mr Two-brain, eh, Temmy. You get me?'

Temmy shook with laughter, took the key off his cousin and did a double dose of powder, two hits up each nasal cavity. White powder coated his nostrils too and Joey stifled a laugh and Temmy nodded hard at Gerard, wanting him to see he understood his bigman cousin crystal clear.

'Gerard,' Temmy said. 'You know I get you.'

Frenchy waved Temmy off and his cousin relaxed. Frenchy came alive. His eyes bulged and the veins in his neck rose. He lurched for his cousin and Temmy flinched and went ashen white. Gerard relaxed instant and howled laughs and grinned at Joey. Temmy turned crimson now and Gerard said, 'Jesus, Thomas. Every time.'

Joey's heart hammered. It got him every time too.

Gerard kept laughing. He stood up and pulled a cassette from the mahogany sideboard and brought it to the table. 'Here, Joseph, this will sort you.' He loaded the cassette into a Hitachi tape deck and hit play, and took the key back off Temmy and loaded up again and offered Joey the sixty-five.

Joey, a faux grimace. 'No thanks.'

Temmy, recovering: 'Frenchy, you've forgotten Mr Brainaic doesn't take coke. Or any fucking thing.'

Frenchy sighed and sat down and threw his cousin a lazy eyed stare and moved this to Joey and put his eyes back on Temmy. 'How thick are you, Thomas? I'm not forgetting anything. Just being polite. It's good manners to have good manners, you anti-brainiac. And you never know, there may come a day when Joseph does indeed partake of the darker arts.'

He winked at Joey and Joey winked back. Gerard did the sixty-five off the key and pointed at the Hitachi. 'You know this tune?'

Joey nodded. The song was Altogether Now by The Farm. He watched Gerard and Temmy sway their shoulders to the beat, eyes half-shut, and he got another surge, an uplifting feeling that came from the melody and the song's title and lyric and the feeling was of something happening, of this, here, right now, and the past weeks of summer and the party at Gildersome to come and the weeks to come beyond that.

A moment that felt forever. Gerard and Temmy keyed more white powder and kids ran in and out of the kitchen from the front room of the chalet and Tina walked through sucking a blue-coloured Mr Freeze and about turned and walked back out. The vocal repeated and the feeling hit Joey more and the feeling hit harder and he flashed on dancing in Sett End and dancing inside the old mills and disused warehouses and abattoirs and of being together. Of high emotion, of morning arriving and daylight through the windows and the party continuing into the first hours of the morn and the party then finally over and the kids departing and going back to their cars and the party only moments ago finished and already a memory and the old mill or warehouse or abattoir where the party took place almost definitely never to be returned to and never to be located again.

The song faded and was mixed into the next one and Joey recognised it. 'Dub Be Good To Me,' he said. 'This a Ducky tape?'

'DJ Nancy something,' Gerard said. He leaned back in his chair. 'You know, that bird DJ.'

'Jesus,' said Joey. 'The lads further up your row, who've always got the barbecue going, were playing a mix of hers too.'

The Romany shrugged and pointed at the pink pills. 'How many of these babies you think you can sell?'

Joey shrugged. 'The normal amount.'

Gerard pushed him ten bags of the twenties. 'Harvey's tonight, the Carleton Friday. What about for Saturday?'

'Haven't served up at a warehouse since Nelson.'

Gerard smiled and took his shell suit top off, muscles dancing through a white vest. He seemed to shimmer. A nineteen-year-old deity. 'Don't remind Thomas.'

Temmy sat down at the table and rubbed his scar. 'Fuck those Mancs.'

Gerard howled laughter. 'To be fair, Thomas, the way you were wired, you needed a blade to bring you down.'

Joey, getting brave: 'I think it gives you character, Temmy.'

A pause. The cousins looked at each other and Temmy locked eyes on Joey. Gerard leaned back in the chair eyed Joey and Joey's s heart thudded.

'You think it's a matter to be mocking my cousin about, do you? Him being bladed by some dirty fucking Mancs?'

Joey's stomach lurched. 'Sorry, Gerard. Temmy I-'

Gerard raised a hand. Telling him to be quiet quick. 'I thought you were clever. Supposed to be?'

Joey's fear was laced with something else. A sense he let Gerard down. Disappointed him. Gerard moved his face to Joey's. The Romany's blue eyes froze. 'Yes,' he said. 'This is a disappointment. You are letting me down. And yourself.'

Joey, stunned: 'How did you know-'

Gerard howled and Temmy joined him and Joey flushed, looked at the Romany, saw what occurred.

'Ha-ha. Very good - you got me. Again.' He waited for them to stop laughing. They did, finally. 'Back to business.' He pointed at the pink pills. 'The warehouse at Gildersome is probably never going to be as big as Nelson, so let's do the same as the party at the abattoir on Halloween.'

The Toces cousins blanked. Joey held up two fingers. Gerard looked at Temmy, nodded and farmed Joey another two hundred pills. He palmed the Es, seeing the stamp on them of a miniature skyscraper. 'Pink New Yorkers,' he said.

'That's right,' Temmy said. 'And remember-'

'You're always watching me, even when you're not.'

Joey broke a grin and Gerard pulled a blade from his pants pocket and arranged two more fat piles of cocaine with it. Did with care. Joey had seen the knife before. Frenchy liked to move the serrated edge across his lips.

'That's correct, Joseph,' the Romany said, and arranged some coke on the blade and moved the blade to his nostrils and snorted it quick, jerking a finger at Temmy. 'Show him our once friend Neil, who thought he was a bad man, Thomas.'

Temmy went to the pile of cassettes on the sideboard and pulled a wallet of photographs. Went through it. Waved one in the air. Joey saw it before. A polaroid of the lad who sold pills for Frenchy before Joey got his gig. 'Here,' said Temmy, 'our friend Neil.'

Gerard shrugged, did more sixty-five off the blade. 'A once friend, Thomas. Once.'

Joey knew Neil was not eighteen yet. The snap showed him freshly cut, a slash down along the side of a cheek, blood seeping. 'We were watching him too,' Gerard said. 'The joker ripped us off three pills, thought we wouldn't know. So Temmy striped him.'

Joey killed a shudder and laughed. 'Silly Neil,' he said. Waited a moment, playing it cool, twirled his shades, told them: 'See you later.' Picked the Head bag up from his feet and stashed the bags of pills in it.

Gerard's eyes blinked. A tic from the coke he did. 'Stay out of trouble, Joseph.'

Joey walked out the kitchen and through the living room, past the kids. Tina held the front door open and smiled. 'Bye.'

'Bye.'

He made the Fiat 127 feeling the sun in its glorious hotness and paused by the car. He saw tiny children playing on grass by their chalets and thought of Tina Toces. He got in the Fiat and motored out the site, fifty yards down Mellishaw Lane, and pulled off and parked behind a large copse and watched the road. Empty. Zero cars or pedestrians. Joey tuned the Fiat's wireless to Radio One and heard Bruno Brookes say, 'This is a record I still like to play. Stakker Humanoid by Humanoid, an acid house classic from 1988.'

Joey tapped a foot, began drifting off.

Now, noise. The washing sound of a car approaching. Joey opened his eyes, looked at the road. There it went, flashing past the trees. The Bentley, cream-coloured, purring, taking the turn-off for the site. Harold Blue's wheels.

It had to be to see Gerard. Harry played secretive about who else featured in his book. Harry got the Second Summer of Love title correct but the secret squirrel act was laughable. Who cared? It was comical yet Joey liked Harry for it. The dude tried something. Despite being in his mid-thirties and nerdy and married with a little girl - he didn't give up on himself.

Joey knew Harry since he was a kid when he played cricket with him in Greaves Park. Joey had his number then. Harry was shy. Before himself. Blushed easy, quick. He seemed to shift once he went to university, getting braver, ambitious for a while. He was a Russia nut, the Kremlin, KGB, Cold War, adored all that stuff. Post-graduating, he wangled a gig on Primrose FM but after a while something turned again, seemed to curdle. Joey didn't speak to him for a long time but caught his late-night show sometimes and Harold always sounded cheesed off, call it frustrated.

The other week. Harry out of nowhere knocked on the door of his mother's house on Lily Grove. Asked if Joey wants to be in the book. Joey said, 'Sure,' and asked, 'Why me?' Expecting Harry to throw a routine about knowing him since a kid. He said, 'Because you're seventeen and are the perfect profile of a young impressionable kid going to warehouse parties as part of your formative experience. I was at Nelson, I saw you there dancing, having a good time.'

Joey waited, said nothing. Realised the dude wasn't going to mention them knowing each other from their games of cricket, from Lancaster being a small town. Joey kind of liking this, too. As he did watching Harry drive in now to see Frenchy. Harry had something that was difficult to decipher, get a take on.

Though why he was at Frenchy's was crystal. Harry must be featuring the Romany in Second Summer of Love, too.

As one of 'three main protagonists', he told Joey about.

Harry tried to keep it secret. It wasn't anymore.

Chapter Five

Harry

The party swung at Gerard's place. They kept putting different sounds on. Mixes by 'DJ Ducky' and 'that Italian bird, we wouldn't mind getting to know'; Gerard and Temmy informing Harry of the latter on repeat. Frenchy ensuring Tina was definitely out of earshot.

Harry refused offers of 'a blade of showbiz', noting the knife Gerard waved around was a Bowie, an expensive one. He kept to his Johnnie Walker Red. He was a narcotics free zone. The diametric opposite of this pair. Kept smiling. Saying no thanks and taking notes. They watched Harry write. Gerard - eyes of blue ice - telling him on repeat: 'No names, remember. No names or,' and waving the Bowie at Harry's nose as Harry told Gerard on repeat: 'Of course not, no problem. That's the agreement.'

Harry wrote down colour for the book. Chapter-and-versed on the 'wide constituency of those drawn to the spectacle, the phenomenon that is the warehouse party.' Using italics/caps: 'This, here, IS the summer of love in all its glorious second coming. Gerard and Temmy Toces, nineteen-year-old cousins, drawn to the sound, vibrancy and vividness of this once-in-a generation cultural shift in the north-west of England.'

Utilising a quasi-elevated, antiquated register for the prose of this section of the book.

There would be no names. No identification of Gerard and Temmy. Sure. But Second Summer of Love would include far more about them than they agreed. Primarily, the nefarious activities they lived as kings off. Harry calculated it this way: Gerard and Temmy could be hoodwinked in the precise same way they got hoodwinked to be in the book. By flannelling them. 'No-one will know it's you apart from you. You can laugh in secret about your starring role in THE publication chronicling acid house, warehouse parties and this new magic pill, ecstasy.'

Harry liked his style and congratulated himself again on choosing the ideal trio. Joey Miller, Nancy Kools and Gerard Toces, the Romany coming with the added bonus of Temmy, who was classic court jester secondary character material.

Gerard broke his reverie, saying: 'What about this tune? Will you listen to that, Harold lad, listen-'

He dialled volume up on the Hitachi, asking Temmy: 'What's this one called again?'

Temmy's accent went thick. Went arrogant. 'I told you enough times Frenchy, for fuck's sake.'

To Harry: 'He's doing this to be the big man, he knows what the fucking tune is called. He's showing off - for your fucking book.'

Gerard grinned, moved slow across the kitchen floor, wavy hair waving. Harry had a sense of Temmy being hunted down. Frenchy deliberate. Let's toy with the captured prey. He reached Temmy and, slower, brought the blade to Temmy's chin.

'You want a second one?'

Drawing the blade across his scar. Frenchy's eyes distant, nearby.

Temmy went ash-white. The scar's dead skin blanched. 'No, Frenchy.' His voice a squeak.

Gerard turned to Harold. 'Sure, I am showing off for your book, Mr Harold Blue, and I'm sure this is appreciated. You want people to actually read it, don't you? Well, I am here to provide some actual personality, charisma, a sense of something happening.'

Harry nodded, eyeing Temmy as he trembled, near quasi-panicked. 'Yes, Gerard. Definitely.'

Frenchy turned back to his cousin and smiled and slowsmooched the tip of the blade of the Bowie, pointing at the Hitachi.

'So, Thomas Toces, this tune, what is it?'

Temmy, squeaking higher pitched: 'Your Love, Frankie Knuckles.'

Gerard laughed. 'It sure isn't Frankie S of Hoboken, for sure.'

He took a step or two away. Temmy breathed out. Tried to recover the thing that mattered, the only thing he put actual graft into: face - not losing it.

'Give us a bit of Frank then, Gerard.'

Gerard thought about it. Said; 'I should charge you.' Cracked a broad smile. Sunshine, flowers. 'Frank is king.' Then began in on the opening bars of a favourite, notes fluttering into the room: 'I've got you under my skin/I've got you deep in the heart of me...'

Harry wrote more notes; Gerard broke off from crooning. 'I am one of Harold's three main sources he says, but he won't tell us who the other two are.'

Temmy read the cue, thought he did. Told Harry: 'Listen to Frenchy. You tell us, for Christ's sake. We miss nothing, you understand? We're watching you all the time, even when you think we're not.'

Harry heard the line from Temmy countless times. Like he observed how Temmy moved from humiliation by Gerard back to default menace, the colour surging into his features again, scar pulsing. Temmy stuck his face in Harry's and Harry read the move, too. Temmy tried to do to him what Gerard just did to Temmy. Harry flinched. Pretended to. Play this clown, like he played them both.

Frenchy pulled his cousin away. 'Thomas - there's no need for this behaviour. Or for us to know who else is in Harold's book.'

'Harold, I was jesting as I do believe Thomas knows.'

Temmy nodded and backed off, and for a countless time Harry mental-noted Gerard Toces was no mug.

Harry wrote in his notebook: 'Gerard genuinely harbours a love of Frank Sinatra and can sing a bit himself, too. Temmy's lightweight - wants constantly to impress Gerard and this can backfire.'

Harry wrote two more paragraphs on what he witnessed.

Capped a final note up.

'GERARD HAS THE MEASURE OF TEMMY AND MOST THINGS.'

Then, in brackets: '(Be careful. Always).'

The more intriguing note Harry made didn't concern the Gerard-Temmy dynamic. It came before Frenchy terrified his cousin/henchman and was contained in something Temmy said to Harry.

The following.

Temmy: 'Harry, do you ever think why the fuck you write this book?'

Frenchy's expression went from the perma-broad smile to bemused. Harry, the same, he got back/wrong-footed. Was Temmy's tone - like he actually wanted to know. Was curious what drove Harry - which was far more than Harry had Temmy down as capable of.

It made him reassess Temmy. And himself. What he knew. What he thought he knew.

Chapter Six

Harry was having a good day that was about to become a far better day. He celebrated in Charles Mua's Golden Fry on King Street; the eatery specialised in fish, chips, pies, sausages-in-batter, mushy peas, curry sauce and gravy. This the Lancaster destination for his fave kind of chow.

Harry took the regular table at the window that gave a prime view of the town main artery. Scoped traffic chug past as Charles brought over chips and mushy peas, a pot of tea. 'Thank you,' he said.

Charles grinned and walked back behind the counter, turned the radio up; he tuned into the cricket - Harold caught a voice blathering about the test series with India - 'Gooch has hit a magnificent record 333' - and tuned it out to background hum.

The Golden Fry filled up; a queue went to the door, tables packed out. The place Harry's de facto HQ; he did regular broadcasts here for his Primrose FM show, vibing on the atmosphere of night-time buses and taxis rumbling along King Street. The show caused a ripple on the local scene - columns were written in the Lancaster Guardian, Harry and Primrose FM proprietors quoted in articles: was the area ready for this? The answer was 'yes'; the show's phone lines got jammed. Harry crowed to Amber of his success and his wife smiled like she was happy and sad for him.

Harry tuned back into the radio; Charles flipped it now to Primrose FM, chart hits blared. The current No 1, Sacrifice by Elton John; Harry played it on his show and shared his thoughts:

the youth frothed over house music and convoys and warehouse parties and the new drug, ecstasy, and what did you know? The midsummer hit record is a middle-of-the-road pop ditty.

Elton was at No 1 and flicking through his notes Harry saw the words 'diversity' and 'charts', and read the following entry: 'Adamski made No 1 for a month from 6th May with Killer' - a house music song. Also, 'Snap, The Power preceded it' - the song Nancy played earlier at the Merchants; and before that it was 'Beats International, Dub Be Good To Me'. Harry put his pad down and munched chips and mushy peas and saw the black Vauxhall Carlton pull up across King Street by the lights.

Here they come - DI Walter Swaggert and DC Brian Ball, each in cheap suits, white shirts, navy-blue ties, black shoes. They dodged across the road and made inside the eatery, took seats opposite Harry. Swaggert pinched a chip from Harry's plate and pointed to Harry's belly. 'Hardly the breakfast of a champion, Harold.'

'It's 5.30pm, Walter.'

Swaggert laughed and took another chip and lobbed it at Ball, who opened his mouth and caught/downed it. Harry ignored them, speared more peas. Swaggert said, 'Shoot then, Harold, we haven't got all day, have we, Brian? Well, we do - but you know what I mean.'

Ball fiddled with his tie.

'Walter, do you play at being Mr Cop or is this really you?' said Harry.

Swaggert looked like he was puzzled or pretended to be puzzled. 'An act, Harold, of course. It all is.'

Ball kept watching - Harry clocked him the shrewder despite ranking below Swaggert. Walter smiled and said, 'Come on, what have you got?' He nodded to Ball - telling him to buy some chips - and the DC joined the queue.

Harold said, 'Before I tell you, you understand what I want? I'm writing a book about this scene, as I told you. Warehouse parties, acid house, the whole nine yards. So in exchange for the information I give you, I want to be able to write about your police operation.'

Swaggert nodded. 'I can get that signed off no problem, but you'll have to be cute. You won't be able to reveal every detail, and you will have to hold back on operational stuff.' He shrugged. 'Before I agree to anything, come on - what do you have?'

Harry ignored him, poured tea, watched a double-decker move along King Street, counted 1-2-3-4 in his head. Then: 'There's a party on this Saturday night in a place called Gildersome, on the Treefield Industrial Estate. It's called Love Decade and with this info you can substantially further your career.'

Swaggert thought about it. 'Where the fuck is Gildersome.'

'Near Leeds.'

Swaggert said, 'Yorkshire.'

Harry sipped tea and eyed Ball return with two plates of chips. He smiled at the DC. 'Charles brings my food over.'

Ball undid his top-button, loosened his tie, looked at the proprietor behind the counter. 'I should get to know him.'

Swaggert applied vinegar and pepper to his chips and forked a few. 'Yorkshire is miles away. Way out of our jurisdiction. We're Lancaster plod. Our biggest miscreants as you know are the local drugs trade joeys, robbers, blade merchants. Small town dickheads in a small town.'

Ball smiled at Harry; like he clocked 100% what Harry got at. Harry said, 'Walter - you win twice here. First off you inform your friends on the Yorkshire police what's occurring - this is precious information - and, so, secondly this is not going to hurt your upwardly rising career.' He sipped tea and ate more peas. 'You heard of Graham Bright?'

Swaggert blanked, Ball nodded.

'He's an MP who last week got his second private member's bill passed through Parliament and into law,' said Harry. Ball nodded more and Harry saw this: Mr Clever is cute enough not to jump in and piss-off his boss with what he knows. 'The bill has a wordy title - of course it does, politicians puff anything up they can - that's what they do.

'The 'Entertainments, Increased Penalties Bill' is the official name and what it's actually known as is the Acid House Bill.

'In a nutshell, Graham Bright, MP, is the kind of kill-joy you police love. The tariff for not having a license and still holding one of these warehouse parties has just jumped from a £2K to £20K fine, plus - you'll really adore this - six months jail-time.' Harry smiled. 'Call Mr G Bright a mini-Maggie. Thatcher in drag.'

Swaggert's eyes brightened. 'So I, we–' - he indicated Ball - '- hand this acid house party info to Yorkshire plod and they close it down and come up smelling of roses, I, we, come up the same, and my bosses think I'm Lancaster and Morecambe's answer to Miss fucking Marple.'

Ball laughed - it played genuine; Harold shrugged. 'Lancashire's answer, at least. This will get you noticed countywide if not nationwide. That's internal. You give me what I want I'll make sure the Lancaster Guardian has a frontpage exclusive splash detailing how the intelligence came from its local constabulary and, namely, its two rising star detectives.' He speared a chip from Swaggert's plate. 'Anonymously sourced, of course.'

Walter Swaggert's eyes brightened. 'One thing I still don't see is how you're going to get any material for your book if Yorkshire plod are handling this. Like I say, way out of our jurisdiction.'

Swaggert chomped a chip and Harry said, 'Was coming to this, Walter. My information is that several people from this area are involved in the party. They're not organising it, but are working for the organisers. Providing muscle for the door, doing the lights, one or two could be DJing, too, that kind of thing.'

Harry flashed on Nancy - using her info to play Swaggert. No way he'd identify her but: she told him the names of other local DJs who played.

Swaggert said, 'Any actual names would be very useful.'

'At the moment I haven't been told any and you know as well as me why. After the raid at Nelson from your diligent Blackburn colleagues, the way these parties have gone, people are wary - and that's before this acid house bill becomes widely known.' Playing Swaggert like a Stradivarius. 'I'm taking a chance trusting you - I hope you see that, Walter? This is my chance to hit it big, too... you two gentleman have to understand that while Lancaster is home, if my book takes off, then...'

Their faces said he lost them; they cast him as oddball, nerdy. Swaggert looked at Harry. 'You're saying we go down there, too? See which Lancaster dickheads we can arrest?'

Harry nodded. 'Follow the usual suspects from down there - it's a shoe-in, you'll get more than lucky.'

Ball fiddled with his tie. 'We only need one result to justify it sir, in fact merely going and doing surveillance we'll be adding to our knowledge of local activ-'

'Yes, Brian, I get it. And call me Walter, for fuck's sake.'

He smiled and looked at Harry.

Harold said, 'We are agreed then? I can write about your operation in the book as long as I'm cute about it.' He paused; to finish off the act - pretend he still didn't quite understand this yet. 'You think you can get your name and Brian's signed off? It'd be great to have you in the book - the two detectives who go down to Gildersome, do the business for our most definitely on-the-case Lancaster and Morecambe Police. Will cast you as local heroes.'

Swaggert got a faux-mean look. 'Are you hearing this, Brian? Give him an inch and what's he do? What all these writers are like. Delusions and delusions of playing god.'

Ball shrugged. 'I didn't realise you had vast experience of 'writers', Walter.' Swaggert faux-grimaced now and Ball continued: 'But, if it's done correct, then we - you, in particular, Walter, will deserve credit. For good honest police work.'

Swaggert thought a moment. Smiled. 'Sounds bootickety. Harry, we have an agreement.' He left his plate of chips unfinished, stood up. 'One other thing – you get any information about who's shifting all the Es around here, do let Uncle Walter S know. Two months ago, there were exactly zero of these silly fucking dancing pills in the area, now some dickhead's got a pipeline going – making a load of cash.'

'Frank Shaw and some of his crew may have gone down but that hasn't stopped these pills flooding the place and being bought like they're a cure for cancer – judging by the number of arrests of kids in possession of them we're doing. White New Yorkers, they're called. Some lowlife has got in on the ground floor and is cleaning up like a Lancaster Pablo Escobar.'

Harry nodded. He knew 100% who was behind the E influx. Uncle Walter Swaggert was the last person he'd tell. 'Sure thing,' said Harry. 'I find out and you are the first to know.' He smiled. 'When I'm out of this place and on my yacht cruising the Med, I will look back on our working relationship as something sweetly symbiotic.'

Swaggert blanked on 'symbiotic' and Brian couldn't resist. 'Two-way, Walter, it means. Mutually beneficial.'

Swaggert faux-grimaced again and Harry thought the DI may not be as dolt-brained as he came off. Still: after the party on Saturday, this weekend, he'd be out. No more watching of anyone in this scheme he designed required. No more creeping around.

Chapter Seven

Nancy

Haverbreaks

Nancy in the garage at home.

She selected records for DJing at Harvey's later tonight. She shared the space with her dad, Paolo. His passion ran two pronged: the VW camper parked by Nancy's Technics 12s and the family eatery, Altobelli's, a pasta-and-pizza joint at the bottom of town. The place was neither high nor low-end - you could dine for £5 and feel a sophisticate or splurge £20 and luxuriate smug in the glow of a gourmand.

Nancy's mother, Sharon, ran Altobelli's. Paolo was wideboy handsome, oversaw the cuisine, libations, and front-of-house stuff; Sharon had echoes of Nancy's beauty, gave her daughter brains. Their home on Haverbreaks estate, an affluent area of Lancaster studded with detached properties in generous acreage featuring apple and pear orchards, rows of strawberry, raspberry bushes, the ribboning Haverbreaks brook linking most of the gardens.

Nancy held a white label 12-inch she bought from Ere-Ere Records in town after seeing Harry at the Merchants earlier. The 12 Airport '89 by Wood Allen - 'a banger'. She kissed the disc and pointed to her t-shirt and laughed. It showed an image of a DJ in action and below this the legend: TUNES TO MOVE YA. She had the t-shirt made specially - the legend her catchphrase. She waved the twelve above her head and giggled.

'This is a tune to move all of us.'

Nancy looked Airport '89 up. It sampled Rah Band's Electric Fling, a song a decade-plus old, Airport '89 an Italo-House number, its sound based on pilfering/sampling the original by Richard Anthony Hewson.

Paolo walked in, said: 'You talking to yourself, bella?'

Nancy pointed at her T-shirt and thumbs upped her dad, saw him smile. Paolo wore slick grey Farah's, a pastel-blue Napoli 10 Maradona shirt. His eyes twinkled. 'You playing records tonight?'

Nancy laughed, put Airport '89 in her record bag for later. 'Yes dad, I told you ten times - in Morecambe at Harvey's.'

He got a look. 'Sorry, your mother-'

Nancy tried to keep quiet. Failed. 'What did she say this time?'

Paolo shook his head and picked up a cloth and started buffing the VW.

'Mummy say daddy silly because he never speaks.'

Nancy and Paolo turned - at the garage door, Esmerelda. The little girl smiled and went for her sister's hand, hair dressed in pigtails like a mini-Nancy.

Nancy lifted Esmerelda high and told Paolo: 'Very perceptive for six years young.' She brought her nose to Esmerelda's. 'You know who you get that from, bambino?'

Esmerelda nodded - this was old news. 'Mama.' She got a quizzical look. 'Mama didn't say 'silly' did she, papa? What she say?'

Paolo laughed, kept buffing the camper. 'No, you are correct, bambino. She say "insensitive".'

More laughs from Nancy and Paolo, the little girl actually bending two fingers to make quote marks as she repeated what her father told her. "Insensitive".'

'I thought you might be laughing.'

At the door, Sharon. She wore a pair of Lee semi-flare jeans, a white smock and an expression.

'We weren't laughing at you, darling,' said Paolo. 'Esmerelda was amusing us.'

'You seem to find it easier speaking with Esmerelda and Nancy than me.'

'Stop it, mama,' Esmerelda said.

'You came in here to hide.' Sharon took one, two steps towards her husband.'

'Mum, please,' said Nancy.

Sharon moved towards her daughters and gave them a kiss. Paolo kept buffing and sheening the VW. Nancy understood why her dad kept quiet.

She should stay out of it but: her mum's expression. 'What, mama - what are you trying to get dad to talk about?'

Sharon's eyes flashed - she'd waited to be asked. 'Everything and nothing - as usual. This particular time it was your dad wanting to raise the price of the starters.'

Nancy caught her dad's sheepish look. She said, 'I thought you didn't want to, papa.'

Paolo stopped buffing. 'I don't - didn't, but your mum thought we should, so I agreed.'

Nancy regretted asking; here - the latest black hole argument that sucked all in the vicinity in. 'The problem is he's gone over the top,' Sharon said. '£2.50 for a Caprese Salad? This is Lancaster, not Milan. We should charge £1.50, nothing more.'

'Sharon,' Paolo said to his wife. '£2.50 is a good price, one hundred per cent.'

Sharon looked at her husband like he infuriated her. 'Point is, Paolo, this is Lancaster, we charge £5 for a main so £2.50 for a bit of mozzarella and basil is not si si, bella, this macho Italian stuff, it's plain wrong. Overpriced.'

Nancy said, 'This is really all over the price of a starter?'

Sharon rolled her eyes and Esmerelda ran out the garage. 'Not really, Nancy. What it's about is what - or should I say - who, changed your dad's mind. After I was trying to get the price dropped your dad was adamant at first - no way was he going to. Then, Cynthia intervenes and suddenly he does.'

She winked at Nancy; Esmerelda came running back in the garage. The little girl held something close to as big as her.

'How is Hoppy this afternoon?' Nancy said. The little girl smiled and walked to her mum and handed a cuddly toy kangaroo to her. Sharon took Hoppy and kissed her daughter. Esmerelda reached forward and out of Hoppy's front pouch took a photo and motioned to her father. Paolo walked to his daughter and took the photo. Esmerelda kissed her father and mother and giggled and ran back out the garage towards the orchard.

Nancy went to her parents, took the photo. It was a picture of Esmerelda as a baby, wispy blonde hair in a pink ribbon. Paolo said, 'The one from our bedroom, Sharon.'

His wife smiled and kissed her husband and went after Esmerelda. Paolo watched her go and got a look Nancy recognised. He started laughing, kept on laughing - the sound bounced around the garage, grated on Nancy. Like he ignored what Esmerelda did - with Hoppy and the photograph. Like he tried to forget as soon as possible.

Nancy said, 'Who's Cynthia, dad?'

Paolo coloured. 'A lady at work.'

'A waitress?'

'Si.'

'A girl?'

'A lady.' Paolo's eyes twinkled.

Nancy said, 'Dad.'

He stopped shining the VW. 'What?'

She shrugged. 'I think you know.'

He smiled. 'Come on - tell me.'

She drew breath. 'Why take Cynthia's opinion more than mama's? Or, any other "lady"?'

Paolo's face fell; like he was being misunderstood - again - but didn't want to say. He moved to his daughter, put a hand on Nancy's cheek. 'Hey, it wasn't like this and is never like this. It's a coincidence only, trust me. Your mother and me were talking about changing the prices and Cynthia, in the restaurant, heard and agreed - with your mother. I was against it, as your mama says, but I had changed my mind anyway because your mother wanted to do it. I was about to say this when Cynthia - at the same time - said she agreed, that mama was correct.'

Nancy looked at her dad, knew he told the truth. 'That's it?'

'What else?'

She nodded and smiled and kissed him on the head and returned to her records, pulled a pink-coloured 12-inch: Dreams of Santa Anna by Orange Lemon. It sampled Babe Ruth's The Mexican which sampled Ennio Morricone's Per qualche dollaro in piu - from the soundtrack to the movie, For A Few Dollars More. She heard the track in her head, flashed on times she played as the warehouse parties began to cook, kids dancing, bouncing with joy, the record bringing all these good memories back-

Her reverie got broken by her dad whistling. She put Dreams of Santa Anna in her bag and pulled another record, Kariya - Let Me Love You For The Night. She looked this one up, too. It was a collector's item in house, an actual original composed record rather than sample derived. Released the same time as Dreams of Santa Anna - 1988 - on Sleeping Bag Records. A tune out of New York. A tune out of the magick of the world.

Nancy heard the track now - the ominous bass-line, the honeyed vocal. Vibe epic, a life event occurring as it pounded from the speakers, made you feel something about yourself, about everything.

Paolo caught Nancy's eye and told his daughter: 'Play the song I like.'

'You say you like them all.'

Paolo reached over Nancy's shoulder and picked out a record and placed it on a Technics, put the needle down, pressed the play button.

'Dad!'

A pretend wail as she loved this one too, as the opening bars of Pump Up The Volume by M/A/A/R/S flooded the garage, Paolo doing a Paolo jig that was a ridiculous rendition of a robot dancing.

He took Nancy's hand - father and daughter moved together, house music playing in the garage, in their ears.

Nancy, though: her dance tinged with regret - mum and dad were not happy; she loved them and yet.

She got the same feeling she got more and more - like she'd outgrown them, like she outgrew home.

Chapter Eight

Joey

South Lancaster

Joey Miller in his house, No 27 Lily Grove, Scotforth. A well-appointed residence in well-appointed Lancasterville. He stood in the hall eyeing the mirror through the sunglasses he permawore. Looking good, for sure. Looking cooler than cool can ever be cool. He got an idea about a girl, a certain girl, so now was the time to be handsome. To shine. Be a small-town, big persona movie star. Be ready when going to Harvey's later because she was going to be there - DJing, being beautiful, being her, having an expression that did something to him, made Joey want to have the same expression, look at the world the way the girl, Nancy, looked like she looked at the world.

Go to Harvey's and try and catch her eye and see what might occur.

He wanted to get out of the house quick, avoid his mum, as per usual; wanting to do so to protect her. The reason simple; his mother didn't know herself, didn't know her son. That was a side-issue - the issue for Joey was this: stop projecting your stuff onto your son.

Too late, here she came now, his mum, Suzie, at last officially divorced from Joey's dad. Except he wasn't his dad, thank God. Tony 'adopted' Joey, except it was more like Tony bullied and terrorised him. Pulled him out of bed for a beating on mornings before school from age eleven to fifteen. What happened twelve months ago - Tony left, Suzie finally had an affair and presented him the evidence, making it non-refutable. It happened at his local, the Greaves Hotel, Tony drumming in his blues band, Suzie walking in with her latest toy-boy. Suzie was forty-seven, Michael Vince, twenty-one. She specialised in younger talent and made Michael the mould-breaker: the first toy-boy she didn't hide from Tony and paraded before him in his favourite drinking salon while doing his fave thing, gigging with his group.

Tony could hit the drums like he hit Joey - with feeling and passion and a sense of depth, meaning. By then Joey had made sure Tony finally ended his child-beating act; the idiot came in his bedroom one morning to smack him about and Joey did the following: pre-empted the move, threw himself on the floor, faux-begged for clemency, saying: 'Tony - please forgive whoever treated you bad when you were a little boy and made you the mess you are.'

Tony stopped dead; Joey kept going. 'Your behaviour speaks of antecedents only you know the full horror of. Maybe get some help - for your own sake.'

The sap stood there astounded; Joey delivered the coup-de-grace. 'That's if you're not too busy wondering why mum goes off with younger, more handsome models. I mean - make sure you have a ponder about what I'm saying here.'

Finally, he started in on Joey, like he had to make it mean more. Temples got cracked, ears bludgeoned. The poor sap - being cuckolded by Michael Vince, a soft-touch lad with zero bad bones - and the end result was how Joey 'Two-brain' planned it: his mum and Tony got divorced and she continued on with Michael.

But, now - Joey became the target of her frustrations: she dug in even deeper about his real dad; would not countenance a word about him. Who his father was, what the story of his absence for all of Joey's life was.

Suzie dug in and Joey vowed not to push her anymore on it. He didn't want to hurt her feelings, his poor and tender mum. Here she came now, through the front door, glammed up - warpaint on. She stood in the hallway, black-and-white and colour photographs of Joey at various ages in frames on the wall behind. 'Where have you been?'

Joey, laughing: 'Where haven't I been.'

'Will you stop saying that?'

He put a hand on his mum's shoulder and squeezed and she threw it off. Gentle, he placed the hand on her cheek and she brushed this off. He got the deja-vu-all-over-again sensation. 'Mum, I'll stop saying that if you stop for a second and realise, I am not him - Tony.' He twirled his sunglasses, dropped his voice. 'You know what I mean?'

Suzie took a step away. 'You say that too much, too. And stop that with your sunglasses - you are so vain.'

'Must get it from you - how much makeup? Talk about warpaint, you involved in a one-hundred-year conflict?'

'Joey-'

'Mum, I'm the seventeen-year-old son, you're forty-seven, and I'm having to point out your frustrations. You did nothing when 'he' was around to stop him beating me up. Terrorising me. You'd say sorry afterwards, then it would happen again. And again.'

Suzie glowered, exited the hallway. Joey followed into the living room she'd furnished vintage. 1930s sofa and chair with brocade finish, doilies on a drop-leaf table, sundial radio with wood panels, the effect near stiff, starched. His mum sat on the sofa and Joey said, 'Now that idiot is gone, has my life here improved? Instead of you standing by while he beats shit out of me, you do the same mentally.'

The bottom-line, this: he was too smart for her. He moved to embrace her and she baulked and he laughed and headed for the kitchen and went to the window where it looked out on the garden, the shed at the bottom, which was his den with a couch, music system, plug-in heater, a picture of a palm tree on a beach in southern California.

Calling through to the living room: 'Mum - tea?'

'Please.'

He nodded, caught the tone - defeated, by herself - and made the drinks, took Suzie her cup and exited through the backdoor, walked paving stones to his shed. He left his tea on the table outside and went in and pulled a mixtape - DJ Ducky playing a birthday party at Vale of Lune Rugby Club, Ducky due to play at Harvey's later tonight, too, after sweet girl Nancy.

The Ducky mix would get him in the mood; Joey pressed play and sat outside at the table in late afternoon July sunshine with his tea.

The garden was well kept. Suzie grew roses - pink, red - and bougainvillea, the bushes running the edge of the lawn. Joey sipped tea and tuned into the record Ducky played - It's Time To Feel The Rhythm by How II House. He asked the DJ about the ditty after he mixed it in. Ducky told him the name and that How II House was actually a dude from Canada.

Joey asked: 'Is it normal, a Canadian doing house?'

Ducky blanked on this and brought the next record in - Pacific State by 808 State, Joey listening to it now.

As the sun burned. As Lancaster hummed on beyond the walls of his mum's back garden. He tried to articulate how the music made him feel. A tenderness? Easy joy?

Ducky faded 808 State down, and brought up Hardcore Uproar. Part of the track recorded at Nelson, the live roar of the crowd inside the warehouse the roar of the crowd on the tune. Joey returned there, dropping back inside the sound of ten thousand kids partying. The sound of something - of something intangible, magick.

The piano solo at the end of the track: wowzers. Hardcore Uproar the song name and apt for how you had to feel, Joey actually on the track as one of the kids hardcore uproaring inside the Nelson warehouse, and here he was now, sipping tea, outside his shed, surrounded by his mother's flower garden listening to the baby.

Being alive; nothing else.

His mum - at the kitchen window, washing pots; clueless about it all. Clueless about herself, her son, the mind-blowing acid house scene that was going on and OFF, each kid their own supernova explosion.

Joey visioning this: Hardcore Uproar - the song and the kids at Nelson. Seeing that night and being only days away from the next party at Gildersome.

There hadn't been a warehouse for months. Not since Nelson.

He re-adjusted his shades. The mix played out.

Silence.

Chapter Nine

'Joey. Joey.'

He opened his eyes. The garden, his teacup on the table, a low sun, and-

Michael Vince. Red-cheeked, as always. Like he blushed at being with Joey's mum, at the thought Joey might think of him being so.

He raised his sunglasses and winked at Michael and threw a Joeyspecial dazzler smile. He never walked in on Michael and his mum, thank god, but heard them once, one afternoon - like they fell off the end of the earth and kept falling.

Michael said, 'How you doing?'

'Great - you?'

Michael nodded. 'Mind if I take a seat?' He sat opposite at the table and blushed more. 'Your mum says you're going to Harvey's later.'

'See you there.'

Michael kept blushing.

Joey tried to hurry this up. 'You working tonight?'

Michael nodded again.

'You can say - whatever it is.'

'Oh- do you want a lift?'

'Jesus. Yes please. Why take so long to ask?'

Joey flashed on Harvey's later, serving up Gerard's pills. 'Actually, you know what, I think I'll drive.' Courier the Es in via his Fiat, not Michael's motor. 'But don't tell my mum, she gets sensitive about me driving - you know, as I'm still on 'L' plates.'

Michael blanked a moment, then threw a goofy grin.

BINGO: he gets it, she disapproves of her son driving on a provisional license with no insurance, driving a rust-bucket motor with no MOT, road insurance, with a faulty handbrake that requires a stone behind a wheel to stop it rolling away when parked on any incline.

Michael winked and Joey twirled his sunglasses.

Now - Suzie walking the paving stones to them. 'Michael - you asked, yes?'

Michael got a scared look.

'You haven't, have you?'

Michael kept blushing.

Suzie said, 'I'll ask. Joey, do you have the £100 you "borrowed" off my kind and generous man?'

Shit. He squeezed this out of Michael for the float that got him up and running with Frenchy a few months ago when Es began flooding Lancaster and Morecambe. His cheeks burned.

'Look, Michael, my darling son's gone red. A first.'

Michael smiled like he wanted to be a thousand miles away.

Joey said, 'Calm down, mother dear. I've got Michael's money you'll be disappointed to learn.' He went inside the shed, reached behind the sound system. The score from Gerard was there - 200 Pink New Yorkers in their twenty-pill bags - plus his cash that still ran to a grand-plus after a splurge at Joseph's for new garb for Gildersome.

He peeled a hundred off plus an extra tenner, went back outside. Handed the ton to Michael plus the ten. 'That's for a drink and to say sorry for the hold-up.'

Joey spread palms at his mum, a tenner a steal to see her face. She smiled. Like she got what he did and admired it. Had to.

He smiled too.

Sometimes, they did connect.

Chapter Ten

Harry

Morecambe Sea Front, evening

Punters came in taxis and cars and buses and vans and on foot from local hostelries that offered pre-Harvey's deals. 2-for-1 bluehued cocktails, cut-price pints of Bass and Red Stripe. Chasers 55p a hit. Morecambe bay twinkled azure; the sea lapped like it had always lapped and always would. Sun kaleidoscoped. The kids were young, buzzed up. The kids fritzed excitement.

What-was-about-to-go-down mainlined.

DJ Ducky and DJ Nancy Kools are spinning the discs! The night's a West End Productions production!

West End Productions the local promo outfit run by Drew Burns and older brother, Davey.

Harry was inside; he took a booth opposite the bar, the dancefloor positioned central and sunk a metre and lit in purple neon. At floor-level, cat's eyes and embedded strip lights that ran rainbow colours in sequence. Balloons hung from the ceiling and jockeyed for space with glitter balls and drapes that trumpeted the name of the night: SUNHAZE AT HARVEY'S. *The DJs Ducky, Nancy Kools plus 'special guest appearance' from the northwest's star record-spinner, Sasha!!!* the West End Productions flyer screamed.

Harry sipped Johnnie Red with coke and ice and eyeballed the scene. He did a feature on Drew and Davey Burns for the

Lancaster Guardian. They were from Ryelands, a housing estate on tough local turf.

Harry clocked them at the bar, recalled what Drew told him: 'When acid house started, I played a Ducky mix-tape at the youth centre on Ryelands and a load of us loved it. I thought this could be a thing - doing nights.'

Now: the bar crowd parted and Harry clocked Joey standing with a woman who seemed familiar, and a beefy bouncer.

A mind-click - the woman was Joey's mum; the bouncer named Maurice or Michael. Joey's mum and the doorman an item. He was twenty years younger, at least. Harry heard the gossip about Joey's dad gigging at the Greaves Hotel and the mum walking straight in with toyboy bouncer Maurice/Michael to show her husband the marriage was finito.

Harry knew the 'dad' wasn't Joey's father. Knew Tony Miller knocked Joey about. Harry admired Joey's attitude in not allowing an item like Miller to kill his spirit.

Entering the club: who Harry came to meet. The London firm. The main dude Frederick Street plus sidekicks, Larry and Wade. Street the brains and something else. The dude possessed a strange kind of enthusiasm Harry never encountered before.

The trio stood by the Burns brothers and Joey and his mum and the bouncer-boyfriend at the bar. The bouncer moved off and stood by the Ladies' to keep watch for dealers, the zone prime E-selling turf.

Frederick Street bought drinks and passed them his sidekicks and saw Harry.

The trio walked over, hit his booth. Cockney-inflected 'all-wight, geezers?' came Harry's way; they scoped him as the fossil he was. Except Frederick - the dude monikered the Fredster due to his status - like he saw who Harold Blue was.

Leaning in now, pointing a finger at the DJ booth and saying: 'Guru Josh - Infinity. Who is the tune meister spinning such choice discs at such a choice establishment you bring us to?'

Frederick throwing an off-kilter sounding laugh. Rich and baby-like. As if Barry White got voice-boxed through a one-year-old's vocal chords. Harry peered up at the booth. 'The DJ is Nancy Kools. And she is definitely a virtuoso.'

Frederick looked at Harry like he might wind him up. Harry tried to weigh the Fredster up yet again. He was late teens/early twenties, Christopher Walken/Ludwig van Bee good-looking. His friends offered a tell on Street. Wade in crimsoncoloured shirt and string-thin to Frederick's built physique, Wade sporting an expression like he was puzzled - by himself. Larry the same age, approaching near-corpulence, having zero to say about zero.

The pair extras in the Fredster show; Street leaning in, saying: 'You sure an extra thousand?' He scoped Harvey's - kids partying on a midweek night. Eyeballed Harold in his smart suit. 'You can really shift them in this manor?'

Harold flashed on his Bentley, the house on South Road, Amber and Lottie. On his need for realisation and something else that was not in Lancaster or Morecambe. Did not reside in this manor.

Second Summer of Love was his shot, after a last lucrative payday via the score off Frederick: an extra 1,000 pills that would make him 15K-plus, wholesaled to Frenchy Toces who ordered them up on tick as always, the Romany seeing a killing at Gildersome.

Then, he was gone, would disappear like the Russians, cold war-style. Post-Gildersome, Lancaster was history, Amber too. Lottie would come and stay with him in London, once settled. Amber mocked him - she could keep doing so while he chased the dream.

To the Fredster: 'Don't worry about the extra order - that's my business.'

Frederick nodded, giving zero ones, and Harold said, 'Dropped the usual place?'

Frederick nodded again, held his hand out. Brazen. 'Payola time.'

Harry felt inside his suit jacket pocket and retrieved/handed over the money for 5k for the 1,000 tablets. The consignment that brought the Fredster up from his east London turf to

Harvey's nightclub on Morecambe Bay.

Frederick indicated Wade and Larry and leaned. 'See ya, Harold baby, and god forbid ever being ya.' laughed the Barry White baby-baritone at his own joke, motioned his sidekicks to follow and they left the booth, Harry watching them walk around the dancefloor, out of Harvey's, into the night.

Harold sipped his Johnnie Red; considered Gerard and Temmy. They had zero idea they got their pills from him; the Es went indirect via the drop system Harry set up. A nerd? The radio show? A penchant for Mozart? Squarejohn suits from Joseph's. Smart cover.

Harry smiled. By Sunday morning, Gildersome would be over and the killer content for Second Summer of Love secured and the 1,000 pills scored sold there by Frenchy who would pay him the 15k owed.

Then, he, Harold Blue, would be gone.

Chapter Eleven

Nancy

Nancy eyeballed the scene from the DJ booth. Harvey's was in full flow, the bar and dancefloor packed out. Harry looked interesting in here in the suit he sported, perhaps the most interesting thing, as he shared a drink with three not quite as interesting lads. The main one emanated a vibe: outre for Morecambe. Possibly anywhere. She played the next track - Meltdown by Quartz - and watched the dancefloor fill more and ruminated on Harry.

He was here researching the book. She admired this, his style; like he didn't give a hoot that he didn't belong. Maybe this was how you began to belong by going to places you didn't. Nancy scanned the record - the needle halfway across it. She kept watching Harry and the top boy. Then, there, past the booth at the bar: the lad, Joey. Two-brain, Too-vain, haha.

Harry said Joey was also going to feature in his book and she had to admit: despite the penchant for preening, he did look quite good; standing there in his shades, not giving a flying - like Harold did, but in a different way.

Joey was with an older woman who looked his near spitting image. Thinking: Joey hasn't come to Harvey's with his mum?

What she saw next - Jesus:

Harry palming the top lad a roll of money that looked thick. Unseen to the rest of Harvey's, though not to her from the DJ booth overlooking the place.

Now - across the dancefloor by the bar. Looking straight at her. Joey twirling his shades, pulling them down slow, eyeballing Nancy eyeballing him and offering a slow wink, followed by a satisfied grin.

Oh dear. He was kind of cute. But the act needed changing. A total and utter revamp.

Chapter Twelve

Harry

Harry pulled the Bentley along the sea front and watched the sun dip over the bay.

He'd left Harvey's, headed right along Heysham Road. The Fredster was an item. His sidekicks fancy-dress, Wade and rotund Larry vacant and not much else. Frederick Street was a different barrel of monkeys. He'd have to watch him with what he plotted. Time to recalibrate.

It had been this: hand the London connection to Swaggert if he got exposed/caught for his ecstasy operation. But: given how smart the Fredster played, he'd find a way to hand up Wade and Larry and leave Street clear. He could not be trusted not to come for Harry if grassed on. Also: the Fredster played bigtime like he was worth nurturing awhile. Insurance for when he hit London.

Harry swung left along Oxcliffe Road motoring three miles, hitting White Lund and Westgate, going right. He hit Windermere Ave, Loweswater Drive, Ullswater Ave, did a left on Buttermere Ave, then Branksome Drive.

Harry kept a house here - No 27. The place disused, boarded up. All the street the same. CONDEMNED plastered on No 27's door. Tape zigzagging across it, the boarded windows to underline the message. Harry got a pal on the council to fix it. He pulled the Bentley up on the pavement opposite. Got out the motor and made across to No 27, walked down along the side of the house. The backyard overgrown, weed strewn. A single tree at the end. Harry made the tree and reached behind to find Frederick's drop: a Sainsbury's carrier bag with enough ecstasy pills to bazooka Lancaster and Morecambe dancing dens and the warehouse party.

Gildersome, Saturday night, 21st July, 1990, is paydirt for Harold Blue. He paused and watched the vista. The panorama took the breath. The sky a burst of colours. The evening sun near-gone. Streaks of gold and yellow across the horizon. Harry smiled, scoped the disused yards either side and walked back along the side of the house and across Branksome, and dropped the Sainsbury's bag in the Bentley boot.

He hit the driver's seat and pulled his pad and watched the sky more and made notes. He squinted, smudging the vista, imagined painting it. The tints of gold and yellow.

Then, plumped for Bach on the CD player for the drive home.

He pointed the Bentley for Westgate Road and hit Shrimp roundabout thirty seconds later, did a three o'clock for Morecambe Road and took this all the way to Lancaster. The Bach had him mind-drifting in the coming dark. He veered right onto Skerton Bridge and hit Cable through town up past Dalton Square. Thurnham became South Road and his place - No 21. He didn't pull up. Kept going, heading straight over the Pointer to Greaves, motoring through Scotforth, past the University and three mile run to Galgate where he parked at the Plough Inn.

The village boozer was last-orders Sunday-eve quiet. Harry ordered a double Johnnie Red and took an outside table by the road and watched the stars shoot light that was twenty-million-years-old his way, and tuned into countryside sounds.

He took a chance. Knew it: rolling around the parish with a load of E in the boot of the Bentley '87. The trade-off, this: he was a one-man band. No-one around here knew what he did. And the pally-pally act with Swaggert offered extra cover - Lancaster plod knew him as Harold Blue, the nerd from Primrose Radio who did regular puff pieces on 'our venerable constabulary' for the Lancaster Guardian, the local rag happy to feature them.

No, it was clear, no-one knew. What he really did. How he did it. He had one client he wholesaled pills to. Frenchy. And the client had zero clue who supplied the Es. It was all done by drops. Like now.

Harry drained his double Johnnie R and walked under a clear moon to the Bentley. He pulled the Sainsbury's bag and turned and walked back and dropped it in the waste-bin by the Plough.

The Es would be collected circa 2am by Gerard.

Harry laughed, hit the Bentley and drove home watching the sky, the stars.

Chapter Thirteen

Joey

Seconds later

Joey pulled the Fiat 127 Extra into the space Harry vacated by the Plough Inn two minutes ago. He sat a moment and watched the road and inhaled the countryside scent.

The sky went from dark to light clear. The moon shone like a silver sun. He found a mixtape and loaded the cassette player and hit play. The mix, a Nancy K offering - ambient, chilled. She looked fine at Harvey's earlier tonight. Looked fine even when she frosted him when he threw her a wink, tried to squeeze a laugh from her, over-playing the Too-vain thing. It backfired, sure; it made him feel a prize-fighter-sized chump. But the truth was the truth: his crush on Nancy Kools was in fine shape. A crush and a sense he could not dodge, didn't want to dodge - like she was smart like he was. Like she was tuned in like he was. Like she knew whatever there is to know about whatever there is to know. And, well, maybe more - far more.

He twirled his shades, lifted them off his eyes - a repeat of the move he gave Nancy at Harvey's. Winked again - this time into the driver's mirror - pictured the expression on her face.

It said: who the fuck is the cheeky lad? But it also said: who the fuck is the cheeky lad.

Nancy. Sweet sweet Nancy K.

NANCY. Why Joey was here, now, outside the Plough Inn,

about to rip off Harry Blue. After what he just saw, what he discovered Harry B did. Why he was embarking on a mad caper he cooked up in three seconds flat. It was Nancy-inspired, Nancy, Nancy, Nancy. It felt stupid and brilliant; do this and go visit her and tell her all about it, see how it impresses. The frost she gave him for the wink at Harvey's was fine and dandy - it only boosted his admiration for her. His feelings. No, this girl would need to be truly impressed, brought out of herself. Do what he planned, and take it to her, show her the play he made and see if this got her going. Defrosted her.

The play this: rip off the bulging Sainsbury's bag of Es Joey saw Harry drop in the bin and see what happens next.

And if Nancy was not impressed, told Joey where to go, this was still win-win. Was fun, would thwart boredom. Lancaster a one-horse town and the nag three-legged. Part of him was definitely ripping Harry off because he shouldn't. Because it would be funny.

How he ended up here happened like this:

Joey left Harvey's after Harry left the club. Got the idea to follow when he clocked Harry inside the club and it chiming wrong, him being there and who he was with. Harry could and would palm it off as 'research for the book' - his fucking catchphrase. But the dudes in his company - three lads emanating out-of-town, big-style. He was sure they weren't Lancaster or Morecambe dudes. The lead one had a look - like he owned the joint and everyone in there.

Interesting.

They didn't vibe warehouse party organisers Harry met as 'research for the book', though they might be. They didn't vibe DJs Harry met as 'research for the book', though could be. They vibed something else Joey could not quite compute. It piqued his interest - big-style.

When the trio split, headed by the lead-dude, Harry waited a moment, then followed. Joey clocked this and told his mum and Michael 'bye' and quit Harvey's too, hit seaside air.

Joey's thinking: Harry might be meeting the three lads elsewhere - discuss whatever they discussed somewhere quiet. Except, no. Joey got outside in time to see the lads motor off in bottle-green Honda Civic and see Harry sat in his Bentley eyeballing them vamoosh. Then, seconds later, Harry put the '87 Turbo in gear and drove off and Joey jumped in the Fiat and followed him to Westgate, Branksome, the derelict house. Watched Harry walk along the side of the place to the garden at the back, saw him disappear, Joey in his motor at the end of Branksome - the road curved so he could park on the corner and take a clear view while being hidden.

Clear enough to see Harry coming back out the garden and down along the side of the house, cross the road with a Sainsbury's bag he put in the Bentley boot.

Joey's hackles going on seeing this - and connecting with other stuff about Harry. He couldn't be sure but the high-end Bentley, the frustration at 'limited Lancaster' Harry mentioned to him, a wife who mocked, his near-delusional hopes for the book. Harry grew large in Joey's imagination. The oddball shtick, the classical music penchant, the Joseph's suits and moribund marriage to a woman who recast herself 'like a glorified stripper', Harry had told him.

Harry back in the Bentley and heading for Lancaster, Joey following. It looked like he headed to his house on South Road. But no - he drove on. Through town, past the university, and out to Galgate where he reached The Plough and parked up.

Where Joey sat, now, in the Fiat 127 in the precise same spot Harry vacated minutes ago. Joey got out the motor and walked to the bin and pulled the Sainsbury's bag. He glanced once/twice up and down the road and hit the Fiat again.

Hand trembles - fear and exhilaration; he buzzed on the stuff. Star shimmer in the sky. Blood mainlining. His heart jumped and flashed. The Sainsbury's bag was taped shut. He shouldn't open it here where the fuzz could get lucky and nick him, hit him with a ten-year-stretch for possession of copious Class As.

But: exhilaration; he saw a thousand possibilities, endings, beginnings. More endings. Beginnings. What might happen if he got caught, what his life would become, where it would go.

Overriding all this: adventure and, of course, her. Nancy.

FUCK IT.

He did the deed; ripped open the Sainsbury's bag and saw countless bags of pills, thousands of Es. All pink. He looked closer. On each what appeared a tiny embossed - yes - Statue of Liberty emblem stamped.

And, the letters: NY.

FLAAAASH!!!

A gargantuan eureka moment. The same Es Gerard had at his place earlier today; the same he gave Joey for Joey to sell at Harvey's, the Carleton, Gildersome on Saturday.

Meaning this: Harry was Gerard's dealer. Jesus. The nerdy Kremlinologist with a back-catalogue of frustration lorded it over Frenchy and Temmy, without them knowing.

'Hahahahahahahahahahaaahahahaha!'

Meaning, too, Gerard ordered a tanker load of extra dancing pills because he knew a killing would be made at Gildersome by his other dealers.

Then-

Shit.

Coming down the road from the Dolphinholme end of the village - car-lights flashing; Joey's heart near-failed.

The motor moving fast towards Joey. He dropped the bag, veered close to panic. It moved closer. Lights dazzling. His future flashed, burned; how stupid to be caught like this as-

The lights - blinding, dazzling, eyes hurt.

And then the motor passed; carried on towards Lancaster. Joey tried to get his breath back, palms soaked with sweat, heart hammering. The road went quiet, Galgate became countryside village again. He scoped the stars and got an idea: the pills had to be stashed, this was stupid, what will not impress Nancy is being caught by the fuzz.

Joey eyeballed the road up to where it reached the roundabout at the top - nothing. The same the other way, going back to Lancaster - quiet. He took the Sainsbury's bag and hopped out the Fiat and went to the boot and opened it. A panel clipped over each wheel-arch. He took the right one off and felt down, inside. A hollow - large enough to stash the Es; this where he stashed those he sold for Gerard. He put the bag in there, pushed it along the arch, clipped the panel back on.

He made the driver's seat and started the Fiat 127 up, pointed it towards Highland Brow and took the hill, drove three miles to Aldcliffe, motoring under a clear sky by the canal. Fear, exhilaration burned. Now, inspiration - that's what he would do.

Nancy.

She lived on Haverbreaks, Bettargh Drive. He'd been to her house once, a long time ago. When they were kids. Joey got a sense then: Nancy nursed a tenderness, a kid-to-kid thing for him. The friendship never took off - Nancy's family had money and seemed stable, while his featured lost idiot Tony and his frustrated mum.

The bridge over the canal to Haverbreaks Road roved into view. Joey pulled the Fiat over, pushed the driver's seat back, kicked back. Calmness surged; Joey got the feeling - like the stars and him were connected, were in him and he in them. He laughed - at himself - at the mad craziness of being alive, mind flicked back to a book he read once: Siddhartha, by Hermann Hesse. The message pedestrian - that life was all about experience. Tell him something he didn't know; pedestrian - like anyone he ever met.

Except Nancy. The thought of her gave a different feeling.

From a kid, Joey tuned into the myth of people, the world. Break it all down you had nothing, and everything, depending.

The world was wondrous or the world was flat, or the world was both and neither. Nancy was one thing only: wondrous. He hardly ever spoke to her since the day at her house when they were young, but he knew her somehow.

So, come on. He fired the 127 back up and put it in first and took the bridge over the canal, took left for Bettargh Drive, driving down the hill until Nancy's house appeared. No 9 had a nameplate on a double-doored wrought-iron gate that read, Haverhills Lodge. The place on a bluff, giving views of the estate and the area and beyond. Lancaster, the castle, River Lune, the lakes across the bay caught vista-wide.

Joey parked over from No 9 and peered in the driver's mirror at himself, hearing the question in his head. Are you really going to do this?

His heart jumped.

He knew the family set-up. Nancy's folks owned Altobelli's, the Italian restaurant in town. Her dad - Paolo - was from the old country and had a twinkle in the eye and reputation for a wandering one; loved the younger ladies, hiring them as barstaff, waitresses. Nancy's mum - Sharon - was local; she and Paolo made an interesting couple for Lancaster/Morecambe.

Joey scoped the house. High-end. Garage complex one side, glass-walled conservatory the other. Two acres of grass, orchards. A rewind to visiting Nancy the day they were primary school age. An image of summer. Being in the garden under a warm sun, sensing then that he and she were more advanced in ideas than others.

The reverie broke; he realised he possessed zero clue which was Nancy's bedroom. The plan: to stand under it and throw a pebble at her window, explain what he did, why he was here.

Now, though, what? The house was double-floored and double-fronted. Attic on top under one of the Rapunzel-like eaves; a fairy story.

Joey got out the Fiat 127, crossed over and walked the hill to

the house, veered left for the property wall and started climbing-
Shit-

A car coming up the road, moving straight for No 9, headlights beaming. Joey scrambled up the wall and dropped down the other side to grass, moved behind a pear tree, eyeballing the vehicle through the twin-doored gate.

A taxi, stopping, parking by the Fiat.

Emerging from it - Nancy. She paid the driver, said something.

Joey hid behind a pear tree and clicked - she was back from Harvey's and whatever she did afterwards, maybe DJing an after-party, playing more records somewhere. He watched her walk the bluff to No 9, feeling flutters, riding the same Nancy-feeling - she's calm, she's the bomb.

Felt this, as well: now is the time; he took two/three breaths, watched her walk through the gate, up the path towards the entrance. The door to Haverhills Lodge styled olde-English, arch shaped with decorative lion's head knocker, moonlight giving Joey a clear view.

He made his move. Stepped from behind the pear tree, and took three steps and said: 'Nancy.'

She kept walking.

Louder: 'Nancy!'

She turned and jumped and in the same moment relaxed, features going from startled to demure as she shook her head - look at this chump - and moved towards him. Like it was normal to see him standing in her front garden past midnight.

'Joey Miller.'

He got more heart flutters, started to speak. 'It is and-'

Nancy held hand up. 'Two-brain.' A smile as if all the world was in her pockets. 'Or is it too-vain?'

Joey flushed hard. Wondered if it showed in the moonlight.

She smiled more. 'Just out of passing interest - what are you doing here? Peckish maybe? Munchies from too much waccy-baccy?' She indicated the pear tree. 'Craving for some vitamin C? Joey?'

His flush went red-hot; senses rushed and the scene soared and it was like his name got lit up when she spoke it. 10,000 watts of arc-lights. His answer - pure braggadocio. 'You can never have enough vitamins,' Making sure she saw him wink. 'Anyway, fancy bumping into you here. What are you up to? Midnight feast time?'

'Very droll. And for your info, the wink-act is seriously cheesy. It was at Harvey's along with twirling your sunglasses and it is now.'

Joey's flush went fuzzy, joy pitter-pattered; she remembered before, brought this up: it had to be a good sign.

'Interesting,' he said and twirled his shades.

'Even droller.' A smile - like she enjoyed herself. 'I get it, don't worry, you don't have to carry on.'

He took the shades off and winked.

She smiled. 'Come on then, what are you doing here in my garden at midnight?'

He drew breath, felt the moonlight, the orchard, this scene pulse, heighten. 'I- I had to see you.'

She pulled a face - mock quizzical and disbelieving and tapped her watch. 'At this time?'

'It took s- some thinking about coming here now.'

'Seems like you didn't think about it at all.'

'Maybe.'

Tapping her toe like she saw something new in him. 'I'm waiting.'

'Eh?'

'Thought you were supposed to be smart. I'll try one more time - what brings you here? You know, to my house - sorry, my garden, which means jumping the wall - at midnight?'

Joey balled his fists. Here he was, where he wanted to be. 'I've got something I want to tell you, see what you think.'

She nodded and took a moment and nodded and pointed at the house. 'Let's walk.'

'What - inside?'

'I live here, remember.'
'I thought my car might be better.'
'I fancy a cup of tea. You in?'
Joey nodded – of course he was.

Chapter Fourteen

Nancy waited for the kettle to boil and when it did, she filled a 1950s-style, white-coloured tea-pot and waited for it to brew and poured them cups. The kitchen was vast. Brushed steel-finish appliances. A double-fronted fridge-freezer. A double-hobbed range. Two sinks. Gleaming dishwasher. Washtub. Dryer. A marble-topped island at centre where they sat. Feeling of light and air.

'Milk?'

'Please.'

She poured from a jug, eased back on her stool and said, 'Shoot then, and this'd better be good.' Her eyes showed a look, like, actually, she didn't care what Joey said; that the point was he was here at all and showing the kind of chutzpah that brought him here. Joey read this, felt more flutters. He was in a movie; this was actually happening.

He said, 'You know a dude called Harold Blue? Harry. Kind of nerdy, does Primrose Radio, writes stuff for the Lancaster Guardian.'

Nancy's features went surprised mixed with something else. Recognition? Joey thought: she's also in the book. Her expression said she had a lead part in Second Summer of Love - as the DJ, surely. That would take Harry inside warehouse parties, inside Gildersome on Saturday a different way, give a differing perspective.

And by the look she gave him she guessed he was in Harry's book too.

Joey said, 'That's right isn't it - you're in the book? Harry's magnum fucking opus.'

Nancy laughed. 'As are you.'

'Harry told you. Interesting.'

'Not as interesting as why you're here - if you ever tell me.' She got a new expression. Disappointment? 'It's about the book?'

Joey smiled, flicked through scenarios, outcomes. This was going to be fun. 'I am telling you why I'm here - trying to. Harry - as I was saying, and no it's not about Second Summer of Love - though, I suppose it is, tangentially.' He took his time, scoped the kitchen. Came back to Nancy, her eyes. 'Everything's tangential, isn't it?'

'I'm all ears. One moment.' She stood up and left the kitchen, then returned with a Sony cassette player and placed it between them. Slower house music started. A smoochy melody hit Joey's ears. Senses fritzed; the kitchen went hyper-real. Nancy had a kind of magic; he felt a feeling like he did not wish to feel anything else other than this feeling again ever.

Nancy smiled and the smile was the music.

Joey said, 'Harry - okay. He's not just writing this book. He's not just a part-time hack. He's not only a nerd, a radio-head. A frustrated novelist. He's something else.'

'This is starting to sound good.'

Joey nodded. 'You've seen his car, right?'

'Who hasn't?'

'His routine to explain how he can afford to drive a £25K motor when he's an after-hours radio jock and all the rest of it is all about his folks. The rich pa and ma who own half of Bentham, who sugar mum and daddy him. This is clever.' Joey tapped his head. 'Because they are rich enough to support him. In fact, they may well have bought the Bentley for him. You see what I mean? Anyway, cut to the chase - Harry is rolling in it and I mean rolling in his own dosh, and it comes from an interesting source.'

'He's a gigolo?'

Joey laughed. 'Not quite. Ready?'

Nancy sipped her tea and Joey got a big flutter. 'He's a dealer. To nutshell it: he's the major source of E around here. Mr Harold Blue is Lancaster and Morecambe's Mr Ecstasy kingpin.'

Nancy laughed, threw him a what-you-talking-about mixed with an actually-you-may-not-surprise look.

Joey told her: 'If I'm right, he buys in large amounts of E and wholesales them to midlevel dealers who get pills punted out at street level by lads at Harvey's, Carleton, Sugarhouse, warehouse parties, etc.'

Nancy cracked a grin. 'Like you?'

Joey blushed. 'Point is he's shadowy and-'

Nancy held a hand up, asking Joey to stop. Her skin, with that sheen. Light shining from her. She is luminous. Then, the smile - incandescent - more light shining through Joey's twirling shades and cool lad swagger act to say 'hi' like there was only her and him. The smile also telling him something he knew she was going to say before she actually said it.

Which was: 'I know you don't get Es directly from Harry because I know who you do get them from.'

'Go on.'

'Gerard Toces. Lives on Mellishaw, the traveller site there, always with his cousin Tommy-'

'Temmy,' said Joey. He tried to take it in. 'How do you know?'

She shrugged and sipped tea. 'I've been DJing around here since I was fifteen - that's two years, starting with this kind of stuff-' Nancy pointed to an album cover on the corner of the island and reached for it and picked it up and read: 'The House Sound of Chicago Vol.1.' Flipped the cover over, scanned the track listing. 'Chip E. - Time To Jack. Fingers Inc. - Time to Love. Mark Imperial - J'adore Danser.' Put the cover back down. 'From 1985, five years ago, when I was young. Point being, this is when you were still going to the YMCA, Baby Crystal T's.'

Joey flinched; Nancy smiled. She said, 'I can remember when it was speed being taken, acid. Who you think supplied that stuff?'

'Gerard?'

She nodded. 'When pills started coming in, they were taken at warehouses first. This one girl, she was selling oranges at a party somewhere by the canal at Blackburn. She would not, I mean would not, stop smiling. And her eyes - wow.' Nancy laughed. 'Like she had strobe lights in her sockets. You know what I mean? I thought she was happy - like, really happy, until someone tells me she's on something - E. Then they reach Lancaster, a few months later. And guess who is one of those who has them, who is supplying them.'

'Gerard,' Joey said.

Nancy, like it was old news: "And guess who's supplying Gerard Toces.'

Looking at him like he had to know. Joey started to get mind clicks, started to feel stupid too. 'Wait a minute - you think, you're saying, what, that Harry supplies Gerard?'

Nancy threw him an aw-shucks stare. 'Did Two-brain grow a third to work it out?' Saying it soft, saying it with her warm smile.

Joey grimaced. Felt more stupid. Trying to think this through - 'Thing is, Harry isn't the only one importing Es into Lancaster and Morecambe.'

But he knew.

Knew she was correct and wanted to know this: why didn't he see this himself?

Nancy laughed. 'Your face.' Then: 'Of course there's others - Frank Shaw, before he got five years.'

'And more.' Joey smiled. 'But, okay, agreed. You are deffo 100% right and I was-'

'Taking your time.'

He laughed. 'Taking my time.'

'You sussed Harry as Lancaster's Pablo Escobar,' she said. 'How?'

He sipped tea. 'Been following him about a bit. Since the

book thing, he got me curious.'

He saw Harry driving into Gerard's place on Mellishaw Lane. Following him out of Harvey's. 'And tonight, when he leaves as you're DJing and I track him, that's when I find out how he works his operation.' He eyed Nancy. 'You're going to like this - it's all done via anonymous drops.'

'Anonymous drops?'

'He gets the pills brought up here, from London is a guess.' A flash on Harvey's. Harry quitting the place soon after the lad he met left with his two friends. 'Then after the pills have been dropped off at the derelict house on Westgate I tracked him to, he collects the pills from there then drops them at another anonymous drop for his mid-level dealers to collect. Which means, as you say, collected - by Gerard.'

'Where?'

'Tonight's the first time I followed him to a drop and it was a rubbish bin in Galgate.'

'Nice choice.'

'By the Plough Inn. You know it?'

'On the main road. You saw him do this?'

'He parked up by the Plough, got a drink, sat outside, it was final orders time. When the Plough closes, he walks to the Bentley, takes the pills out the boot - they're in a Sainsbury's carrier bag - and drops it in the bin. A load of Es in a plastic bag hidden in a load of rubbish in a bin on the street for Gerard to collect.'

'Then you watched him drive away from the Plough and pleased with your detective work came here? Like Sherlock Holmes with cheaper sunglasses.'

Joey faux-grimaced and twirled his shades. 'This is precisely what I did. Followed Harry, then came here. If you ask me why...' Joey shrugged. 'I read detective books when I was a kid and loved them. I wanted to be in them. Be the detective.'

'Interesting.'

'What's better than being in a made-up story? Being in a real-life one. Otherwise, it's boring, isn't it? Life. You have to make it exciting. But you weren't quite right in what you said. I mean, I did watch him drive away and came here. But I did something first.'

He saw Nancy's eyes widen.

'No.' It was the first time she looked concerned. 'You didn't take them?'

Joey flashed a smile, did a scan of the kitchen. 'You know what, fucking sue me.'

'You steal hundreds of ecstasy pills for an adventure?'

Joey shrugged.

'Now what? You expect me to join you in your adventure?'

He looked at her.

'No way.'

'You haven't heard my plan yet.'

She sighed and broke a smile. 'What is it?'

Joey gave her a goofball look. 'I don't know.'

'You don't know?'

Laughing; he couldn't help it. Nancy's expression and the ridiculousness of what he did.

'I haven't a clue.'

Nancy shrugged. 'Great. As in brilliant. Forget Sherlock Holmes in sunglasses, I've got it now. And forget Two-brain. Well wide of the mark. You're Einstein reincarnate. You steal a batch of ecstasy and come here to get me involved in a masterplan you've yet dreamed up. Sheer unadulterated genius.'

'Yet,' said Joey. 'Yet.'

'Yet?'

'Yet.'

She formed quote-marks with two fingers of each hand. '"Yet". This is great. It really is. Wish I'd made some popcorn to go with the tea, you know, to really enjoy The Joey Two-Brain Miller Show.'

He told her: 'Embrace this. I am. "Yet" is how life should be lived. "Yet" is how stuff, including plans, come to fruition. You understand?'

Nancy wrinkled her nose. 'Do I understand? Oh yes, I understand. That is for sure. I have never understood anything more.'

She stood and went to the sink, filled a glass from the tap, turned and smiled at Joey. 'I have a plan. I just thought of it. Ready? Why don't you get back in your car and drive back to the Plough Inn and put the Es back before it's too late.'

'No way.'

Nancy sat back down. She said, 'You didn't let me finish. My plan is one you're going to like. A lot. You simply drive back and return the Es before they're discovered stolen. Possible?'

'Why would I take them back?'

'We wait to make sure Gerard comes and collects the pills as we expect. When he does, we hatch a plan about how we're going have some real fun when we do actually take the pills.'

Joey got flutters on "we". Her plan, thinking intoxicated too. 'Jesus, I do like it. A lot.'

Nancy's eyes lit. 'Let's go then, while we still have time to put the pills back.'

'You think we have time?'

'We're about to find out.'

Chapter Fifteen

They hit the Fiat. Joey's heart pounded. Scary and crazy; here it was, the adventure he yearned for. A glance at Nancy in the passenger seat. He had zero plan beyond going to her house and seeing what happened. He didn't think about what would happen if she agreed. He got caught in the moment - the thrill.

They both did.

Now, no doubt: this is on.

Nancy pulled the cassette out of her dungarees front-pocket. She retrieved it from the garage on the way to the Fiat. She loaded the motor's tape and pressed play. A piano house tune they heard countless times flooded the car; it still felt fresh, still carried a sadness, too. Like the melancholy that tinged life and waited for them one day was present in the drum beats, the hopped-up electrification of the piano. The way the vocal hit high notes and echoed and re-echoed, re-re-echoed, each new echo the same and yet different as the one before. A madrigal coming at them through the Lancaster night.

Joey swung the Fiat out of Brettargh Drive and joined Haverbreaks Road, steered on to Ashton. Caspian Way became Ashford. The dark surrounded - light-blue streaks lit the sled. Joey went right on Scotforth Road and headed for Galgate.

Nancy kept quiet. They passed the university. Joey piloted the Fiat on into Galgate as the tune got mixed into an ambient seashore sound; the madrigal no more. He slowed and parked the Fiat a quarter mile down from the Plough.

The railway bridge loomed two-hundred yards ahead and just after it the pub and the waste bin. He lifted her hand and slowly brought this to his lips and kissed her fingers lightly.

'I don't care.'

She moved her hand away slow. 'We will if we get caught.'

Joey shrugged. 'First, we won't get caught as I have the perfect plan. Second, there is no "we" in this. If this gets serious, I take the blame, and I mean all of it. If what I say to try and get us out of it isn't believed, then what I'll say is you knew nothing about why we were here until we got here.' A sunglasses twirl. 'And that once you realised what was going on you tried to persuade me to stop - as simple as that.'

Nancy leaned back in her seat. 'Who knew cheesy lines delivered in real life might sound good.'

Joey winked. 'Comes natural.'

Nancy took his chin in her hands and kissed him on the nose. 'My prince of cheese.'

Joey moved forward and Nancy raised a hand.

'What's the plan?'

Joey turned the key in the Fiat and fired the motor up. 'Simple.'

He reached above the driver's mirror and took a pair of shades that were mirrored and gold-tinted, priced 99p from Woolworth's. He swapped these for his aviators and twirled them and flashed Nancy a cheeseball Two-brain smile.

'The plan if we're caught is –that as you smartly suggested– we are only returning the pills.'

She looked up towards the Plough Inn and back again at him. 'For what reason would we return them unless we took them in the first place?'

'Good question. That I haven't figured out yet.'

He put the Fiat in gear and blew her a kiss like the coolest dude Nancy Kools and Lancaster and Morecambe ever saw. Like the world wasn't ready for what was coming.

He loved this. It was life. Adventure. He felt the prince of the world and she the princess of his world, of their real time storybook caper.

Chapter Sixteen

Fifteen seconds later

Joey pulled the Fiat up before the railway bridge. It was arched, straddled Main Road. On the other side The Plough Inn, waste-bin in front. 'Come on - let's do this.'

He reached for the door.

'Joey.'

'What?'

'You're still wearing the shades.'

He cracked a grin. 'Tell me something I don't know.'

Nancy sighed. 'Christ.'

'Come on.'

He got out the Fiat and Nancy followed and they met at the boot. Joey flipped it open and took the cover off of the wheelarch, pulled his sunglasses down his nose, twirled them, shades catching moon-glint. He felt inside, along the wheelarch, found the bag, and pulled it.

'A Sainsbury's plastic bag. You weren't joking.'

Joey caught a first wave of nerves. His stomach lurched; fingers trembled.

Nancy saw. 'What happened to movie star in his Hollywood blockbuster called Life is Yet?'

'Still here. Just about.'

Nancy smiled and leaned forward and kissed him.

A wowzer sensation. Starbursts. Chemicals going off. A sense of another life unfolding here and now. What existence should be.

Nancy, now, saying Joey's line: 'Let's do this thing.'

She took his hand and they moved forward, walking under the bridge, trying to stroll at normal pace. 'Keep like this. Like we're out for a moonlight walk and don't care about anything else.'

'We don't.'

She smiled, clasped his hand tighter. Joey spoke in a low tone. 'I'm going to drop the bag in the bin, then let's turn back for the car like you say, natural.'

They reached the bin. In one action Joey dropped the Sainsbury's bag with the Es into it. He felt his heart ratchet up and pulled her to him and in the moon-glint kissed her.

They broke and laughed and turned and held hands and strolled back under the bridge towards the Fiat. As cool as that. Nothing; no cars, zero other traffic. The sound of the countryside, the sound of-

A motor coming up Main Road. Careering across the concrete.

White, familiar. A white Sierra.

Gerard's motor.

Joey gripped Nancy's hand tight. 'Keep going.'

Nancy threw a smile. 'And talking.'

The car flashed up to them and past in light-dazzle. They kept walking and behind them the sound of the Sierra. The sound of it stopping.

'Fuck,' said Joey.

They made the Fiat 127, got in, Joey pulled the keys, fingers trembling. He fired the car up, put it in reverse and eyeballed the scene ahead: Gerard's car parked up, headlights full-beam, pointing at the bin. Joey did a U-turn, eyeing the Sierra. Coming out the car, two figures silhouetted.

'That's deffo Gerard. Almost deffo he's with Temmy.'

The Sierra's lights lit the scene like Close Encounters. Voices, movement.

'Come on.' Joey pulled the Fiat out and turned it around and away from the Sierra, pointing it towards Lancaster.

Nancy said, 'Stop.'

He touched the brakes. 'What?'

'This is exciting. Like you say, why we are doing this. Turn back around - let's drive past.'

'What?'

'Do it. Drive up there. It will be funny as in hilarious.'

'No way. Frenchy is dangerous.'

Nancy shrugged. 'And? Come on Joey, do it.'

He considered a split-second and then he did a U-turn, facing the Fiat up Main Road again towards the Plough and said, 'let's go,' and hit the throttle and got up to speed quick, driving the Fiat hard and fast along Main Road and under the bridge, towards the Sierra.

Now, turning at the sound of the Fiat, thinking it could be the police, Gerard and Temmy staring at the headlights, the car coming at them. In a moment it gained to where they stood and Joey veered the Fiat 127 Special, near hitting them. Joey hit the horn once making a sound that had them jumping back in a fright and had Joey turning to Nancy and they shrieked in unison as they flashed past the Romani and Joey drove them on up through Galgate and towards Dolphinholme and for the back lanes to turn in these for Haverbreaks, for Nancy's house.

Chapter Seventeen

Brettargh Drive

Nancy led Joey up three flights of stairs to the top floor. She had the whole attic space, spread across the span of Haverhills Lodge. Her folks refurbed it with bedroom and en-suite, living room, large skylight windows.

Everything powder-blue. Wallpaper, two plush sofas, cushions, bean bags, her second set of Technics, these the original 1200s she saved up for when she was fourteen, saved and bought and showed her father and mother she was serious. The pair in the garage were 1210s, a birthday gift for her sixteenth from Paolo and Sharon to say sorry for doubting her.

On the walls - posters, flyers from nights at Park Hall, Hacienda, Monroes, Blackburn warehouses - green and yellow Live the Dream tickets, some of these billing Nancy on the line-up.

Joey sat on a sofa and took a look, trying to take in where he was. Nancy Kools's bedroom. She cued up the sound system, found the tune she wanted.

'I'm house music all the way but this song is-'

She pressed play and a pogoing rhythm entered the room.

Joey recognised it instant. 'Jesus - Tiffany?'

Nancy cocked a hand on a hip and did a slow dance towards him, singing along. 'We're certainly alone now.' A laugh. 'Fluffy pop - listen.' She put a hand to an ear, waved Joey to do the same as on the record Tiffany crooned: 'I think we're alone now.'

Nancy offered the hand and Joey took it and she pulled him up from the sofa and led him in a dance across the carpet. She was close to breathless. 'Don't you think music has magic? Makes you feel invincible. Any of it. All of it.' She paused. 'You ever taken E?'

Joey shook his head.

Nancy did the same. 'Me neither. That's what they do from what I see when I'm out, what my friends say. They connect you with the music, open up a mainline from you to the music and its magic. It's different for me. When I listen to this - pop - it's like listening to house or anything that makes me feel this same way.'

Joey understood. The way she talked was a magic music.

A new song came on and Nancy said, 'How about this - you know it?'

They'd stopped in the middle of the room; they still held hands. Joey listened. 'I don't think so.'

'Don't Stop Believin' - listen to its epicness.' She raised his hand, made it an imaginary microphone, mouthed the words while keeping her eyes fixed on his.

Joey got tingles. The way she looked at him as if she saw how alive he felt. The song peaked and faded and she led him to a sofa. 'Beer?'

'Yes please.'

Nancy went to the small replica fridge in the corner and pulled two Red Stripes and popped these and handed Joey one and sat next to him.

He flushed. 'Have to admit, the cheesy pop was fun.'

Nancy sipped beer. 'Fluffy pop you mean. And it is fun. As will be this.'

'What?'

'Whatever we do next.'

Nancy kept eyes fixed on him and she curved her back and slid off her dungarees and dropped them to the floor, going to t-shirt and underwear. Joey went bright red. Followed with a face that went rictus in embarrassment at blushing.

Nancy laughed

Joey kept looking at her.

She leaned forward and kissed his nose. 'Guess what?'

Joey gulped. Nancy laughed again. 'No, not that.'

She reached for her dungarees on the floor and from the front pocket pulled a bag with two pink pills inside and held the bag to the light.

'What the-'

He took the bag from her. 'Pink New Yorkers.'

Nancy nodded. 'I thought it'd be funny if we kept a sample. Put your sunglasses on.'

'What?'

She looked at him.

'Sure.'

He pulled them from his jacket.

'Put them on and then why not you and I enter a whole new world of ecstasy?'

The room reverberated, the space between them electric.

He put his sunglasses on, opened the bag and handed one of the pills to Nancy and took the other one.

She split her new yorker in half. 'Open your mouth.'

He did.

She placed the half on Joey's tongue and Joey took the other half from Nancy and placed this on her tongue. He lifted his can of Red Stripe to her lips and she took a drink and downed the half, and Nancy lifted her can of Red Stripe to Joey's lips and he took a drink and downed his half an E.

Their eyes gleamed; excitement surged.

'Now,' Nancy said. 'Let the party begin.'

Chapter Eighteen

Three minutes later

Nancy told Joey to finish his beer and pulled two fresh ones from the fridge. He veered between swooning and excitement. She walked in the bedroom and told him to follow and put a mixtape on the cassette player and sat on her bed. The space twice the size and more of the living room. She pointed at herself. 'Why don't you take your jeans off? I did my dungarees.'

He didn't say a word. Did what she said. Sat on the bed beside her. From the cassette player, the opening record of a mix Nancy did. She watched him. Like she waited to see the moment he recognised the song

'Is that what I think it is?'

She nodded.

'Take On Me?'

Another nod.

'First Tiffany, now A-ha. What's going on with DJ Nancy Kools?'

She shrugged. 'My little sister loves this song - I put it on here for her. She was in the garage when I did the mix and asked if I would. How could I refuse?'

Joey nodded.

'Esmerelda and mum and dad. I love them so much. But our family is together yet somehow apart due to mum and dad.'

'What?'

'They don't really talk properly. Like they can't.'

Joey nodded. 'Families.'

'Families.'

She moved from the bed to the cassette player and pressed pause and stood and looked at him. 'Subject change.' She smiled. 'Not only do I like pop, I fancy myself a singer, too.'

'Really?'

'All girls of a certain kind do, don't you know?' Speaking in a candy voiced American 1950s style accent. Like she starred in one of the Saturday matinee movies her mum watched on BBC. Seeing Joey as young as she was in all the ways they could be young. Seeing them together for a long time for a first time.

Seeing the way it could be.

'I have to admit, this is a surprise.' He saw she was happy again. Had forgotten her mum and dad.

'Tomorrow night it won't be a surprise.'

'Tomorrow?'

'At the Brown Cow. There's a kind of cabaret night - for girls, women. Organised by Amber Blue.'

'Harry's wife.'

'Yes. I'm singing. Come along. You can mime or sing and I'm doing the latter.'

Joey cracked a grin. 'I wouldn't miss it for being able to pilfer all the ecstasy tablets in Lancaster, Morecambe, Galgate and Heysham.'

'What I wanted to hear.' Nancy sipped at her beer. 'And to get on my soap-box for a moment - those who don't like pop are missing out.'

Joey drank from his can of Red Stripe. 'Go on.'

Nancy smiled. 'My theory is that you hear pop everywhere so it gets inside your head and starts to mean something. Whether you like it or not.'

'Pop to affect the senses. Why not…'

'The imagination.'

She unpaused the tape and the A-ha song faded and the next track faded in. 'Magic. The name of this one. Proper house. Just listen to that beginning.' An air-raid siren sound. A visceral sense. The world concertinaed. Nancy began skipping around the bedroom. She stopped. Pirouetted on the spot. Blew Joey a kiss. 'It's from 1987 and from the future. Listen to the vocal.' It soared. The night outside and the two of them in the bedroom. A sense of another life. Myriad lives. All made real by the way the tune sounded. The song moved to the end and on the tape the next one was mixed in, mixed in by Nancy one day and one time in her garage at the foot of the big house when she and the music that was a balm and triumph and a passion came together in a communion mixed as a one-off artefact record forever, or as for as long as the tape could be played, and here now she and Joey communed again with these moments and she clicked her fingers and said, 'Here comes the next one.' Double thumbs-upped him, threw them at Joey like a gunslinger and said, 'Ker-pow-pow-pow. Ker-pow-pow-pow.'

He cracked a grin and Nancy danced over to him and she kissed him and here came a feeling that came fast and out of no place known before and was like the half a pink new yorker could be starting to work. Nancy got the same, a sensation of butterflies in her fingers, an off-kilter sense, as if the walls of the bedroom contracted and she felt a push and pull sensation come at her body and her head and her mind.

'Fuck.'

Joey looked half-scared. 'It's working?'

'I'm-' Nancy held her hands out; watched them flutter, felt her arms go light. Something in her eyes, too. Heart. Senses. Mind and brain whirling. A frightening yet wonderful kind of psychosis started in.

Joey - wide-eyed: 'You're shaking.'

Nancy clocked the walls, the posters and the flyers. There - Thursdays at Park Hall, the club by Charnock Richard services.

On it her name - DJ Nancy Kools, the date last Easter. She did it straight. She did all her gigs straight.

Zilcho drogas.

She was starting to feel rather very far from straight. From zilcho drogas.

Telling Joey: 'I never wanted to do pills before, never fancied it. I see what they do all the time when I'm out DJing-' She felt the flutter swarm over her. Like limbs took off and like something else too: like every part of her twinkled and shone.

'What?' Joey said. "What do you see them doing?'

Nancy smiled and the smile felt centuries old and the stars streamed out of her. She started to speak; speaking felt hard, speaking felt amazing. She giggled. 'You must see it yourself, Mr Two-brain. What Es do. You sell enough of them.'

'I do - and I like what I see.'

'Really?'

'What's not to like - everyone cuddles, declares never-ending love for each other and dances and enjoys themselves. Enjoys being themselves.' Joey thought about it. 'To be honest I'm not sure why I've never done one before.'

They smiled and a flashbulb popped between them.

'When you describe it like that...'

Light - cascading. Nancy - overtaken by a sensation like she was drunk, kind of. Her legs and arms quivered. More stars and an undeniable age-old wisdom that silliness was contained in everything everywhere. Difficult to speak. As if her eyes grew and widened. Everything grew - the room and walls, music. Joey - how wonderful he was. He has no clue how wonderful he is. He laughed and waves emanated, moved through her. Something loomed over them.

Joey laughed at something and there were more waves, a cartoon sense and he sounded silly. Funny-silly, E-silly. Nancy forgot her whole life in half a second and remembered it all again and in another split second she heard him say something and the words boomed down as if from a 1,000-floor skyscraper before it was like it may never have happened. Joey was still speaking. She tuned back in. Tried to.

Wow - his face-

'That's the thing with an experience,' Joey said. 'Until you try it you don't know why you would like it so why would you? Try it, I mean?'

The room got vibrations, quivers. Joey's face roved in and out and the ceiling whoooosed and the carpet was the most dazzling colour.

Time and space.

Being sucked in.

And-

A fairground ride like the heart is a big dipper and the world wheels on moons bursting and the music playing is suns and dawns and dusks and this is like jumping from a gorge into a deep-blue sea that is never coming.

Never com-

Nancy tried to speak and couldn't and she relaxed.

Just relax.

WHOOOOOOOOOOOOSH.

Chapter Nineteen

Later

This is all of what all is.

Nancy fixed eyes on Joey. Joey was hypnotised. How long were they like this? Time shifted - years stretched slow and fast. The room jagged, eyesight blurred. Nancy moved to the cassette player and found a tape and put it in and hit play.

A woman singing a solitary word. 'Alright. Alright. Alright.' Nancy twirled, waved Joey to his feet. The vocal changing. 'Ecstasy. Ecstasy. Ecstasy.' The vocal changing. 'Rock to the beat. Rock to the beat.'

Like the stars stream light, the sun races to the end of the universe. Nancy started kissing Joey and the world collapsed and was remade and she said, 'Our lives are only beginning.'

The half a pink pill kept coming. Heavy metal crash and burn. Rushes hit hard; electricity bolted.

The planets aligned; they were celestial. Constellations. The sun. The past and future.

Us.

They fell into each other's arms.

'This is amazing.'

'You are amazing.'

Pink new yorker rushes became caresses. Soft pillows.

Joey said 'What next?'

Nancy held his hand. 'Adventure, of course. Starting

tomorrow.' Her eyes flashed.

Joey remembered. 'The Brown Cow.'

'Amber Blue's revue night. Harry will be there to see his wife's show. And I will too, singing pop, and you too, watching me sing pop.' Nancy's eyes strobed. Like she an ethereal alien come to earth only to let him know how special he was and always would be. 'Let's forget Harry. And start this.'

'What?'

She kissed him and they fell onto the bed and it was like the bed centrifuged and it was like they did too and it was more than this.

It was something else.

Chapter Twenty

Harry

No 21 South Road

Harold woke late in his studio after sleeping on the Chesterfield. He placed the sofa direct under the skylight for a view of stars if he slept up here - like he often did. Like Harry did last night after the drop of the consignment of pink pills in the wastebin by the Plough, getting in late, not getting into bed with Amber.

He heard her. Downstairs with Lottie, their daughter soon to go to school. The floor below had his and Amber's bedroom, plus Lottie's. Harry's studio took the whole third floor. The studio a den, hideout. He made notes on Second Summer of Love at the Herman Miller desk, playing classical on the Marantz sound system. Notes scribbled with silver-plated cross fountain pens. Harry was Lancaster Royal Grammar School educated. The LRGS way that their pupils write with quill style pens.

He flipped, played Mozart and hit the ensuite and took a hot shower with plenty of suds and got out and brushed his teeth and got dressed and took the two flights to the ground floor. A living room, study, dining room. Kitchen at the rear of the house. The garden overgrown. Apple trees, wild rhubarb. Halfway down, a beat-up shed. At the bottom, a forgotten greenhouse. By the kitchen, a chicken run with a black rooster, three red hens.

Harry walked into the dining room. Lottie sat at a plate with eggs and buttered soldiers, ready to dip. The girl had ringlet curls and clear blue eyes and wore her Bowerham Primary School smock. Her eggs were blue-speckled. Harry pointed at them.

'Pauline's?' The little girl giggled and tossed her curls. She was six and knew her dad's sense of humour. The joke was that Pauline was the only hen who could lay eggs so they had to be hers.

'Yes, daddy.'

Amber came in from the kitchen and Harry saw she did her hair again in blonde tints that lit up in the dining room lights. Amber had a BA in History and a MA in Dialectics and lectured part-time at Lancaster University, and it wasn't enough. She knew what she wanted, which was to get back out there and enjoy the night as she did when she a younger woman. She told Harry and Harry understood. He was frustrated too. Came alive at night too. The radio show, pill drops for Gerard, the book on the Blackburn warehouse parties. Amber wanted to sing cabaret so she started an evening for women she knew who felt the same.

The evening was tonight at The Brown Cow. Harry saw Amber on stage under the smoky red and blue lights and he saw the pub crowd braying as she and other women sang and performed.

A pang. At what he missed with Amber. He could relate to what his wife wanted but relating to Amber herself was different.

She said, 'You were late in and now you're up late?' The colour rose in her cheeks.

'The two are related,' Harry said. 'Late in at night, late to rise in the morning.' He moved to kiss her and she moved away. He counted on her doing so. He played the passive husband act 24/7. He had zero other option. The pang faded, turned to hostility.

'Why were you?' Amber said.

He ignored her and sat down opposite Lottie and scanned the table. A cafetiere of fresh coffee, orange juice, a jug of milk, a pot of tea. China cups, knives, a rack of toast, jars of peanut butter and marmite. Amber passed him the cafetiere and Harry poured a cup.

'Do you not like having breakfast with us? Time with your

daughter before she goes to school? When Lottie's back you'll be out at the radio, no doubt.'

Harry smiled. 'Thanks for the coffee.' He reached across the table and tousled Lottie's hair. 'Of course I want to see my darling girl. Why I'm taking her to school this morning.' He fixed a smile and sipped coffee, smothered a laugh and snuck a peek at Amber.

'How come you've got time to take her?'

'Because I worked late last night to make the time to take Lottie. That's why I was late in and late up.'

'I see.' Then: 'Is this going to be a regular thing - taking Lottie to school?'

Harry nodded and looked at his wife and beyond her and saw the younger one who had dreams for both of them. Now, only dreams for herself. Where did the woman go who laughed at becoming Amber Blue when they'd marry? Silly name. Two colours.

She said, 'Did you hear that, darling? Daddy's going to take you to school now every day.'

Harry sipped coffee. 'Not every day. I didn't say that.'

'But some days, daddy?'

'Yes darling, definitely.'

Amber said, 'You coming tonight? To the Brown Cow?'

He pretended to think about it. 'I've been promising to come along and tonight feels like the right night.'

Amber smiled.

Lottie dipped the end of a soldier into her last egg and ate it. 'Come on, let's go.'

They left the house and Harry picked the little girl up and fastened her into the child seat in the back of the Bentley and fired the '87 Turbo on and pointed it up South Road towards Bowerham.

Chapter Twenty-One

The Brown Cow

The townboozer rated close to packed out. The crowd classic Brown Cow evetime demographic. Lancaster University/St Martin's College lecturer and student types. Dole-ites, dope smokers, speed-devotees, Brown Cow regulars cheesed off at the swollen numbers attracted by Amber Blue's women only revue evening she called Night Creatures.

A saloon and bar room. The saloon at the front, large/near-cavernous. Stage to the right. An old-style bar on the left with mirror across its span carrying letters etched in a bygone time: 'ALES AND BEVERAGES SIX-PENCE'. Pumps did pints of Guinness and John Smith's and Skol. Tables, booths dotted the saloon. Punterati mobbed the bar. They were two, three drinks in. The place started to jump and raise noise.

The stage got lit cabaret-style under Amber's order. A single spotlight shone on a single microphone on a stand. At tables by the stage - groups of women garbing costume: burlesque, heart-throb singer, Vera Lynn wartime done-up, sixties beehives, other regulation, one-pony-town glam-attire.

Harry got roped in by Amber to help once he confirmed attendance. When Amber said, you can do the lighting, the intro/outro music, Harry felt a new sensation - a warmth. She involved him.

Also, this: he had business to consider. He left a message at the note-drop - a place he used on the Marsh Estate, where

Gerard could leave messages if needed and Harry could collect anonymously, retain his cover.

Gerard left one this morning, about last night's pill consignment he left in the bin outside the Plough. The note from the Romany said, 'This is two pills short. Let me know.'

Harry chuckled and weighed it up. His merriment concerned this: two pills? Two??? Gerard 'Frenchy' Toces was certainly professional and parsimonious. You had to hand it to him, counting out a batch of 500 pills to find 498 - two short - showed keen business-sense; flagging it up via the note a quasi-Scrooge act.

Having to weigh this more seriously: Harry knew the batch was not two short when he delivered it. He didn't count the pills out - he weighed the 500 Pink New Yorkers on scales so it was bona fide bomb-proof the 500 drop was 500 and not 498.

So, what then? Did Gerard lie? Was he trying to be clever? Rip off only two tablets and pull a huckster act and see what happens? Maybe to prepare the ground for a bigger rip-off of a future pill drop - the next one, for instance? Harry could picture, hear Gerard, in his Romany-brogue, telling his cousin: 'Let's keep two of these sweeties back, see what our man does. You with me, Temmy?'

Let's see.

Harry stood at the back of the saloon controlling the lighting rig: a console on a table with three switches, lights. He controlled the sound too via a decade old tape player amped to speakers. He had a Johnnie Walker Red and coke going, refilled it surreptitiously from his pocket-bottle.

Harry slugged the brew and extrapolated on Gerard, the missing pills.

Three options.

1: Buy what GT said in the note, re-up the two New Yorkers, chalk it off as simple oversight, wait and see what happened next.

2: Call Gerard's bluff - the pills were there - this is on you, Frenchy Toces.

3: Pretend to buy it.

No 2 didn't feel right, and No 1 was the same as No 3. So, write a note, offer apologies for the 'oversight', re-up the two tablets and see if it happens again.

If it did, he had a plan. He had to for this potentially happening. Pills were new in Lancaster/Morecambe but the market was established quick. Es got snaffled like candy by the kids making the trade a money tree.

Pre-Harry hooking up with Frederick Street, no one heard of them around here. How it began - Harry and Amber and Lottie went to Rhodes Island last summer for a break. He met Frederick and his chums in a Rhodes Town bar one night on the strip. Frederick was nineteen, his eyes lit like twin moons. Demeanour something else. Vibrant, dark. Harry's Kremlinologist antennae perked. They got talking - business, eventually. Frederick S had Es couriered in from Amsterdam - thousands and thousands at dirt cheap price. Supplied them to something he called 'raves' in London that took place around the M25; cockneys went mental for them. On them.

Frederick was young and rich from the E trading - plus other ventures, Harry's antennae told him.

Harry wondered why the Fredster let him in on this. Then, worked this out quick and it unnerved. Street saw something in Harry that Harry didn't realise was in him. Palsied ambition.

Frederick saw a new market opening up - the north-west. He saw Harry as franchise holder of the Lancaster/Morecambe branch of the Frederick Street E trade. They kept chatting post-Rhodes and the rest became backstory leading to today, to this: Gerard Toces apparently missing two Pink New Yorkers.

'Harry.'

Amber broke his reverie.

'Stop daydreaming. We're about to start.'

He smiled. 'I was dreaming - of Russia, kind of.'

She grimaced and she smiled. He swung between wanting away from her and the precise opposite feeling.

'You ready?'

'Am I ready to turn a dial and hit play on a cassette?' Harry said. 'I am primed with a 100-font capital italicised P.'

Amber tossed her tints, turned for the stage area. She wore a Mary Quant skirt purchased from a Penny Street charity shop, ankle high red boots, a grey fur with showy lapels that went to her knees. She called it 'Amber Glam' and Harry rated the costume as apter than apt.

The Saloon Bar entrance opened and Nancy entered with Joey. Holding hands. Star-crossed lovers. A turn up for his book. Harry chuckled. Second Summer of Love would benefit from two of the main players having a 'thing'. The whole world had a thing. No thing, no world, no anything. That was the thing.

Amber waved to him - press the button, play the music, throw lights. He did - opening bars kicked in, Sinatra's version of That's Life. The stomping defiance. The soaring voice. Tones of honey and Hoboken and Sinatra laying down the track in '66 at United Western Recorders at 6000 Sunset Boulevard, Hollywood.

On cue, Amber hit the stage and drew copious applause. Harry dialled the lights into a wee-hours, neon-tinged red spotlight on his wife. Nancy and Joey hit a table near the stage. Harry's eyes moved from them back to Amber and she said, 'Ladies and gentlemen and-' She faux-peered out into the dark lit saloon bar room. 'Sorry, I should say, night creatures. That's the name of our show and, I think, an apposite description for all of us here.'

Amber fielded a heckle. "Apposite?' Speak English, woman.' Followed by a raucous cackle.

Harry peered through the smoke-filled saloon and caught a bee-hived-bewigged revue participant pulling at a cigarette.

Blue smoke twirled in the light.

Amber said, 'That's enough from you, Lacey - or should I say, Cilla.'

The crowd group-chortled - there's Cilla Black, ready for her turn.

Amber smiled; let it play out. Said, 'As I was saying before being so "rudely heckled" - we are night creatures and this is our night.'

Amber pointed at the sign placed at the back of the stage. "NIGHT CREATURES" spelled in glowing purple neon bulbs. 'Our first night creature will be 'Talented Talulah' doing a favourite of hers. Let's hear it for her, please.'

The Brown Cow broke to applause, Amber signalled Harry and he flipped the Sinatra cassette out, replaced it with the cassette on which were recorded the numbers for the acts in running order. Talented Talulah hit the stage. She wore a sparkly get-up - blue dress, gown, scarf, sparkly blue heels. Short hair bleached white.

Harry hit play. The first notes lifted the mood - Erasure's A Little Respect. It was a backing track, ran sans-vocals as Talulah took the mike. A demure figure with a vocal range that held on high notes. She crooned 'I hear you calling, pleeeeeeeeeeeeeeeasssssse'. Smalltown, big emotion vibe. The Brown Cow saloon bar got to its feet. Tables in the by-stage area emptied as they danced.

Joey and Nancy. Young love. How long would it last? As long as the hot months? As long as the summer of love of Harry's book? All was ephemeral, was it not? The Erasure track moved towards denouement; the saloon bar crowd ratcheted to feverish. The boozer recast as mutual adoration parlour.

Coming through the crowd - Nancy. Her eyes. Ethereal. A kind of magic you wanted to be touched by. She wore a trench coat that went to her knees and she smiled and she offered Harry a hand and he got a picture of DJ Nancy Kools playing acid house records at a warehouse party. Sending the kids elsewhere. To a heaven transient and elusive. Only found at the parties. Harry made a mental note re his book. Watch her at Gildersome on Saturday. Capture when she opens the warehouse party as the first DJ. Write lyrical about the moment this will be. What her music does to the kids.

She said, 'Harry - fancy seeing you here.' A nod towards the stage. As if Nancy knew Amber was his wife so why would he not be here. He felt her vibe again. She was who she was.

'It's a small town.'

They laughed and Nancy pulled a tape from her trench coat and said, 'If you can play this later, please, that would be great. After your wonderful wife's show has finished, I mean. Just the first song.'

'I can't, I mean- I'm not sure.' Feeling himself burn red. He dialled down Erasure, ejected the tape, put the one with That's Life back on, hit play, dialled volume back up, doused the stage lights and raised the house lights.

He saw Nancy observe him and saw something else. Her appearance/features. They showed a sheen different from their usual luminosity. Over Nancy's shoulder, Joey at the bar. He waved, made a drinking action with a hand and Harry said, 'Nancy, what would you like to drink? Your boyfriend is asking.'

Her eyes glittered.

'You are then, how should I say, an item?' Harry said.

More glittering eyes. 'An item? Kind of. Let's wait and see.'

Harry nodded, pointed over her shoulders. 'He's still waiting - what do you want?'

'He knows what I'm having - he's asking you. What do you fancy?'

'That's very kind.' Harry held his glass up. 'A Johnnie Red, please.'

'Sure,' said Nancy. 'Back to the music.' She waved her cassette. 'As I said, could you play this after the show, please?'

'The landlord might not be up for acid house.'

Nancy smiled like she understood Harry, the landlord, herself, the world. 'It's disco - the women will get up to dance to it and if the women dance the boys will follow.'

Harry could buy that. He'd buy anything she sold as truth. 'Sure.'

She pressed the cassette into his hand. 'Thanks. Think I am on next.' Her smile and the sheen and the glittering eyes. She headed back to the stage and Harold was transfixed and Joey moved over from the bar holding the drinks, palmed Harry his. 'Fancy seeing you here, Harold.' He raised his pint. 'To you, to your book and your artistic endeavour, and, really, your way of existing.'

Joey: is he on something? His mantra is never touching anything. They chinked glasses. The kid had the same sheen as Nancy; maybe it's a goofy, we-just-got-together thing. Or, maybe, they did take something.

Not something.

A specific thing: E. That's what the sheen, the vibe reminded him of.

And yet.

Joey and Nancy told Harry they didn't take E or anything else. Plus, this is a rainy night in Lancaster. He pushed the thought away. 'That's very kind, Joey,' Harry said. 'I salute you, too.'

They chinked again, Joey twirled his shades, walked to the by-stage area and Nancy. Amber threw the signal and down went the volume on That's Life and the house lights, up came the red spot hitting the stage. She had the mic in hand. She said, 'Our next night creature is Dusty Springfield-'

Harry tuned out, looked for the running order tape, loaded it up, waited for Amber's cue. His wife saying, 'Here she is - Dusty Springfield!'

Stepping on stage - Nancy. Harry double-took; Nancy ditched her trench coat to reveal full Dusty S regalia - florid pink dress, a platinum wig, heavy make-up a la Springfield. Amber handed Nancy/Dusty the mic, signalled Harry.

He hit play and bars of prancing notes kicked in.

Then, the vocal.

Nancy mouthed to it and Harry realised he knew the song.

'Since you've been away, I've been hanging around-'

The crowd went nuts, on their feet, jigging, whooping, singing along, Dusty's voice angel-like.

The track wound down, Nancy/Dusty stopped singing. The Brown Cow exploded applause, the bar was mobbed, punters desperate for more drinks. Harry hit the house lights, switched tapes, put That's Life back on.

Saw Nancy/Dusty leave the stage, take Joey, the two walk to the bar.

The saloon entrance opened - in came Gerard and Temmy Toces.

Interesting.

Very interesting.

Why were Frenchy and his cousin here?

Chapter Twenty-Two

Thirty seconds later

Nancy ran a post-performance flush and buzz. She downed Red Stripe at the bar with Joey - hurled the stuff back. They both felt last night's pink pill linger; wallowed in a post-new yorker wonderland. An ambient sense - like they/the Brown Cow floated. The booze they drank cocktailed with the post-pink pill linger, the brew an elixir; they could not stop smiling. They'd slept at Nancy's from early morning to mid-afternoon. They'd woke to a quiet house - the rest of the family at the restaurant. They showered, ate zilcho, came here.

Now - Amber on stage, calling the incoming night creature up.

Nancy: 'Fun - that was fun.'

'And everyone else is having fun too. Why that song?'

'Dusty Springfield's a legend. Pet Shop Boys are legends too. What Have I Done To Deserve This is perfect pop.'

'I see.'

'Jesus.'

'What?' said Joey.

Nancy looked past Joey. 'Don't turn around but guess who just walked in?'

Joey twirled his shades. 'Frenchy and Temmy.'

Nancy double-took. 'You are sixth-sensed.'

Joey laughed. 'I have to admit - wow - I was only joking.'

Nancy watched the Toces cousins hit the far end of the bar, waited to see if they saw them. Chinked her pint glass with

Joey's. 'Are we to find out if they saw us at the Plough last night?'

Joey drank Red Stripe. 'So cool, Nancy Kools.'

Her eyes glittered like hers only could. 'This is our movie, our adventure. We are cooler than cool.'

Joey smiled. 'Movie stars.'

'The heroine and hero.'

'I know what the next scene is.'

'It's where Gerard and Temmy walk up and say hi and we are cooler than cool. More heroine and hero than heroine and hero.'

Joey nodded. 'Here they come.'

Gerard and Temmy Toces moved towards them. Each wearing their particular smiles.

'Remember I peddle their pills so there might be chat about that. If so, play it all natural.'

'Don't worry baby,' Nancy said. 'This is our movie. This is our summer.'

Chapter Twenty-Three

Gerard bought a round. He teemed bonhomie. Eyes blue as blue, blond hair shining in the saloon bar lights, coiffured, extra-wavy. Like he'd had it salon-ed.

Red Stripes for Nancy and Joey, Guinness for him and Temmy. A bottle of champers in a bucket for whoever fancied a glass. Gerard threw money around. The Romany's patter went this way: 'You only live once; you know what I'm saying? I know Temmy knows what I'm saying. I know Joseph here knows what I'm saying. And as for the young lady, I'm sure she knows what I am saying too.'

Nancy nodded and weighed Gerard up. He's the brains, the brawn, charisma, everything else. Temmy's along for the ride and a ride it certainly is with Frenchy. Temmy is not as cut-throat as he projects. Like he got trapped in an act.

They took a glass of champers each, Joey pouring. The barman double-took at Gerard ordering the bottle: buying champagne in the Brown Cow in midweek in Lancaster? Whatever next? He made a show of palming a bar-towel and dusting the bottle off. Popping the cork. Punters who took in the show whooped.

They swigged and downed the fizz and Gerard refilled their flutes and the bottle got killed. Nancy sensed Gerard wanted to say something. Here he came, leaning forward. Saying: 'You have an interesting look.'

She got propositioned 24/7. Her take on lads, the male sex in general: they lacked class. Not all, sure. Some were cool, like Joey. He had looks and class. Most lacked the latter while having the former, which was a shame. For them.

'I don't mean anything by this, you with me?' Gerard continued. 'I mean, you look Italian, you must have Italian folks. That's unusual for these parts, right? Do you get me?'

Nancy got wrongfooted; Gerard indicated Temmy. 'He's got his own look, too. You get me?'

A pause. Temmy shook his head; he heard it umpteen times. Gerard bellowed laughs, Temmy joined in - what else could he do? - and Nancy too. She still tried to decipher Gerard. Joey saw. The Romany was nineteen going on ninety-nine.

Gerard eyeballed them curious. 'You two on something? You've got that - what me and Tem call it - the look.'

Temmy nodded.

Nancy felt a chill - where's this leading? She said, 'We may be having our own party. You know what I mean?'

Gerard nodded at Joey. 'I thought you didn't "take those things".'

Temmy crowded in. Getting interested.

Joey, smooth: 'And you'd be right to think that because it is - was - true. Until last night.' He leaned in; got a bashful look. Played up to them. 'You know what we mean, gentleman?'

A pause.

Nancy laughed; Gerard and Temmy baulked at 'gentleman' - the effect comic, a near-blush from both. Like the word came from a language, a world they got reminded of existed and did not like.

Gerard found a smile. 'I will drink to that. You two taking your first pills and it's those fucking pink pills. Rocket fuel, aren't they? You with me?' He split a grin like he was on one of the pills now. Or several. The grin warm, manic. Like Gerard saw stuff in Joey and Nancy that amused the fuck out of him. 'And do I mean, rocket-fucking-fuel.'

Temmy eyeballed them. 'Lovebirds? How very romantic.' His eyes woozed; the look he fixed on Nancy was like he could do what he wanted with/to her. Nancy smiled - she received the look umpteen times; knew she'd spend her life throwing this off.

But, Temmy: the scar, the eyes, the sense he subconsciously sensed he was Gerard's patsy made him, what? Mean, sure. Also, vulnerable. Which meant kind of sweet. She raised her glass to Temmy's and they chinked and Joey and Gerard followed.

Grins all round - Nancy got an "interesting" vibe from Gerard: the dreamy look in the eyes - like he fielded stuff. 24/7.

They drained their glasses. On stage Amber made way for the latest night creature. 'Here is Rhonda Streisand,' she told the saloon, and moved out of the spotlight as a Yentl-era Barbara S, cropped hair, garbed as a 1900s Jewish boy appeared. Nancy saw the movie more than once; identified with Yentl's girl-has-to-be-boy storyline from DJing thc lad-heavy circuit.

Rhonda Streisand started crooning Yentl - from the movie soundtrack. The crowd whooped, they were copious drinks and other substances in. The Brown Cow saloon bar approached fever pitch. Like the night would not and could not end ever. Must not.

Gerard said, 'You two would know this far more than Thomas here-' A forced grin from his cousin, understanding Frenchy rated him as thick, uncouth, uncultured. Knowing only the first of these adjectives but smart enough to know how he was viewed. 'This is the kind of place,' Frenchy said, 'that Sinatra would have started out in when in Hoboken. You with me?'

A blank from Joey and Nancy.

Gerard, grinning: 'You know, New Jersey, where he was from, where Ol' Blue Eyes started his fucking crooning.' A nod in Harry's general direction. 'That's Life keeps being played, I notice - what a Frankie boy classic.'

Joey said, 'A place like the Brown Cow in New Jersey? I'm not sure-'

'Hoboken. To be specific.'

'Don't get him going,' Temmy said.

Nancy wanted to get Frenchy going. 'A bar is a bar, a pub a pub. I get it, Gerard. Sinatra would definitely have fit in here, a night creature 100%. He basically invented this kind of thing.' The boozed-up saloon, the crowd lost to the evening. The glitzy-costumes and low-slung lights. The after-dark hours sense. She said, 'Never mind Hoboken, looks like a bar in Las Vegas and correct me if I am wrong, but didn't Frank practically invent Las Vegas, too?'

Gerard chortled - he took a shine to Nancy Kools. 'That, Frankie boy did.' He pulled a bag of pink pills. Did a faux-concerned is-anyone-watching scope of the saloon bar. The Es sparkled in the lights as he palmed four, dished them out. He and Temmy necked theirs instant with slurps of Guinness. The New Yorkers got chased with the black stuff.

Nancy exchanged a look with Joey and told Gerard: 'Thanks, but it's no thanks from us.'

'Yeah,' said Joey. 'Very kind of you but no thanks. We want to keep last night special.'

Gerard flashed a silver/gold toothed smile. 'How sweet.'

'Touching,' said Temmy. 'Touching.'

The Toces cousins slurped Guinness. Nancy and Joey kissed. The Toces cousins raised their pints to the lovers.

'The reason we're here is not only for a laugh,' said Gerard. He indicated Nancy and addressed Joey. 'Since you're together I can say what I have to say in front of the good lady?'

Joey got prickles. 'That's cool.'

Nancy knew what was coming, fixed vacant eyes Joey. A flicker moved across his face. He hoped he killed it.

Gerard said, 'We may or may not have been ripped off last night.' He smiled his smile. 'Now, I won't go into the details except to say we were two pills down.' He grimaced - like the loss personally hurt.

Joey knew how to play this. '200 pills is a lot to be down.'

Gerard scowled. 'Two.'

Joey kept playing the act. 'Two?'

'You mutton jeff,' said Temmy.

Nancy laughed and joined in Joey's act. 'You're down two

pills? Hardly the Great Train Robbery.'

Joey bellowed laughs. 'Yeah, come on. Could just be a mistake? An oversight from your supplier.'

Gerard kept smiling his smile that was no smile at all. 'I know that. But, on the other hand, maybe not.' The smile became a stare he fixed on them. 'Why we are here.'

Temmy said, 'When collected them the bag was open. It's usually taped up.'

Joey got chills. 'Go on.'

'Go on,' said Gerard, 'is we're wondering if someone planned to rip the whole lot off then for whatever reason decided not to. This time. You know what I'm saying?'

He stared at Joey. He stared at Nancy.

Joey nodded, shifted the act he played. 'Fucking hell.'

'Oh yes,' said Temmy. 'Fucking hell.'

Gerard drank his Guinness, kept eyes on them. 'Reason we're here, reason I'm telling you this is simple - keep an ear out, you hear someone saying they'll be in business soon, serving up pills on our turf, or saying they can get a job-lot, you know; if you're interested in serving up for them - let me know.'

Joey nodded. 'Of course.'

'Trust me,' said Gerard. 'If this is what's going on, we'll find out.' He ran a hand through his long hair.

Joey pretended to give the matter thought - wondered if this was all a coded message to him.

Gerard moved a hand through his hair, the coiffured mullet bouncing in the saloon bar lights. Told Temmy: 'Come on - let's leave the lovebirds alone. Nice to meet you, Nancy. Joey, look after this young lady.'

Temmy put a finger to his lips. 'Sssshhh. You know what I'm saying. Do not be telling anyone you shouldn't about this.'

'Sure, of course.'

They moved away into the saloon. Joey and Nancy watched them take a table.

Joey, low voice: 'What do you think?'

'That you played them sweetly and, no, I don't think they suspect. I do, though, see that neither of them are stupid. Especially Gerard.'

Joey nodded. 'I hear you.' His shades were hooked to the top of his T-shirt. He took them, placed them on, and Nancy laughed. 'Too-vain is back.'

Joey, cheesyball-tone: 'He never left, baby. But never mind Too-vain, did you clock Gerard's hair? I'd bet serious fucking dollar he's had that done. I mean I know he's a natural blonde but the more I was looking at that mullet of his in these lights, the more I'm thinking it's tinted.'

Nancy laughed. 'Semi-permed, too.'

'His curls are natural too.'

'You think?'

'To be honest I've never asked and don't plan to.'

Nancy pointed. 'Look, on stage. Amber.'

It was her turn on the Night Creatures bill - Amber's get-up a female Barry Gibb, Saturday Night Fever vintage. The soundtrack started in; Amber belted out Staying Alive in a Barry G-falsetto. It was actually higher - the effect comical. She sang live, no mouthing. She sang for laughs and joy, and the laughs and joy showed.

Nancy and Joey howled.

Joey saying, 'Jesus. The windows could go here.'

Nancy was in pieces - as if she'd die from laughter and what a way to go: how high is Amber pitching her pipes voice??? 'Where the hell did she get that voice from? An interesting wife for Harry. He's the dark horse who keeps getting darker.' She took Joey's hand. 'Going back to Gerard for a moment - forget the smile and the hair, those eyes tell the truth. Talk about blue and icy. I think he suspects anyone and everyone. It's his nature. Default setting. It may "only" be two missing pills but it's a matter of pride and honour for him.'

'You think he'll find out, then - that it was us?' Joey took his shades off so they were eye-to-eye. 'That it was me, I mean. No way are you anything to do with the dastardly plot of the missing pills of the Plough Inn wastebasket.'

Nancy smiled. 'If we're in this together, we're in this together. None of this macho, valour, saving the damsel stuff. You want to be my hero, you forget it now, you know what I mean?'

Joey caught her tone. 'Sure. No problem-o.'

She took his shades, fitted them on. Put a finger to his nose. Laughed. 'Good. I believe you but what I don't want to believe is Gerard and Temmy - they are frightening.'

'I know.' Joey took his shades off her, put them back on. 'Gerard has given me an idea, though - with the offer of an E.'

'That we rejected.'

'The right thing to do.'

'Go on,' said Nancy.

'Let's spread the E love about.'

'Go on.'

Joey took a look around, dropped his voice to a low whisper. 'We still have the other pill we pilfered from Gerard. You split yours with me so I still have mine. I've got it with me. So-' A wink. 'Let's drop tiny fragments of it into a few drinks. See what occurs when the night creatures experience a little of the pink new yorker love.'

Nancy smiled and it was the smile of this summer and the smile of them. She scanned the saloon bar crowd and how it lapped up Amber's Bee Gee night creatures turn and fuelled the raucous vibe.

'I like it. A lot.'

'And,' Joey said, 'so will they soon.' Pointing at the crowd.

Nancy giggled and kissed him. 'This,' she said, 'is going to be hilarious.'

Chapter Twenty-Four

Five minutes later

They stood at the back of the saloon with Harry. He was No 1 on the list: the first nominee to enjoy E. Get on the waltzer-ride and strap-in.

Small talk ensued - about Harry's book; how Second Summer of Love took shape, the centre-piece Saturday night's warehouse party. Harry told them how the book would start. A "split" opening chapter that moved between the drive to the warehouse/getting inside and feeling the 'rhythm of the night' - this the kind of "poetry" that "non-fiction" could be. His eyes lit up - they saw a different Harold Blue, one of a vibrancy creativity gave.

Harry continued to work the lights and music for the cabaret. The latest night creature was "Molly Parton", who wore a padded-up bra, Texas longhorn boots, a rhinestone skirt and blouse. She did nine to five in jangly notes, the place hitting booze-fuelled post-10pm and the certainty the revelry would never end.

Joey nudged Nancy. 'Now.'

Harry ducked under the table to sort the right cassette. Nancy broke a tiny sliver off the pill, dropped it in Harry's glass of Johnnie Red. The fragment fizzed and dissolved and Harry came up with a cassette and took the glass, and drained the rest of the drink.

Nancy said, 'We're getting another.' Tapped his glass. 'Want one?'

Harry smiled. 'Yes please.'

They made the bar and Joey ordered Red Stripes for them, Johnnie Red-and-coke for Harry. Two glammed up women drank turquoise-coloured cocktails and faced away from the bar, watching the show. Nancy said, 'Excuse me, I haven't got my glasses.' Indicated her eyes. 'Can you tell me if those crisps are cheese and onion or ready salted, please.'

She pointed behind the bar, the pair swivelled and looked and Nancy broke off a fragment of pill and broke this in two and laced their cocktails. Bubbles swirled. The fragments dissolved, the pair turned and one said, 'Cheese and onion, love.'

'Much obliged,' said Nancy. 'I only like ready salted so I'll leave it.'

The women nodded and she and Joey walked back off towards Harry.

Joey said, 'Those bits were a crumb. I know those Es are rocket-fuel but I'm not sure they're going to work.'

'Have you forgotten how we felt last night?'

'Good point.'

They reached Harry and Joey gave him his drink and Harry grinned kidlike. As if he knew something was happening to him and wasn't sure what it was. This the genius of lacing drinks with minuscule bits of E. Who could be precisely sure what was occurring? Harry turned the grin on Nancy. 'You wanted your tape playing?' A glow - like he was a child again and the world waited for him. Eyes deep and warm, connecting - no evasion. 'Well why the hell not?'

Toning confidence, ease, Harry in Cary Grant mode. Hilarious the effect confidence made. Nancy killed giggles at birth; those eyes - like all the tension he lived with 24/7 dissipated, like he got a glimpse of the different person Harold B could be and got wowed by him.

Nancy said, 'That would be cool - thanks.'

Harry's eyes shone like two suns. 'Cool for Nancy Kools,' he said, and the cheeseball joke made Nancy laugh.

On stage, the final night creature finished, left to applause and cheers. Amber took the mike. 'Thanks to everyone who performed and came to be an amazing audience. Same time, same place, next week.'

Amber stepped off stage to wild whoops and yells; the Brown Cow saloon bar pure noise. Harry took Nancy's tape and slotted it in the machine, hit play. A DJ Kools disco-mix started - punters were obliterated; the tunes hit instant, Harry eye-gleamed and moved from the table, his grin broadening.

But: he got a self-conscious moment, wondered what occurred, palmed his glass and said: 'The Johnnie Red is potent tonight.'

Joey stifled a laugh, avoided eye-contact with Nancy. At the bar - Gerard watched on - he wore an expression: goof-balled from pills and something else: like the Es he did bazooked him his own way, making him more cunning, abreast of everything. Temmy roved into view with fresh drinks and gave Gerard his latest Guinness and the Romany raised the pint glass to Joey/Nancy/Harry. They raised their drinks back; Harry kept smiling, had his own look - benevolence, calculation, fixed this on Gerard and Temmy.

Joey read it this way: Harold Blue might know his drink's been mickey-finned with E, might think Gerard did it for a chortle. Further: he might wonder if Gerard was actually two New Yorkers short last night or if, actually, the Romany played a game.

Harry turned the look on Joey; like he hoped to x-ray Two-brain's mind. Joey kept smiling - fronted it out.

BUT: the mad effect of the drug - how the E seemed to work on Harry. Like the sliver of pill stripped back filters, gave Harry a sixth sense; Harry seeming to see something Joey didn't want him to see. Despite Joey's smile.

Like maybe Joey was behind the two-pills-being-missing-move. Or, maybe, not.

Joey felt a surge: this is your movie - yours and Nancy's. And, inspiration - the movie could be called, The Stars In Us. Yes.

The Stars In Us. Because that's what it's about, this is what this is.

The spell broke. Harry said, 'My round. Same again?' They nodded, watched him hit the bar. 'Jesus,' Joey said. 'Did you see the way Harry looked at Gerard, then me?'

'No.'

'Like he started to put two and two together and was getting a large Eed-up four.'

'Four?'

'Like maybe he thought Gerard spiked him with E. And, wondered if Gerard was genuinely two pills short last night or if Frenchy is trying something.'

Nancy thought about it. 'That would suit us.'

'But then Harry looked at me the same way, you know what I mean? Like, did I somehow find out about his pills racket and he was thinking: "Did you do me over - did you take the two pills??".'

'Sssssh,' said Nancy.

Here came Harry - bussing over their pints of Red Stripe, his Johnnie R-and-coke. Still with the look - like he became the older brother of himself. They chinked and drank, and Joey and Nancy eyed each other and felt the same fluttering sensation.

Harry caught this. 'Don't let me detain you any longer. Go and enjoy yourself - looks like the stage is a dancefloor now. I'll be in touch about the weekend and may be at the Carleton before - see you in action, Joey, doing your salesman of the year act there, providing your pills and powder service.' He grinned the all-is-sweet-all-of-a-sudden brand-new-Harold Blue grin.

Joey said, 'See ya,' Nancy said, 'Bye Harry,' and leaned forward, kissed his cheek, which Harry loved. It brought cartoon-wide, hopped-up E eyes out of him and they tried not to laugh. They moved off through a crowd 12,000 sheets to the wind. Drunker than drunk, fever pitch and beyond. They hit the stage; Harry got it right - the night creatures show was ancient histoire, a jive zone replaced it.

They started to dance.

Nancy pointed at Amber. 'There, look. Only fair to make sure husband and wife are on the same level - could make it "interesting" for them later.' Joey laughed and they danced over to Amber. She did a half-blitzed jig, a glass in one hand, smoke in the other.

Nancy played decoy. 'I really enjoyed tonight, Amber, thanks so much. I've got something to ask - I'm thinking of doing a jitterbug next week and need a partner - would you do it?'

'A jitterbug?' Amber looked at Joey. 'Do you know what she's talking about?' Her dress fell open - Joey copped an eyeful, shook his head.

'Here, I'll show you.' Nancy took Amber's glass and palmed it Joey and pulled a here-we-go face. She took hold of Amber's hands and started jitterbugging. Joey tuned into Nancy's disco mix and the Brown Cow vibe. He visioned the place otherworldly. What he yearned for - adventure. Mid-week Lancaster became Jupiter and Mars. He felt in his pocket, broke another slither off, dropped this in Amber's glass in one movement.

Threw Nancy a thumbs-up.

His girl smiled - eyes teeming brightness, possibilities; the place swirled and vibrated. Here they came, Nancy jitterbugging Amber. Harry's wife caught her breath, dress still open, Joey got another eyeful of the woman she was, and he palmed Amber her glass and she said, 'I need this.' Joey and Nancy watched her hurl the drink back. 'Cheers.' She slurred. 'We ssshould definitely do this next week. The bitterjug, wittersmug.' A leery look at Joey. 'Whatever it's called.'

She cocked a half-closed eye at Nancy and told Joey: 'Hold on to her - she's a good one, especially for round here. This town is beautiful to look at - buttssssss -' She zoned out, back in. 'She's a keeper.'

To Nancy: 'And as for him, your boysssfriend - I mean, have you seen my husband?' A point towards the bar where Harry gassed with Gerard and Temmy. 'Like comparing Tom Cruise with Eddie the Eagle.'

She gurgled laughs - they were infectious, Amber was infectious - Joey and Nancy laughed - you had to like her.

'I'll take Tom Cruise,' said Joey. 'But isn't he a little short?'

'Not where he shouldn't be,' said Amber and leered like a navvy and went for Joey's crotch and he threw Nancy a well-whadda-you-know grin and intercepted her hand and twirled her instead. Nancy gave Joey a raised eyebrow behind Amber's back and told her as she came back around: 'Hey, you know he's got a point, Amber - Joey is Tom Cruise for looks but six-foot-plus for height.'

Amber looked Joey up and down like she wanted to go up-and-down on him. Booze-dazed: 'See ya, then - I've got other people to dance with, you know' - and staggered off and Joey said, 'I think the pill is starting to work.'

'Amber is like me - she doesn't need any chemicals to see how beautiful you are, inside and out.'

'Wow - no-one ever told me anything like this before.'

Nancy pointed over his shoulder. 'I wonder what they're telling each other.'

Joey turned and saw Harry, Gerard and Temmy still gassing. 'Hilarious isn't it - Harry supplies pills to Gerard and Temmy but they don't know it. Gerard and Temmy are trying their hardest to find out if they've been done over by their mysterious supplier. Or if they've been ripped off by someone else. And they talk right now to their mystery supplier who is also wondering the precise same thing - if he's been done over.'

Nancy smiled. 'Come on - we need to spread more pink pill amor. How much of it is left?'

Joey grinned and felt the pill in his pocket. 'Just under half, I reckon.'

Chapter Twenty-Five

Harry

Harry kept on feeling the feeling. It was odd, it was disconcerting, it was gooood. Like his toes fizzed, arms buzzed. Like Gerard and Temmy could never ever have ripped off the two pills. Could never ever have fed him a line.

Why? The why was simple - the why was because of the feeling, the way Harold Blue felt. The Romani were too nice. What a simply lovely pair. They really were. Gerard 'Frenchy' Toces and Thomas 'Temmy' Toces twenty-four-carat salt-of-the-earthers with the largest hearts once you knew them as Harry was certainly beginning to, on this wondrous night, in the amazing Brown Cow, surrounded by all these vibrant people he could easily hug for joy due to the way he felt about everything and everyone.

Wow - what a thought process; Harry grooved on how clear his thinking was, particularly on Gerard and Temmy. Romani as a people, a culture, could be slated, slagged. He had never done that and never would.

And now there was a connection. A direct line between Harold Blue and Gerard T and his people. An understanding, an accord. He got them. He congratulated himself for making Gerard one of the players in Second Summer of Love. What foresight and prescience. A seer-like vision. This is your gift, what you bring to the table: a second, third, and eleventh sight.

He never felt as pure of vision. He never saw before how he

could see this way. X-ray, transparent.

Like, now: as Gerard and Temmy gassed about the party on Saturday, how they thought the 'pigs would be keen to raid it', Harry saw his tome in 3D; himself in 4D. Second Summer of Love was going to create and define the genre of Acid House culture and he would be its soothsayer, its magi. The oracle on warehouse parties and rave music and the young and the older who got lost in and loved into it. WERE it.

He told Gerard: 'Have to be honest, I won't be heartbroken if the police do raid the warehouse. It made the party at Nelson. Without our constabulary in their riot gear breaking in at 7am that party would not have the profile, the notoriety it has.'

Temmy's eyes golf-balled from E; he flashed a gold-toothed grin, rubbed his scar. 'You're saying you want the place to get done by the pigs? Have you heard this, Frenchy? Tut-tut. These writers, they always have to be different, don't they? Thinking they're clever.'

Gerard flashed his own metallic grin. 'They are clever, Thomas. And what do you expect - that's 'artistes' for you. Let's leave the thinking and the writing to Harry and we'll do what we do best, gobble pills and inhale the white magic.'

He and cousin spewed laughter; Harry did the same - laughing never felt so amazing. He said, 'That is actually very poetic.'

Gerard's eyes went E-large. 'Don't patronise me, Harold.' His eyes bunched, and in his slow manner he straightened his arms out and placed them on Harry and lifted him off his toes and held and watched him, biceps bulging in his shell suit.

Harry shit 10,000 bricks and Frenchy placed him back down slow and guffawed and his cousin joined in and Gerard said, 'Temmy's the philistine. Not the Frenchy. You see that, don't you? I mean, for your sake, you are with me?'

Harry, eager to please: 'Yes - sure.' But Gerard disconcerted. Confused.

Temmy's grin was E-crazed. 'You calling me a kiddy-fiddler,

Gerard?'

'Philistine. I said philistine.'

Frenchy shook his head at Harry - conspiratorial: my cousin, eh? Temmy, clocking this, leaned into Harold, an aftershave/ Guinness aroma hitting. 'I ask you Harry lad, do I look rum?'

Harry smiled, went for the register that would connect with Temmy. 'Rum? Who knows.' A shrug. 'Nothing wrong with being a touch rum if rum means being your own man, Temmy.'

Temmy got a surprised look - Harold showed a little attitude.

Harry grooved on the way he spoke. Words spilled, resonated. He kept on getting feelings - butterflies, meadows, being at one with all. Significance, meaning was everywhere; Harry hit a full-blown E-haze, Gerard and Temmy were travellers from millennia-steeped lineage. Their Romany ancestors trod the world in noble regard. They were actors in this thing named life, as was everyone. There was no blame, malfeasance - only the simple way of being and moving through each moment, day. Temmy's 'paedo' outburst cast him so sweetly naive yet understandable due to the forces that had evolved and were at play and no-one truly understood.

This thought-stew hitting Harry as Temmy slurped endless Guinness; the Romany's eyes oscillated and went a dark black. Temmy drained his pint and leaned in again on Harry - more aftershave/beer odour - and said, 'What we want to ask is what we asked Joey and the bird, you know, who's called...'

Gerard nodded and half-staggered forward; Harold got a click on him and Temmy: they're on E, look at those eyes. A further click - on himself, was he on E?

If so: HOW?

'Nancy,' Gerard told Temmy.

'That's the bird, yes. You know our business, Harry boy.' Temmy eyes kept whirling. 'This goes no further, like we told bird and her boyfriend Joey - we are light.' His tone hardened. 'Some shithead ripped us off. Two pills. We want to know who and why.'

'The why doesn't matter.' Gerard smiled at Harry. 'It's who thinks they can get away with it.'

Harry felt serene. 'Two pills? Doesn't seem much.'

Gerard's smile was mean. 'Two pills, twenty, two hundred - it's all the same.'

'How did it happen? Someone came to your place and took them?'

Temmy laughed. 'I won't be giving any secrets away by saying nothing is kept in the house.'

'Keep this to yourself, Harry,' said Gerard. 'Keep it to yourself like you tell us you're keeping our names to yourself for your book. We stash stuff once we get it. But we lost the pills well before we got to stashing them. They were missing when we picked them up.'

Gerard slurped Guinness and eyeballed Harry. Harry felt like he surfed the South Pacific under azure skies. The world swirled and the world went faraway. "Picked them up"?'

'What Frenchy is telling you,' said Temmy.

Harry's mood shifted from bliss to a glee he hugged close. He supplied the pills. A fat hahaha on that.

Gerard said, 'We collect the stuff. Pick the pills up. You understand? But we don't know who supplies us, drops the gear - it's done in different places. So, we collected the drop last night and it was under. Two pills.' Frenchy's eyes whirled. 'Have to say, it is rum. Being only two short.'

'How d'you know it wasn't under when you collected the drop? As in your supplier didn't count right?'

Gerard flashed a grin. 'Sure, we're considering that too.'

Gerard swigged Guinness and brought a generous bag of cocaine out and bumped some up a nostril. Waved Temmy on and his cousin did the same. Said, 'T, Harold has a way of speaking, all these words and phrases, some we know, some we think we know. And through doing that he has his thing.' Gerard's eyes gleamed. 'His thing being a certain kind of control.'

Temmy's eyes gleamed from the coke. 'There was us thinking he was green. How green of us.'

'No, Thomas,' said Gerard. 'Green of you. I'm thinking the opposite. Knowing it. Have known it since I first met Harry. Harold - you are, in your own way, smarter than smart. Tracking us down, persuading me to be in the book.' Frenchy's eyes glittered, hardened. 'Question is - what we want to ask - is how do we find out who?'

Harry missed zero beats. 'Ripped you off?'

Temmy leaned in and Harry got an E-fuelled, split-second sight of him. Frustration and a sense of himself as a mug. 'What Frenchy is saying, Harold, is we want to know how to find out who our supplier is. I don't mind saying it isn't the best arrangement we've ever had. I told Frenchy at the start. And now I've been proved right and with this happening, we need to know.'

Harry surged satisfaction. They thought he could help. Actually, reached out to him. A load of laughs, for sure. And more prescient: what Gerard and Temmy did showed they had not pretended to rip him off, that the two Es were genuinely missing.

PLUS: they still had no suspicion he was their supplier. Inspiration hit, a 10,000-watt Eureka moment; he knew how to pitch this, extract the maximum. 'Sure, no problem,' he said. 'My studies of the Russian mind, its approach to intelligence, espionage, means I do, indeed, have an idea.'

He leaned in and took control. Grandstanded. Felt his body fritz, the mind buzz, reverberate. 'What you do, is tell the supplier that the whole consignment has been taken.'

Gerard and Temmy blanked; Harry knew they would, of course. A Russian chess grandmaster play, Kasparov and the gang. 'Think about it,' he told them. 'If that doesn't flush your supplier out then what will?'

Gerard got a crafty look. 'You're suggesting we lie? Tell him that it's all gone when it hasn't?'

Harry shrugged. 'You have a better idea, let's hear it.' A faux-huffy tone. Take it or leave it.

Gerard sipped Guinness, eyeballed Harry. 'Don't be sensitive, Harold. No-one's saying your idea isn't good or we've a better one. I'm thinking about it. The thing is we have been left short or ripped off - genuinely - so I'm not sure we need or want to lie about anything. You with me?'

'Yeah,' said Temmy, catching his cousin's shtick. 'Like Frenchy said, why should we?'

Christ - Gerard and his mini-me Temmy are stuck on the honour-among-thieves thing. Some twisted sense of what's right/wrong.

'You do surprise me - I mean, it's a pleasant surprise, but the last thing I thought you wouldn't be up for is to play smart.'

Gerard smiled and Harry felt a surge through his leg and his chest and he was certain: the feeling he rode was induced. Everything at this moment was. The way the Brown Cow saloon bar vibed, Gerard and Temmy, the possibilities contained within all and everything.

Artificially induced. Chemically. And wow did it feel sweet, not how he thought it would. Someone must've dosed him, laced his Johnnie Red - the old trick. The KGB doctored drinks, a joker in here did the same.

The question was - who?

Gerard, breaking Harry's reverie: 'There's smart and there's cute. You know what I mean?'

Harry smiled. 'That's smart. And cute.'

Temmy leered. 'You saying we rip off the supplier and say we've been ripped off?'

Harry tried not to laugh - the way he manoeuvred this, moving the Toces into place to rip him off - their pill supplier - if he kept playing them this way. The real question remained, though: who dosed him? Amber? The kind of stunt she'd pull to mess him up. But, no. She didn't do drugs, wouldn't know what E was. Harry watched the stage, his wife dancing. He had to concede this - her evening tapped into something. Night Creatures had a kind of carnal energy. A visceral electricity.

The crowd parted and Amber saw him watching her. She broke a smile; Harry did the same and double-took big-time.

Her eyes.

Shit - like she's on something. Time to reassess her being out the picture on lacing his drink. If she was on E, she could've scored some and thought she'd mess him up while getting messed up herself. Would fit her night creatures/mid-life crisis routine.

Harry mind-whirred.

He got this.

Two-brain punted Gerard's pills; maybe he sold Amber one tonight.

He filed his wife under 'possible', moved to Gerard and Temmy. Did they lace his drink? Gerard was capable of anything - could order his cousin to do it and stand back and enjoy the show.

He filed them 'possible', too.

Who else? Nancy, Joey. Two-brain punted pills and was difficult to get a handle on; a character of differing characters. And check the family history. His mum a loose cannon, the (real) dad absent. Throw in Nancy - she read people, the world, yet remained innocent somehow and she just got together with Joey. Suddenly they're lovebirds, Siamese twins. It would be a wheeze for them to mickeyfin him. Maybe.

File them the same as Amber and Gerard/Temmy.

Who else? A random punter - possible but less likely.

Temmy said, 'You deaf, writer-man? You really think it's a "smart" to tell our man we've had our whole supply ripped off?'

'Can you think of anything else to flush him out?'

Gerard said, 'There's no guarantee this will.'

Temmy's cheeks reverberated, like the pills and coke placed him in a personal wind tunnel. He brought a handful of Pink New Yorkers out and palmed Gerard one. 'Frenchy has it right.

Here.' He offered Harold a bar snack. 'Feel like breaking your cherry?'

'No thanks,' said Harry and felt his limbs go billowy. He grooved and grooved and grooved on. Temmy laughed and threw back Guinness. Harry told Gerard: 'You're right - there's no guarantee. But,' giving them the grandstand finish, 'what guarantees are there in anything? Now, gentlemen, if you'll excuse me, I see my lovely wife coming over.'

Gerard caught his arm. 'Not so fast, Harold.'

The grip was hard, what the-

Gerard smiled straight into Harry's eyes. 'I've got something for you - for your book. You can have this for free. If you want it.' His tone wavered. He kept on looking straight at Harry. It might've been the pharmaceuticals he did or something else. 'Before we came in, we were across the street at Lankys. Stood outside, me and Temmy having a drink in the sun and - what's the Chinese across the street called?'

Harry thought about it. 'Red Chinatown.'

'Whatever,' said Gerard. 'We're having the drink and we see this old fella walk up with a cane, stood by the window.' Gerard wheezed a laugh, 'You remember him, Thomas?'

Temmy nodded.

'Then up walks another old fella and stood by him - it looked like he was his mate. Next thing a man pushing a pram is by them, by the window. Then two lads, about fifteen, sixteen came up, stood by them. By this time, we're starting to laugh, aren't we Thomas, like what is going on here? Now it's a couple, holding hands, the bird lit a gasper. From there, what Thomas, you think another five, six, seven other fuckers walk up. It's a regular crowd scene, you know what I'm saying Harold? All outside the fucking takeaway.'

Gerard kept staring straight at Harry.

'And then guess what happened?'

'Go on,' Harry said.

'They all stood there for a few more seconds as we're drinking. Then they started to walk off. The man with his pram first, then the old fella - the first one who got there - then the lads, the rest of them.

Gerard sipped his pint and watched Harry. 'What you think about that?'

'I'm don't-'

'Interesting, right? I mean, whoever sees that? First, they're strangers, then they're a crowd, then they all fuck off and they're strangers again.'

'I see-'

'Stuff is something and then it's not. You know what I mean?' Gerard smiled. 'Lots of things like that, isn't there?'

Harry stared at him, broke away.

'Here comes the wife,' said Temmy.

Gerard, on repeat: 'Lots of stuff.'

Temmy, indicating Amber: 'Look at those fuck-me-quick eyes, Harry. She's not coming for you with those, is she? What's your secret, you wily fox?' He hooted and Gerard gave Harry a smile and eyeballed Amber.

Harry tried to forget about Gerard, what he said. What he might get at. Who it might be directed - as in Harold Blue. Here, indeed, did come the wife - and Temmy was right; Amber headed straight at him, with eyes large and inviting. She had to be on something.

Didn't she?

Chapter Twenty-Six

Harry

South Road

Amber told him they should hit Harry's studio. A turn up for the annals - she never really entered the place when he was there. She never really took an interest in what he did there.

The walk from the Brown Cow to South Road took three seconds flat. That's how it felt - they floated along.

Their house loomed, was overlarge; it bulged and marshmallow-ed. Like something from a Looney Toons flick. They made inside and took the stairs to the studio. Bounded up them. They were young again. Very. Call their age about ten-years-old. Lottie was at her grandma's; they had the place to themselves. Amber sat on Harry's Herman Miller chair and palmed a notepad from the desk. 'SS1 - what's this?'

He didn't tell her about the book; Amber retained zilcho interest in his work, his dreams of the future. He gave it a whirl, now.

Telling her: "SS1" is title of a book I'm working on. The pad has notes in it.'

"SS1"?'

'Second Summer of Love. "1" means the first pad of notes for it.'

'You didn't tell me you were doing this. You don't think I'd be interested?' Saying it with shining eyes.

Feeling the same shine. Feeling the words he spoke next shining too. 'You're never really ever interested in anything I do.'

'That's unfair of you, Mr Blue.'

'Unfair, true - what's the difference?'

Amber's eyes popped. 'A sage, are we?'

He laughed. 'I always have been.' He had to ask her. 'Amber - you on something?'

Her face showed no surprise. 'What, you mean?' A giggle and a glass-to-mouth hand gesture. 'You going to pour me one?' He pulled a bottle of Johnnie Red from the cabinet, popped a cola and poured, added ice brought up from the kitchen, handed her the drink.

Harry watched her throw it back. 'How you feel?'

'Great.'

'Different at all?'

He understood at last. She didn't know she'd taken something. She got mickeyfinned too. Interesting.

'How you mean?' She scoped the studio. 'What - because I'm up here?'

'You never come up.'

'I clean the place for you.'

'You never come up when I'm here. You know what I mean.'

She kept at the JR-and-cola. 'Put some music on then.'

He reached for the racks of classical stuff as usual and stopped. Play something different - the cassette Nancy gave him. He found it on the desk and read the label: 'AFTER HOURS'. Put it in the tape deck, pressed play. Nancy's voice, flooding the studio: 'I don't like DJs who talk, so all I'll say is these tracks are for when you get back to yours and want to dial it all down.'

Harry liked that - 'dial it all down' - could use it on his late-night show. 'Residents of Lancaster and Morecambe, dial it all down time.' Nancy's voice evaporated; the first track played. The tempo was down, the mood smoochy.

Harry took another stab. 'Amber - you do feel different, don't you? Come on.'

Her eyes twinkled. 'Thought we'd discussed this and, as usual, we reached the conclusion I'm right, even if you don't admit it.'

Harry said, 'Like you've taken something.'

'Yeah, booze. I nearly drank the Brown Cow dry.' She gurgled laughs. 'Milked it dry.' More gurgles and Harry saw her different for the first time in a long time. Remembered her: the girl he met, the girl he knew so many years ago. He smiled. Said, 'What I'm saying, what I mean is something - chemical, pharmaceutical.'

Amber, clicking on his tone: 'What do you mean?' Like she realised she did feel different. 'Like what, Harry?'

He pointed at his eyes. 'Can you see these?'

She scoped them. Their eyes met and connected. Grew and pulsed in unison.

'Jesus.'

'Exactly,' Harry said.

'What? What happened?'

'I think we've both had something put in our drinks at the Brown Cow.'

'What?'

'E.'

'E?'

'Ecstasy.'

'Jesus, Harry, I know what E is.' She said, 'Why?'

Harry shrugged. 'Why does anyone do anything?'

'Mr Sage - where you been hiding all these years?'

He'd normally be needled by her. Not tonight. The opposite. He grinned and felt a thousand days drop off him. Time tip-toeing away. 'What I think is someone thought it would be funny to spike people with E who don't normally take drugs. You see what I'm saying? People like those at the Brown Cow, at your night.'

Amber, even wider-eyed: 'Housewives and mothers? Someone thought it'd be funny to mess up women who have kids at home and are on a midweek night out because they have kids and need an escape from lives they're probably bored of?'

Harry shrugged. 'Wasn't only housewives and mothers there.

I spied the male of the species too.'

'Don't be pedantic, Harold.' Amber saying it as her smile lit 1,000-watts and more. 'Who did it, then? Come on - who?'

Harry shrugged. He got an idea. 'This is the six-million-dollar question.'

Amber's smile full-beam E-wattage now. She didn't give a hoot. Give it to her. Say: 'We could, you know, have a top up.'

Amber, like she played coy: 'A what, dear?'

'A top up. A little one.'

'Of E?'

He nodded and grooved on the look on her face. He hadn't seen it for an age; it vanished one day after their marriage. The look, this - a vulnerability. A desire. And, something else. Adventure. Mark it as a sense of unadulterated adventure.

He said, 'A little one, like I'm saying.' He pulled a pink new yorker and Amber's grin lit up like Las Vegas.

'So, you do drugs now?' she said.

'What do you mean - now?'

Her eyes widened. 'What are you telling me?'

'I'm joking. Point is: how would you know.' Smiling.

'You really do need to drop the ignored husband act.'

Sure, I probably do.' He broke the pill in half, then half again. 'If you drop this, I will.'

He handed her the quarter of E.

"Drop'?' said Amber. 'You young and trendy too, now?'

'Just take it.'

She held it to the light, gave Harry a sideways expression and gulped the quarter pink new yorker, chased it with Johnnie Red-and-coke. Harry grinned and did his quarter. Amber said, 'Who were the couple you were talking to in the pub - good looking boy, good looking girl?' She thought a moment. 'I talked to them later.'

'Joey Miller and his girlfriend, Nancy - Nancy Kools, she's a DJ.' He pointed at the speakers. 'This is one of her - mixes. As they're called.'

Amber's cheeks gleamed. "DJ". "Es". "Pink New Yorkers". "Mixes". "Nancy Kools, the DJ". What is happening to my Harold? Has happened. You're trendier than trendy - how come none of this gets featured on your radio show? I actually quite like this music.' She pointed at the sound system.

'Maybe it should - good idea.' He didn't care she teased him - this went great. He tuned into the Nancy mix; the music did give off a definite early-hours vibe.

Amber, clicking her fingers: 'Hello, anyone there?'

'I'm most definitely here... you make an interesting observation - like I said, maybe I will feature Nancy on my show. And as for all the terms you're teasing me about - what do you think the subject of Second Summer of Love actually is? How do you think I know Nancy and Joey? Where do you think I got this pill we're sharing?'

Amber smiled on.

'Joey sells Es.'

A line in bull, of course; the pink new yorker was his.

Amber looked at him and she looked straight past him. Near-blitzed; the quarter E they did started working. 'You're saying the two kids are in this book?'

Harry nodded.

Amber's face fizzed 'How long is this tome?'

'I'll know more or less after the weekend.'

'Go on.'

'By then the focal point of the book, the story, will have happened.'

'Which is?'

'You really want to know all of this?'

Amber's eyes fizzed. She uncrossed, crossed her legs. Harry got a flash of thigh and felt a rise. His gander got goosed. She saw this, she saw him. She said, 'Before we get amorous, come on - the focal point of this magnum opus of yours?'

Harry hazed. The room flashed black-white, flashed 3D colours. The last time they got amorous felt like never. He said, 'There's a rave this weekend, an acid house thing. A warehouse party. It's near Leeds, a place called Gildersome. It's the first of these warehouses since the last one was raided by the police in February, at Nelson, which is near Blackburn. The raid more or less killed the parties off - the police went in with dogs, in riot gear, the lot. People I've talked to about it for the book say the raid was frightening, terrifying, though some say it was fun.'

'Who said being raided by riot police is fun?'

'Joey is one.'

'Interesting boy - I saw the way he looked at me.'

'Any male of the species looks at you that way, Amber. You are one hot lady.'

Amber's chin juddered. Harry eyeballed this, didn't know what the hell he looked at, then felt his chin and felt the same thing happening. Floaty. As if in his studio on the top floor of their house and he was elsewhere, as if he heard his wife speak and he made all kinds of sense of what she said and he heard his wife speak and made all kinds of non-sense of what she said.

'And you know what,' Amber was saying, 'I think he was right.'

'What?' Harry's head dizzied; his palms sweated up.

'I think Joey was correct in the way he looked at me because the way he looked at me was that he saw the way I looked at him, which was that I liked the look of him and he knew it.'

Hearing this and understanding Amber meant she might like to bed Joey Miller, seventeen years old, and not caring and not caring because of the quarter-pill they took that was hitting far harder than the E his drink got mickeyfinned with at the Brown Cow.

Amber, like she tuned into him: 'I think the pill is working - it's much stronger than I felt before.' Gasping, now: 'I feel like my body's being taken away from me.'

'That's a good way of describing it,' Harry said, and he reached for a notepad and he palmed a fountain pen from his desk and scribbled: 'Feel like my body's being taken away from me.'

'It feels strange but I like it. I'm going to get more comfortable.' She stood up and a whoosh went through Harry. The sight of Amber going down to her slip and knickers. The whoosh whooshed more.

'Wow.'

'What?' Their eyes connected. A fizz going back-and-forth. A fizz comical, a desperate yearn for the other. Harry knew what was incoming. Knew what she wanted.

Now - here it came.

'Where is it?' Amber said.

Harry grinned and pulled the bottom drawer of the desk open. On top - papers, a book, 'Samurai Chess'. He delved down and came up with what she wanted. Placed it on the desk.

Amber - transfixed. Harry - like his mind and body was one never-ending organ of love. Amber's hands moved to her knickers. 'The Big One. How long has it been?' Answered her own question. 'Too long.'

Harry eyed the Big One - a 12-inch dildo they bought in an Amsterdam sex shop on honeymoon. Christ, they'd had fun with it. On it.

Harry got emboldened. The pill and the vibe. Her hand at her knickers. 'I have fantasies 24/7. I don't know what to do with them.'

'Fantasies?'

He knew she knew what he meant. It was part of their play, frisson. An excitement surged. A sense he'd never been so alive. His heart as if it could crush the world.

She said, 'Come on.'

No more words.

She picked the Big One up. The old routine. They got into it straightaway.

'Oh my. O-H M-Y. Harold. Harold.'

Harry heard his voice speak. 'Amber, my honey dew.'

"Honey dew"? What the actual fuck, Harold?' She hooted laughs. Harry the same. They cracked-up together bigtime.

They got back into a rhythm. Pleasure and wonder. Like the walls marched through them. Pink new yorker utopia. This mad pill. Ecstasy.

Amber bucked and bronco-ed.

Nancy's mix played on.

Amber recovered, extricated herself. Said, 'Come on, Mr Blue.'

Wow.

WOW.

Part Two

Movie Stars

Chapter Twenty-Eight

Joey and Nancy chomped fry-ups at Bellybuster on Dalton Square. Morning traffic washed by. A warm sun streamed its incandescent nuclear fusion-ed burning plasma starlight through windows. Shafts lit the vista. The world seemed like it might always seem, as long as they were together in this groove. In their groove.

Joey plumped for double bacon, double fried egg, sausage, black pudding, baked beans, fried bread, toast, a pot of tea. Nancy the same except she drank coffee - black. Joey asked an umpteenth time: how sexy is she?

They slept until 9am, post the shenanigans at the Brown Cow. Crashed at Nancy's again, her folks leaving early for the restaurant - preparing Altobelli's for the lunchtime trade after taking Esmerelda to school; Nancy telling Joey about her sister as they strolled the twenty minutes from Haverbreaks to Bellybuster.

This, a first proper repast since the half a pink pill. Since the rest of their lives began. Joey put two rashers of bacon between fried bread and wolfed it, chased with tea.

He had a plan. Knew how they could make their movie an unadulterated glitz and glamour flick. If it had a name, they would call their glitz and glamour flick this:

Adventures in Love.

He watched Nancy fork black pudding, his girl eating like a navvy. His girl glowing. His girl all the girls in the world and his. He told her: 'Nancy, I've been thinking.'

She drank java. 'I would not expect anything else, Mr Double Brain. Shoot.'

He pulled his shades up, let them drop. 'We're going to "acquire" the next drop from Harry. Take all the pills, see how it falls.'

Nancy scrunched her eyes up: this is your grand plan?

He read her instant; knew she'd react this way.

Said. 'This will make our picture a blockbuster.'

Nancy leaned back in her chair, watched Mr Bellybuster - the owner, Alfred, dish up a plate of toast and tea to a pair of older dears sat by the counter.

'I know this is going to be good. Shoot.'

Joey smiled. 'I peddle pills for Gerard, right? This is how we can have some real fun. It's the perfect front for knocking out all the pills we rip off from Harry's next drop.'

'I don't quite see-'

'Simple, baby. If I didn't already punt pills and then a load is stolen and I pop up, suddenly starting to sell the same issue of pills that were ripped off, then I'm a walking advertisement as the one who ripped the load off. So, because I sell for Gerard, who will know that I - we - have the extra ripped off load that we're selling at the same time I'm selling my usual supply?' He did a sunglasses twirl. 'Which if we sell them all, by my maths, is going to be a serious earner.'

'Go on.'

'The drop we put back in the bin at the Plough was fifty bags of twenty making 1,000 Es. Pills go for £25 a pop. That's 25K.'

'Wow.'

'Wow and double wow.'

Nancy thought about it. 'You normally sell for Gerard at Harvey's and the Carleton.' Harvey's the other night, DJing, Joey standing by the bar, Harry sat in a booth with the interesting appearing dude. The night this all started. She said, 'Harvey's has been and gone for the week, and the Carleton is on Friday - I'm no E selling expert but I'm guessing wildly there is zero hope you can sell a thousand, 500, 250, there. The crowd is too small. Holds, what, maybe 150?'

Joey bit fried bread. 'I'm not arguing.'

'Point is,' said Nancy. 'You - we - may have a front, beard, for selling a thousand pills if - and it's a massive if - if we manage to rip them off. And, as I say, there's no guarantee we can do that. But we don't have a venue to sell them if we do. Or we do - Harvey's and the Carleton - but it will take weeks, maybe a month, two months, meaning more the chances we get caught. We do not want Gerard after us. Even before Harry gets involved.'

Joey looked through the Bellybuster windows, saw a magpie flit and turn in the spiralling sunlight, circle Dalton Square, fly off and away into the ether. Nancy made sure Joey saw her looking at him. 'Well, don't worry because we do have a venue.'

As soon as she spoke, she he started to see it too.

Nancy said, 'An epic party on Saturday night in a place near Leeds called Gildersome. I'm DJing, first on, opening up. From around midnight.'

Joey laughed and leaned across and kissed her. 'Brilliant. It will be filled with kids gagging to trip the light fantastic.'

'And we'll have a large supply of pink pills to sell them.'

Joey's eyes danced. In an instant their future unfolded. 'And if we pull this off, guess what?'

Nancy waited.

Joey said, 'Our movie can end how it should.' He smiled a dazzler. 'Let's take off. I'm seventeen, you're seventeen. We have precisely nothing to keep us here and we have our whole life before us. Let's take the money and head for the sun.'

Nancy's features lit. 'Wow.' Then: 'You think you can sell 1,000 pills at the warehouse? In one night?'

'Sure. But even if I only sell half of them that makes 12k. That will keep us in cocktails and beach loungers a long time.'

Nancy flashed on home, leaving mamma and papa, leaving Esmeralda. It would be sad, it would be exciting, it felt simply right. Maybe this was why her folks were frustrated with each other. They were yet to truly live.

Joey said, 'We're on?'

'We have never been more.' She kissed him. 'You and I. Us.' She whooped and Bellybuster diners rubbernecked, and she whooped again and held up a hand to apologise and Joey laughed. The diners went back to their plates of fry.

Nancy's eyes twinkled. 'Where you want to go?'

'Good question.'

Her eyes twinkled more. 'Really? No clue? Come on, think about it. Where can we party and I take my records and DJ? It's July, the middle of summer.' She kissed him again, longer this time. 'Ibiza. Where else, baby? Party central. Disco, house music, Balearia. Sunshine and days on the beach. Cocktails and beach loungers, you say? Sunsets, midnight swims, early morning walks on the sand, too, I say. Amazing times. Amazing times we'll never forget. That will live for always.'

Joey looked at her and never wanted to stop. The way she was, the way she thought - selling the pills at the warehouse, jetting to Ibiza. Nancy embraced his hopes for adventure and turned them to living dreams. He took her hand and squeezed it and said, 'Thank you. For being you. Never ever stop being that. Though I know for sure you will never not be who you are.'

They kissed. Lifetimes of sensation fizzed between them. They kept kissing. Bellybuster diners started to notice, they put down knives and forks. They looked away and they looked back at Nancy and Joey. They kept on kissing - never-ending, the two old ladies sat near the counter started to clap, the rest of the place heard and saw them and caught on and joined in. Alfred the owner delivered Bellybuster Specials to diners by the front window and he joined in. Still Nancy and Joey kissed. As if joined together forever. As if this was it, because it was it.

Take the sun and place the sun in our hearts and never let the sun leave. As all the Bellybuster diners applauded them, applauded Nancy and Joey, Bellybuster diners rising to their feet, their ovation going on and on as they stamped their feet and banged the tables. Joey and Nancy kept kissing until finally they broke and Nancy stood and took his hand and together, they bowed and laughed and hugged and sat back down.

The place - slow - went back to normal. Bellybuster returned to greasy spoon cafe land.

'Wow,' Nancy said. 'I feel dizzy.'

'Me too. All we have to do now,' Joey said, 'is pull this off.'

'That's the fun bit.'

'The fun before the fun in the Ibiza sun.'

'We're young and it feels great,' Nancy said.

Joey looked at his girl; the only girl he would ever want. He knew this, felt it. 'Are we - in love?'

'Of course we are.' Nancy giggled and took his hand and lead him towards the door out of Bellybuster. She turned to him - sunlight framed freckles, her features. 'Let's go 'acquire' those beautiful 1,000 pink pills,' Nancy said. 'Get our one-way tickets to paradise.'

Chapter Twenty-Nine

Harry

Harry at his window seat in the Golden Fry. He chewed on the Gerard/missing pills situation. Only two, sure, but Gerard and Temmy were antsy about it. He knew he hadn't miscounted; knew the drop was the number it should be.

So: if Gerard and Temmy didn't scheme something, and the drop was genuinely light when they collected from the Plough, who taxed the two Es?

Charles Mua delivered a plate of fish, chips, peas, gravy, a pickled egg on the side, sausage in batter. Harry went the whole hog. He got a hunger on, post the frolics with Amber. He grinned at the memory; him and his girl and the Big One: old times, new times. Nostalgia played and created memories. They fell asleep eventually, hand-in-hand, woke up smiling. Knowing they'd taken E a first and last time. Knowing they'd loved it. Nostalgia became the present again. Created real-time magic between them. Harry felt a bounce, a skip in the step. It invigorated his thinking on the missing Es. He would out-Russian whoever the Russians were who pulled the two-pill rip-off stunt.

Charles sat down opposite Harry with a mug of tea. The chip-shop proprietor took the sugar pot and poured it and swigged hot tea. 'How are tricks?'

'Tricky.'

'You want to talk about it?'

'I am - with myself.' Charles Mua: Harry went to school with him; Charles was Lancaster-born yet his Chinese heritage attracted racist bull. Harry flashed on their friendship a 1,000th time - sticking up for Charles when they were kids and matriculated at the town grammar school. LRGS a split of eleven-plus day-boy entries and fee-paying boarding pupils. Scholastic stew of clever poorer kids there on brains and posh lads with family dosh. Harry had his sole fist-fight in the second year when the form's hardest lad, an item from Halton village, racially abused Charles. Harry got a sound beating and respect - the tough befriended him for his spirit - and Charles M signed up as lifelong loyal to Harry.

'You can always speak to me,' Charles said.

Not on this he couldn't. He changed up - asked, 'What about you? Your wife still agitating for this breast augmentation?'

Charles smiled. 'Tit job, Harry, save the posh words. And I see what you are doing, switching the subject.'

Harry speared a chip. 'Answer the question.'

'Dolores never stops chuntering about it.'

'You tell me you told her she's already large.'

'What I tell her all the time.'

'How did she find out she could even have an op?'

'From Dynasty, Dallas, all those shows - shoulder pads and suits, you know what I mean. She starts dreaming, like Dolores does, next thing I know she's got to have D-cups.'

Harry flashed on Amber last night - how she shimmered in his studio. How they shimmered. They were high on themselves. Getting back to the kids-in-love they'd been pre-marriage. He speared fish and mushy peas and ate and chopped the battered sausage, and ate more and light-bulbed an idea. Maybe Charles could help if Harry kept it cute. Use his shrewd mind obliquely. He said, 'You want to find something out about a person without said person knowing - how would you do it?'

Charles laughed - the sound of a man finding humour in

something you missed. 'Don't tell them you're trying to find out whatever you're trying to find out.'

Harry grimaced. 'The only way I think I can find out is via the self-same person.'

Charles watched the door open, a customer enters, make the counter. 'Not sure I understand.' Charles pointed. 'Business calls.' Pointed at them. 'To be continued.'

He made the counter and turned - inspiration hit. 'What you do in a situation like this, anything like this, what you do - what you need, is a distraction. You understand, H?'

Charles to the customer, 'Yes please.'

Harry chewed on what he said.

Then, lightbulb flickering bright: how about if the distraction was to play it cool? Take Gerard at his word. Do the next pills drop, then hang around. See what happened. Either he'd see who came and tried to repeat the pilfer act. Or if no-one turned up and Gerard told him the delivery was light again, Harry had it wrong: it was Gerard swindling him.

So, do this: change the location of the drop, see how that played. Leave the Es for Gerard in the new place and hide and wait.

Simple.

Harry pulled his pad and wrote out a note. Then, told Charles, 'See you and I'll always like to be you.'

Left the Golden Fry and headed for the '87 Bentley. Events were about to be jump-started. Events were about to be turbo-charged.

Chapter Thirty

Harry parked up the hill, on High Street. He walked to the sled, hit the driver seat of his motor, loaded a Wagner compact disc and pressed play and drove onto Meeting House Lane and hung left. The Wagner the Tannhauser Overture; Dickie W recast Lancaster as epic event-shattering, universe-centre. The right from Meeting House onto Station Road became 1,000 funerals occurring at once. The marching of the pallbearers and the mourning fancy in their finery. Harry heard violins, trumpets. He curved along Station onto West and visioned Lancaster as the fields and meadows the town, the hamlet it once was. Willow Lane became the retreat from Moscow. Napoleon marched through Harry B's mind and he hit Chestnut Grove.

There was nothing else.

Nothing else, apart from what he did; what he wanted to do. He pulled the Bentley up and parked and walked the corner to Sycamore and hit No 21 and dropped the note he wrote at his window seat in the Golden Fry in the letter box; the letter box actually a shelf where the note could be retrieved if you reached through to it. If you knew to reach through to it.

He turned around, scoped the street. Deader than his ability to turn his ideas and imagination into anything approaching art. A whole road of derelict houses - one of the many that made the Marsh Estate the Marsh Estate. The note he wrote read this: 'New drop is bin by the Sugarhouse - Thursday, 11.30pm.'

Harry re-hit Chestnut and the '87 Bentley and pressed play on Dickie W. The great man's fervour flooded the sled. Harry put the motor into gear and zoomed off. Let's see how this goes down.

Trumpets and flowers and nothing else. Nothing else.

Chapter Thirty-One

Joey and Nancy

Thirty seconds later

Nancy and Joey watched Harry turn his motor off and away from Sycamore onto Chestnut, hit Willow Lane, and go left towards the River Lune back towards town. They drove here in Nancy's VW Golf. Chose this rather than Two-brain's Fiat 127; Harry knew the car, if he clocked it they were smoked.

They tracked him from the Golden Fry. They tracked him yesterday, too. That came to nothing - Harry took his little girl to school, went to the Golden Fry then too, ate an early lunch, jawed with the proprietor at a table by the window, returned home, went out the evening to do his Radio Primrose show - the studio two rooms above the Ring O'Bells boozer on Prospect Street, at the bottom of Bowerham.

Today: the same routine, until bingo - full house.

They pulled up on Chestnut so they could see Sycamore but Harry could not see the VW, see them. Hid by the angle of the street. Clocked Harold walk to No 21 Sycamore and put something through the letterbox, then drive off.

Nancy saying: 'Has to be a note - I bet he's telling Gerard about a change of location to pick up the pills.'

'Mind reader, are you?'

Nancy smiled. 'Think about it, what else would he do - if he's trying to flush out what's going on? If he thinks it's Gerard or

161

someone else.'

Joey did think about it. 'Change to a different bin.'

'What a load of rubbish.' Nancy pokerfaced for a long second, then cracked up.

'That's bad - so bad it's funny.' Joey cracked up too.

'Come on,' Nancy said. 'If it is a note for Gerard then he must be able to retrieve it which means we can, too.'

'He may have a key,' Joey said. 'Could be a lock on the letterbox.'

'Time to find out.'

They left the VW, hit pavement and rounded the corner from Chestnut onto Sycamore. Walked the path to No 21 and the front door. Joey scoped the street - derelict houses both sides. No soul around. Nancy put her hand through the letterbox, felt the shelf - bingo! on that - and the note. She took hold and brought it out.

'Showtime.'

She opened the note and held it so they could both see. Joey read: "New drop is bin by the Sugarhouse - Thursday, 11.30pm."

Nancy refolded the note, put it back in the letterbox, back on the shelf. 'Harry - what an item.'

'Jesus,' said Joey. 'You are a mind reader, you read Harold Blue perfect - change of location for the drop.' He kissed Nancy. 'I'm supposed to be the smart one.'

'Maybe I'm Nancy ten-brain.'

'You are.'

'Come on.'

They walked back to the VW and took their seats. Nancy kicked the engine on and looked for a tape to play. 'Here,' she said. 'My latest.' She pulled a cassette, showed him. He read her writing along its side: 'Gildersome, 21st July, 1990.' Looked at her. 'Eh?'

Nancy shrugged. 'Come on, silly - in celebration, of the night to come, the night of our lives. What this is all about.'

She loaded the tape and hit play.

Then: 'Shit.'

'What?'

'Look.'

In the rear-view mirror - coming towards them, the white Sierra Cosworth.

'Fuck,' said Joey. 'Duck. Quick.'

They bobbed their heads down. The Sierra moved up the road, coming from Chestnut onto Sycamore the other way, pulling across from No 21. Coming out of the motor now - Gerard and Temmy. 'Tweedle-dum and Tweedle-me-me-me,' Nancy said, cracked up.

Joey laughed, dropped his voice. 'This isn't going to be funny if they clock us.'

'Yes,' said Nancy. 'It will. Who cares? And why you whispering?' She winked, took his hand and Joey grinned and they watched Gerard and Temmy walk the path to No 21, Gerard stooping to the letter-box, pulling the note out.

Joey said, 'How you want to play it if they do see us?'

She shrugged. 'We are playing it.'

'It's not a Hollywood ending if they catch us.'

'Sure it will be - our Hollywood.'

Joey smiled. 'Looks like they're going.'

'As long as they don't drive this way, we're clear, 100 per cent.' She thought a moment. 'But if they do drive this way, pray.'

Gerard revved the Sierra up - now-

Shit, this way - here they came.

They ducked down more. The sound of the Cosworth coming along the street: slow.

Too slow?

Now - right by the VW Golf. The purr of the sled's motor.

Now - slow - pulling away.

A wait of eight, nine, ten, fifteen seconds. Then, a joint phewwww.

Nancy saying, 'You think they saw us?'

'If they did, we are history.'

They sat back up in the seats, taking their time.

'If they only saw my car - we're okay. They don't know it.'

'Smart not to come in mine.'

Nancy nodded, put the Golf in first and pulled out and along Chestnut, hit Willow Lane. 'What we've got to work out now is how we "acquire" the pills from the bin at the Sugarhouse because you can bet your bottom dollar Harold and Gerard - plus Temmy - will be watching to see what happens.'

That was smart too.

Chapter Thirty-Two

Harry

Thursday, 11pm

Harry parked the '87 Bentley in St Leonard's Gate carpark. It was an hour until midnight, half an hour until the pink new yorker pickup. Town was busy - night revellers kicked the weekend off with pub crawls, 50p a-shot libations at Brooks International, the fleshpot dance and pick-up joint across from Dalton Square.

Harry's plan: drop the taped-up bag of 1,000 pills in the bin by the Sugarhouse, hit The Moon in the Stars opposite. From the juicer he could scope what went down - if Gerard picked the drop up clean. Or if someone beat him to it. If Gerard got the pills and left a note saying it was light, Harry was in business: he'd know 1,000% Frenchy ripped him off.

But: if someone beat Gerard to the drop, Harry was in business too. He'd clock who it was and they'd be paying for it sooner than something that came very soon. The beauty of the plan, this: The Moon in the Stars a regular haunt. Harold Blue had every reason to be drinking Johnnie R-and-coke in the place on a Thursday if seen.

He walked the eighty yards from where he parked to the bin. You reached the Sugarhouse down a series of steps and through a tunnel that opened onto cobbles. Here, now. Harry walked to the bin, dropped the Sainsbury's carrier bag of pills into it and hit the Moon in the Stars. The pub packed out. This hot summer night reached for apotheosis. The juicer's lights sparkled; punters were merry. What else could there ever be than to be right here on this eve?

Harry soaked the ambience up. The odour of existence - fag smoke, stale ale. Older men eyed up student girls. A fruit machine paid a barrage of 10ps out in cacophony - silver glinted, the juicer rubbernecked: look at the lucre being won on the fruity.

Harry ordered a double Johnnie R on ice with coke and snagged a stool by the window. It looked out at the bin - a prime spot. It looked out too at the sky - a vault of sun going blue. The northern heavens streaked white as another day died. The moments of existence ongoing.

Harry settled in to discover if anyone messed with him. And if so, who this was.

The time - 11.07pm; twenty-three minutes before Gerard was due to collect the tablets. The by-bin scene: students lining up to hit the Sugarhouse and dance to indie tunes and swig cut-price Pernod-and-blacks and revel in their youth and revel in being them.

Harry sipped JR and heard: 'Harold, Harold!'

He turned. Trevor the barkeep held the blower up. 'Call for you.' Harry quit his stool and made the bar and took the handset. 'Harold Blue.'

A voice, muffled: 'Your car's a Bentley?'

'Who is this?'

'Parked in St Leonard's Gate, across from the Sugarhouse.'

Harry, starting to suss what went down: 'Who is this?'

'If I was you, I'd get out the pub and get to your car.'

Harry stiffened - this had to be a trick. Decoy time - they had to think he was stupider than stupid. Time to play this like Mozart on his grand piano. 'Why,' he said, 'might that be, then?'

'Because your beautiful cream Bentley Turbo 1987 is on fire.'

The caller hung up. Left Harry hanging. He had to admire the front of whoever fucked with him. Whoever called and muffled their voice. Then threw him a line about his motor being on fire. Hahahahahaahahaha.

Like he'd fall for that. Like he'd panic. He was Harold Blue. Compared to the Russians, the Kremlin spooks he studied, Mr Your-Bentley-Is-On-Fire was a clown. He handed the phone back to Trevor and scoped the juicer and did a slow walk towards the door.

Get outside, turn left, walk two or three steps and you could see under the tunnel to the car. No way the Bentley was going to be on fire. But let whoever was trying to pull the trick think they got him. He walked out The Moon in the Stars and hit hot air and did a left.

He took three steps and looked through the tunnel, up past the steps to the carpark, and his motor.

There it was - his beautiful cream '87 Bentl-

Shit and Jesus.

It is.

On fire.

He started doing something Harry didn't do since a kid. A young kid.

He started running-

Chapter Thirty-Three

Joey

St Leonard's Gate carpark - a few minutes before

Joey hit the phone kiosk.

It gave a clear view through the tunnel down to the Sugarhouse. It gave a clear view of the parked up '87 Bentley. Harold B's sled. The phone box gave a clear view of something else, too:

The fire Joey lit by the Bentley.

How he did it, this:

Just before 10pm and closing time, he hit Sainsbury's - with Nancy. They cruised aisles, passed rows of fruit and veg, booze, kitchen accoutrements, frozen fries, arctic rolls, tubs of ice-cream, and reached home supplies. There - a new fad, they just came in: disposable barbecues. They took two - the plan needed two, plus a box of matches. They hit the checkout, paid, and skipped back across Cable and North Street.

Then, split.

He left Nancy at the bottom of Sugarhouse Alley - preparing for her part. They kissed long and parted. Exhilaration bolted. This is on. This is splendiferously wunderbar.

10.30pm: Joey hid by the corner of Lodge and St Leonard's Gate. Waited.

10.59pm: bingo - here comes the cream '87 Bentley - only one owner of this high-end motor in Lancaster. Out stepped

Harry, he headed down Sugarhouse Alley - to drop the pills. Joey followed, clocked him do the drop, clocked him hit the Moon in the Stars across the way.

11pm: Joey reversed, hit the phone booth on Upper St Leonard's Gate, and waited a few minutes, thumbing the listings book. Found the number for the boozer, dialled this, asked the barkeep when he answered for Harold Blue, put his sleeve over the phone, muffling his voice, told Harry when he took the receiver: 'If I was you, I'd get out the pub and get to your car.'

When Harry asked why, Joey hit movie-star mode. 'Because that beautiful cream Bentley Turbo 1987 edition is on fire.'

Now, 11.15pm: Harry comes running. Running and wheezing and panting and puffing. Joey held his sides, howling - look at the state of that. Hilarious with the H of Hilarious lit-up in movie premiere, red carpet arc-lights.

Under the Sugarhouse Alley tunnel, towards the fire here he came. The fire that isn't actually the cream-coloured Bentley '87 on fire.

Joey kept holding his sides; could not stop howling, watching this from the phone-booth. Upper St Leonard's Gate carpark raised, allowing a bird's eye perch to eyeball Harry reach his motor in panic.

Joey wishing he packed an Instamatic - Kodak this priceless for all-time moment.

As Harry made the sled and saw - it's not alight; there's a fire BY the Bentley - the throwaway barbecues are flaming.

Joey close to creaming himself at the sight.

Harry stopping and trying to take it in.

What the-

Scoping the carpark - seeing revellers walk into town, hitting Sugarhouse Alley on the way to the club.

Joey creaming himself Nth-degree at this: the lightbulb in Harry's brain hitting 10,000-plus volts. Realising: the E drop, the pills: fuck's sake - this is a decoy, you have been mugged off biiiiiiiig-time.

Harry turned, puffed and wheezed back towards the alley, down the steps, under the tunnel. Towards the bin and the 1,000 pills he dropped off there.

Too late.

Too late, that is, if Nancy was as quick and slick as she told him she would be.

She would be - wouldn't she?

Chapter Thirty-Four

Nancy

North Road - around the same time

Nancy felt a thrill. Her legs fluttered. Arms went pins-and-needles. Her imagination raced, drew vistas of possibilities never before her before. This is on, showtime, movie time. Now time. She clocked Harry - he left the pub opposite the Sugarhouse, ran up the alley, under the tunnel, took the steps, disappeared from view towards the carpark, towards his car.

They worked it all out, her and Joey. The time from when Harry vanished out of sight to reaching the Bentley, realising his car wasn't on fire, would be thirty secs, forty tops, factor in another ten, twenty to get back to the bin, and Nancy had a minute - TOPS - to pull this off.

Here, now.

This is on.

She sprinted up the alley. Tried not to look conspicuous running full tilt. Tried not to laugh while doing so. Forget it: she definitely looked conspicuous; in fact, scratch that, she blared odd-and-the-gang. As in, odder than odd to be doing what she was doing while donning what she was donning. A mask. A Lynda Carter-as-Wonder Woman mask.

She swerved round punters hitting the Moon in the Stars. She headed for the Sugarhouse.

For the waste bin.

There it is–

Looking past the bin, up the steps, through the tunnel, to the carpark beyond.

No sign of Harry.

Great, now – come on.

Breathless, heart hammering. Nancy/Wonder Woman made the bin, peered in: there's the Sainsbury's bag. She grabbed it, looked round. Revellers rubbernecked, clocked her. They blurred in, out of vision.

Shit– there, coming down the steps, through the tunnel. Harry's legs, feet. Suit-trousers flapping.

She clutched the Sainsbury's carrier to her chest and–

'Hey!'

Coming from somewhere out of view – from someone. Harry?

No time. The pub – run in the pub. The passage raced by, faces jumped and blurred. She hit the Moon in the Stars, heard another 'Hey!'

She was being followed, knew it had to be Harry. She scanned the pub, the joint jammed. Punters rubbernecked – behind her the sound of the door opening. She didn't dare turn; a thousand thoughts raced.

She'd been in the place once before – a long time ago, as a kid, with her mum and dad, before Esmerelda was born. She scanned the place for the Ladies'. Hearing shouts and laughter.

'It's Wonder Woman!'

'She looks younger than the American tart!'

Clocking the Sainsbury's bag.

'Shopping for some meat and two veg, love?'

There – the Ladies'. She crashed through the door and hit a cubicle and knew Harry would follow. Shouts, yells. A voice. 'Wonder Woman's in the tart's khazi!'

She had to escape – somehow get out before Harry caught her. The door ran floor-to-ceiling, she bolted it shut – solid metal, that gave her time.

But time for what?

She turned - there, behind the cistern, a small window - big enough to squeeze through?

Nancy heard the Ladies' door go, heard pants and gasps. It had to be Harry.

Now:

'I know you're in here.' He hammered at the door. 'I know you just ripped me off. We both know what I'm talking about. Give me it back and I'll let you go. I haven't seen your face - that mask means you can walk away from this and I'll never know.'

Nancy killed her breathing to a hum. She smothered giggles - listen to the way Harry spoke - 'you can walk away from this and I'll never know'. Like he was in their movie. Gerard and Temmy - everyone else - too, in their beautiful caper. When she should be scared - she was scared - she saw the name of the film starring Nancy and Joey, co-starring Harold and Gerard and Temmy. The name Joey gave it.

Adventures In Love. She saw something else. The 'e' at the end of 'Love' should be capped up making it 'LovE'. Making it: Adventures in LovE.

Why?

Well, because, after all…

Flashing on this while hearing Harry hammer at the door, trying to force it. The flash turning to desperation. Have to escape. Nancy gulped air and out-of-bodied. The door held firm. A silence started and built. Only their breaths between them. Only a floor-to-ceiling length of metal between them.

Harry, laughing: 'Come on, open the door. This is ridiculous. You are going nowhere. You've locked yourself in but we both know there's only one way out. Open up, give me the bag and let's end this.'

Nancy scoped the window. A fifty/fifty hope or impossible to get through? She tip-toed over; the window was small and rectangular and smoked glass so what it opened onto not visible.

Behind her - Harry: 'If I have to break the door down-'

Nancy flashed on the 1,000 pills he wanted back; Harry had to be careful - if he got caught in the Ladies he could be ejected. And if his cover was blown on 1,000 Class As in a Sainsbury's carrier bag he was pursuing, the police could be called.

It would escalate.

Nancy pried the clasp off the window and opened it and saw:

Six or eight feet of drop to bushes, a grass verge. The sky fading to dark - the boozer's lights offering sight, showing the way down, the jump to freedom.

Harry: 'Play it your way then. I'm breaking down this door - and don't worry I know who you are, the Wonder Woman mask is no good, you can't hide who you are.'

Nancy froze; if he knew-

'Tina, it's you, isn't it? Makes sense now. I don't know why I didn't see this before.'

Nancy refroze a different way, if that was possible. Tina? Tina meant Harry didn't know this was her.

'Come on, this can still all be okay. You haven't seen me, you don't know who I am, but I know who you are. Gerard's made you do this, hasn't he? Eh, Tina? I am right?? It's - Tina Toces. That's okay, too. I only want what is mine back.'

A pause, a silence.

Nancy computing: "Tina Toces". "Gerard". He thinks Wonder Woman is - Gerard's wife/girlfriend/sister/cousin? She drew a breath, surged relief. Their cover wasn't blown.

Not yet.

Harry said, 'Play it this way, then. I'm going to have to break in and that means you're going to see me, which means the ramifications - consequences - are going to be worse for Gerard. Far worse.'

Confirmation. Tina is surely Gerard's girl.

Harry started hammering at the door once more. Nancy

moved quick, got up on the cistern, stuck a leg through the open smoked glass window, then the other. Started squeezing through it, clutching the Sainsbury's bag. Clutching the bag as the doorframe started to splinter; getting herself all the way through the window apart from, now, her head. The window wedged up against her shoulders and jammed and she got desperate, pulled at the bag, hit this against the window, un-wedged herself.

But–

The Wonder Woman mask, the elastic snapped, and off it came: fell off Nancy's head and spiralled down to the grass verge. Her face got exposed; desperation became panic – she dropped the bag after the mask, thankful it was taped shut, no spillage of ecstasy tablets when it hit and she watched it swirl and hit ground – grass – as Harry kept battering the door, more splinters breaking off.

Another few seconds and–

He will be able to see me.

Nancy reached the edge of the ledge and weighed up the drop to the ground.

Behind her, coming around the side of the door – the middle of the door: Harry's fist. 'Fucking hell Tina, it doesn't have to be this way.' Nancy killed giggles – Harry's fist bled; crimson ichor spattered knuckles, fingers reddened and bunched, turned and twisted and felt for the bolt. Last sunshine glints through the window, lit these seconds. July air stilled. There was a moment, an actual moment when Nancy felt a pause. A freezeframe. Like she took in what occurred and time concertinaed and stretched. Time became something at the end of years. Became meaningless. Its potency and constant presence fell away and all that remained was Harry on one side of the door and Nancy watching him.

And, then–

Fingers found, turned the bolt, slid it free and the door opened. Harry – coming through the door.

Nancy - now or never - do or dying - like the last tune you play at a warehouse. The end of the night or the start of the dawn.

Drop-

NOW…

Dropping.

The ground hit hard. She felt her knees go, tried to soften the impact by putting a spring in her legs, bouncing with the landing. Shit-

She didn't have the mask on anymore. She had to hide her face. She saw two trees off left and grabbed the Sainsbury's carrier bag and ran for them and dived for cover and heard:

'STOP WHERE YOU ARE! YOU WON'T GET AWAY!'

Nancy hugged herself and laughed. She had got away. Pilfered the pills undetected. Enough to sell and for them to go and live on the profits in the sun for a long time. Hit the Mediterranean a long time. Ibiza.

The rush of all this could be invigorating.

IF they didn't get caught. Between now and Sunday morning. Go to the warehouse at Gildersome, peddle the pills, then scarper. For the beach. Their future. For them.

Harry, out the window, from behind the window to keep his identity hidden. Harry shouted: 'Tina! I know where you live - I know where Gerard lives!'

Nancy faded him out; a thought flashed: pack passports and a bag and head straight for Manchester Airport after the party. Do not come back here first. Once past customs, have a celebratory drink or three in departures. Then, fly.

Fly, fly away.

Ibiza, here goes.

Chapter Thirty-Five

Nancy and Joey

Friday morning

Bellybusters again.

The plan this:

The pills couldn't be stashed at Nancy's or Joey's place - too chancy. Their move hit Gerard AND Harry - twice the heat. And, factor in the number they pilfered - 1,000: if they were caught by Gerard or Harry, it's game over; if they were caught by the fuzz, hurl the key away big time.

Call it three times the heat.

They kept them for one night at Nancy's; 1,000 pink pills stashed under her bed, like they were kids in a fairytale, not kids dicing with serious danger, then came to Bellybusters for a pow-wow; discuss where to stash them until Saturday and the drive to Blackburn in Joey's Fiat 127 Extra, find the convoy, follow it to the warehouse.

Except, they wouldn't. Only Joey would; Nancy would go early - she DJed first, playing the first set at Gildersome, the warm-up spot at the acid house party that was the fat two-fingers to what the police did at Nelson: up yours to the plod, the authorities.

Nancy DJing as the place filled with kids.

It gave her an idea.

But first: where to stash the pills.

Joey speared black pudding and kept his voice low. 'Best place to hide the stuff is where no-one would think we would think to stash it.'

Nancy in her flower power garb, July 1990-style. A button-down shirt decorated with daisies. Faded dungarees, Kickers sandals. Taking her time, cutting her fried bread. 'You have me intrigued.'

Joey said, 'Sugarhouse alley.'

'Sugarhouse alley?'

'More precisely - the bin where you pinched it from.'

Nancy, starting to smile: 'Where Harry left it for Gerard.'

'One night only - Friday.' He pointed at the sun that shone all month. 'On the Lancaster Riviera.'

Nancy said, 'The bins aren't cleared tonight?'

Joey pointed out the Bellybuster windows. 'Friday morning. As in now.' Across Dalton Square, two refuge trucks loading up bins of trash.

Nancy brought the pills from under the table. They ditched the Sainsbury's bag for a white one, masking tape sealed it. 'Come on.'

They hit the Square, turned right towards Sugarhouse Alley. Five minutes and here came the steps going down under the tunnel. Joey said, 'How does it feel, Wonder Woman, being back at the scene of the crime?'

Nancy put her hand in Joey's. 'Wonder Woman feels weird because it's not weird. It's morning, the sun is shining again and I'm not being chased by a middle-aged man who becomes stranger the more I think about him.'

'I hear you.'

They walked down the steps, passing the morning strollers. There - the bin; they walked up to it, Nancy dropped the bag in, and they kept on, down the alley to the junction of North Road.

Joey said, 'Now what?'

Nancy said, 'It's midday - a drink or two ahead of tomorrow?'

'Great idea.'

She pointed at the King's Inn along North Road. 'There. We can get a bite next door later.' Ali Baba's Kebab House was two doors along.

'We just ate.'

'After a few Red Stripes we'll want to eat again. I mean, this is a magical summer but even hunger can't be cured by a Bellybuster heart attack special. And Ali Baba's lamb pitta with chillies - mmmm.'

'Let's do it.'

They hit the King's - two old geezers played chess by the windows, drank ale and chuffed woodbines. Smoke hung thick in bars of sunrays. They clocked Joey and Nancy and went back to their game.

Joey told the bargirl, 'Two Red Stripes, please.' The bargirl pulled the pints, walked off, and they sat right there, at the bar.

Nancy sipped lager. 'This time tomorrow.'

'We will be starting the day - the day of our lives. A day to start all the others.'

Nancy's eyes gleamed. 'Our endless days.' She leant and kissed him and Joey said, 'What about your folks?'

She shrugged and swigged Red Stripe. 'I've thought about it - they could probably do with the space and I'm not the girl who says no to an adventure.' Another shrug. 'I'll be back - one day, with you. This is what being seventeen is for.' She chinked her glass with Joey's. 'What about your mum?'

Joey pulled a face.

'You feel like that now, but...'

'I'll be back - one day.' Joey smiled. 'Is it possible, though?'

'What?'

'To do this. Go there and live in the sun on the beach in Ibiza, swimming in the Med? Cold beers. Partying at night. You DJing the island. Sounds like paradise.'

'An endless holiday.'

'Yes.'

'So,' said Nancy, 'why not?'

'Yes,' said Joey, 'why the fuck not?'

Nancy eyeballed the bargirl; she was dressed student style, gave off an attitude of cheesed off cool. 'Why should we be stuck in Lancaster during the best years of our life?'

'You ever think about any of this - before?'

'Before?'

'You met me.'

'Too-vain is back and I like it.' She laughed. 'I did think about it, my life, future. DJing - I want to do it forever. I only see house music getting bigger.' She drank more Red Stripe. 'Think about it: something you love doing for the rest of your life.'

Joey smiled. 'I thought you wanted to be a pop singer.'

'I don't want to be a pop singer but I like singing pop - I'm sure there'll be plenty of bars in Ibiza with nights like Amber's.'

'How can you be so sure?'

'Of?'

'Sure, you want to DJ for the rest of your life.'

Nancy laughed. 'How can anyone be sure of anything?' She wrinkled here nose. 'Another way of answering - I don't know. But, I know.'

'I so want this to be true.'

'Believe it, it is. Anything is.'

'Thought I'm supposed to be the smart one.'

Nancy drained her Red Stripe, signalled the bargirl two more. 'What's smart? What isn't? Anyway, you're the same as me. You think endless days are possible, living the dream is possible.'

'With you - sure.'

Nancy laughed hard. 'You see, super-smart.'

The fresh Red Stripes came and Joey said, 'Most people will spend their whole lives not realising what they want, what they should do.'

'Which is?'

Joey laughed. 'Easy. What we want. What everyone wants.

We all want the same. Sunshine, beaches, sun. Doing nothing apart from what you want to do. How many go for it?'

'You're seventeen and you're going for it.'

'You're seventeen and going for it.'

'Feels great,' Nancy said.

'What if we get caught?'

Nancy threw him a look. 'Bonnie and Clyde. Nancy and Joey. We get caught chasing our dream, well-' She looked at the old men chess game, looked back to Joey. 'What a thing to be caught doing.'

'Like the movies.' Joey pulled an envelope from his jeans and waved it. 'One-way tickets.'

'To Ibiza.'

'Don't,' Joey said, 'forget your passport.'

'I won't.' She laughed. 'Make sure you don't.'

Nancy walked over to the chess game. Joey watched her.

She said to the woodbine smoker A: 'You're black? Watch out.'

Woodbine smoker B said: 'Ssssh.'

Woodbine smoker A studied the board. What Nancy saw. 'I don't see any danger.'

She winked; she moved to the jukebox, fished 50p from her pocket and fed the machine, moved back past the chess game to the centre of the pub, waved Joey to her, the song on the jukebox starting in.

Piano flooded the King's Inn. Nancy took Joey's hand and ballroom danced him, led her man, slowly, making the bar twirl, sunrays sparkle in their eyes.

They danced until the song finished. Until the music faded to silence.

The chess players watched.

This vignette. They would twirl in other rooms, on other days all along and across the year.

Chapter Thirty-Six

Harry

Harry had a problem. The biggest since starting his Lancaster ecstasy graft operation.

He sat in the Golden Fry the day after being ripped off the thousand and chewed on a girl in a Wonder Woman mask heisting the drop from the Sugarhouse bin.

Tina Toces did a number on him, big-style. Who would believe it? He couldn't. He'd been primed and ready, wanting the pills to be taken as he waited in the Moon in the Stars. Jesus.

Charles brought him a chip barm and a pot of tea and clocked Harry's face and walked off. Harry watched King Street - buses, taxis motored by; a Wagner tune hummed around his head. Failed to recast the world, as per usual. He couldn't get past this: Gerard using Tina to steal from him last night. A sucker move and he fell for it.

Harry already heard from the Romany post-last night. He left a note in the letterbox at the house on Sycamore; Harry unfolded it now, read it again. 'Nothing there. I never saw them and now you gonna say I have to pay because of the agreement. We go splits, I owe for 500.'

How thick did Gerard think he was? The Romany playing this act - like he knew zero about the pills vanishing from the bin by the Sugarhouse. Like Harry didn't suss Tina wore that ridiculous mask to steal the thousand.

Now Harry was being taken for a patsy twice by Gerard. The

Romany tried to make this work by saying he'd be liable for 500. That way he got 500 free pills that would pay off his bill for the other 500 and still make a fat profit.

No way.

Harry plotted how to catch the prick and decided on this: don't answer the note - let Gerard stew; maybe his mystery E-supplier went for the idea that the Romany should only be liable for 500 or maybe he didn't.

In the meantime, Harry started thinking. If he carried on as normal, arranged another pill-drop, and if Gerard pulled the same trick, then what?

He weighed it up, saw a plan.

It came to him when he dropped Lottie at school this morning. Play Gerard at his own game, reverse fucking ferret him. Pull a Kremlin move. Agree to another drop and leave a bag of aspirin, paracetamol - dummy pills. And whether Wonder Woman turned up again to rip them off or Gerard collected them as normal - do this: trail Wonder Woman/Gerard and see where he stashed his stuff. Find that out and Harry could break in, take back what he was owed - plus more as compensation - and get Gerard scrambling the way Gerard had him scrambling.

He knew this day would come. Here it was.

This complicated the book. Or, it made Second Summer of Love richer, more complex. One of the central characters ripped off his supplier. That's how Harry could write it up. And because Gerard didn't know Harry was his supplier, he still held the ace card. Wonder Woman/Tina never saw him, never turned when he chased her. She escaped out the back window of a cubicle in the Ladies of the Moon in the Stars without knowing who he was.

So for Second Summer of Love, if Harry found a way to "know" about the pills being ripped off, he could include it in the book by bringing this up in front of Gerard. Get him to speak about it - Frenchy unnamed in the book after all. Get chapter-and-verse, author-to-central character.

Time for an ambush, an impromptu visit. Dress it up as a final chat about the tome. The central event about to happen - the warehouse at Gildersome - Saturday night and Sunday morning. The book was an ode to youth and vibrancy, and if Harry played Gerard like a Stradivarius, he could play up the crime element, too. Look at this atavistic happening. All of life is drawn to Blackburn Warehouses. To Acid House. Moments of joy, fun, ecstasy, reflection among the kids. The dancing and the dodging of the police.

Crowbar the Romany being ripped off into the narrative of Second Summer by talking to him about it. Say he heard what happened, that a large delivery of pills never appeared. Then, put Gerard on the spot: tell Frenchy to tell the tale to Harry like it happened to someone else, and Gerard was accused - wrongly, of course - of ripping the pills off and saying he never saw them.

See how Gerard squirmed, watch how he felt no choice but to play along.

A good start. A good and cunning and venal and sly way to start in on the revenge that would be Harry's. For what Gerard 'Frenchy' Toces did.

Harry finished his chip barm and waved goodbye to Charles and walked outside into more hot July. He turned right, did another right up the hill. Made the '87 Bentley and pointed the sled towards the Morecambe border.

Started off for Gerard's place.

Let's see how he played this.

Chapter Thirty-Seven

He pulled on the Romany site and scoped the scene. Kids playing, horses and ponies grazing, families outside their chalets, a barbecue fired and grilling meats, beer drunk in the sun, a radio playing chart music. Somewhere further off, the sounds of house music sounds Harry got familiar with these past days.

He guided the Bentley over gravel and grass and parked it up by Gerard's. One of his tots opened the door and here came Gerard and Temmy through it. Like they expected him. Like they wanted a word. Harry started to get out the Bentley and got leaned back in by Temmy; the cousin showing that grin of silver/gold canines he adored. Harry went to get out the motor again and Temmy leaned back this time, let him pass.

Harry knew his face showed fear.

Now, Gerard: standing by the front of the Bentley and smiling. Saying: 'Harold, my man.' Putting on a cod-posh accent that made him sound rougher. Harry threw Temmy a look Gerard read instant. 'Don't worry about him, you get me? Can't be too careful these days - especially after the events of the past few days.'

Winking at Harry.

Harry trembling and thinking what the-

Maybe Gerard's about to lay the whole thing out, with zero prompting because he wants to tell the writer about it. Feels he can and the secret will be safe. That would be good. But: the look Gerard and Temmy wore. As if rumbled.

A flash on Tina - where was she? Did she guess who he was

from the chase yesterday?

They looked at him. Harry said, 'What - what's happened?'

Gerard looked at Temmy; Temmy looked at Harry. 'Come on, Harold, don't give it that. We know you know what's happened.'

Harry trembled. The scene started to build. Kids stopped playing, families stopped talking, the chart and house music went quiet. Harold flashed on something scary: what if Gerard and Temmy watched last night. Watched Tina. Watched him chase Tina. If so, he was finished. Gerard and Temmy would beat him up bad - or worse - and warn him off: we're taking over your business - you got an argument with that?

He said, 'Good stuff for the book, maybe?' His voice a squeak.

Temmy's face went smug. Sometimes he seemed smarter than the dumber Toces cousin stereotype. 'This guy's always thinking of his "writing", isn't he, Frenchy.' This was not a question; this was a statement of some incriminating fact that was yet to be revealed.

Gerard studied Harry and grinned. 'You know what, Thomas, I don't think Harold does know what happened.' The grin broadened. 'I really don't.'

Gerard indicated Harry sit at the table outside the chalet door and Harry breathed and the scene dissolved.

Now -

Tina coming through the door. She dished out Red Stripes, smiled. 'How are you?'

'Good thanks, T-Tina.' Harry looked at her and relaxed. He had to stop stuttering. Would give himself away bigtime if not.

But it was true: nothing - zero vibe she recognised him yesterday.

'You here to talk about your book again?'

Harry nodded and Gerard said, 'Me and young Thomas Toces here are just debating if he does know what the fuck's going on. What, with his connections and all the fucking rest of it.'

Harry pulled a pad, kept the act up. He started to understand where he stood. 'I'll take notes, if that's okay, Gerard? You going to tell me now what it is you thought I should know?'

Gerard lowered his voice. 'Last night, when I went to pick up the pills. They weren't there.'

Harry faked a surprised/quizzical look. One Oscar-winning big fecund, eh?! Then said the right line in the right tone with zero stutter. 'Two more?'

'Two?' said Gerard, then understood. 'Not fucking two, Harold. All of the fuckers.'

'Wow. How many?'

He looked at Temmy. His cousin shrugged and Gerard said, 'A cool thousand.'

'Jesus,' said Harry. This time he made his voice squeak.

Gerard studied Harold. 'Exactly.'

Temmy leaned in. 'Someone's having a laugh - thinks it is funny to mess us around. The deal we have, even though we never saw the pills - never mind touched them - means we're liable. You know how much that is?'

Harry shook his head.

'Best part of 12K. That's money we don't have fucking to hand-' Gerard watched Harry pull a slow oh-you-are-joking-that-is-bad expression as he took notes; pretending this was news and vital stuff for the book.

Gerard said, 'We get the stuff on tick. You know what that is? We pay for the stuff by selling the stuff. Via Joey punting them out. Point is, last fucking night they weren't there - they're gone. We're not sure if the pills were ever there, or if they were and someone took them.'

Harry, pretending: 'Last night?'

'Outside the Sugarhouse,' said Tina. Looking at him straight, no flicker.

Harry took a moment, going slow. Like he worked this out as he spoke to them. 'So either your supplier never dropped them off and is trying to rip you off bigtime, or they did and then they were taken, so you were ripped off bigtime that way?'

Gerard nodded. 'Because we don't know, I'm gonna tell our man that we're only liable for half of them - you know, 500. Call his bluff. You with me?'

Harry, slow: 'You think he goes go for it?'

Temmy grinned. 'Probably not.'

Gerard's eyes brightened. 'Who gives a fuck.' The Romany shrugged in the direction of the sky. As if only the heavens knew what Frenchy Toces was capable of. Gerard nodded at Harry; the pen paused in his mitt. Harry stopped taking notes at this juncture. Another party of the Harold-Blue-Is-Thrown-By-This-News act.

'You want to put this in the book? I bet you do, Harold, knowing you.'

Like he fell for Harry's act or maybe Gerard thought about this before and wanted it in the book. Harry played it cute. 'I suppose. If you think it's a good move?'

'You tell us,' said Temmy and looked at Tina.

'Was my idea,' she said. 'Me and Gerard discussed it. We decided, why not?'

'What do you think, Harold?' said Temmy.

Harry got the creeping sensation again. Like they tried something and he wasn't sure what. Maybe this: they did suspect and were seeing how he reacted. 'To be honest,' Harry said, 'I'd be disappointed if you didn't want this in the book. This is kind of why I asked you in the first place - why I wanted you in it. You add glamour, like I've said to you many times, Gerard. The glamour of crime, of the outsider. That's why I bill you as precisely this in the book - as The Outsider.'

Harry just made it up. Right now. Riffed on this as he spoke, inspiration hitting. Harry snuck a look at Gerard: ooh, the Romany kind of blushed, vanity took hold. Bullseye: direct hit.

Temmy, clocking his cousin: 'Fuck me, Frenchy, don't fall for the blarney. Harry, this isn't a fucking movie.'

Harry, cheeky: 'No, it's a book.'

Temmy shrugged at Frenchy like Harry had less than no fucking clue. He said, 'I'll let that one go. But don't be fucking cheeky again. Some dickhead is playing games with us and we don't like it.'

Harry took the cue. He manoeuvred this whole scene precise the way he manoeuvred it. 'Sure,' he said. 'But Gerard is saying he and Tina have discussed it.'

Gerard nodded at his cousin. 'This is Harry, Thomas. The writer who you say is all about his book. What they - whoever they is or are - say is an artist type. An artiste.' Gerard put his face in Harry's - the Romany's blue eyes glassy. 'What I will say is, you hear anything you tell us all about it.' Gerard shrugged. 'Call me the Outsider in your book, call me what you like. Just make sure you do me right.' He offered a hand and Harold took this, and Frenchy grasped and shook. Slow. 'You get me?'

'Sure.' Harry fought new trembles off. Gerard dropped his hand and Harry smiled and made a note in the pad.

Temmy's smile showed his silver and gold gnashers. 'What you writing, right now?'

'That "the Outsider asks the author for help".' Harry tried to forget Gerard. His face, the warning - and kept smiling, tried to move this up in the smile category to the kind of dazzler Nancy did natural. 'Think it's a nice hook for the reader. They might not consider that he - the Outsider - would do that. Pride and, you know, the reader knows he's a Romany, is aware Romani, Travellers, are a tight community.'

'Shows our human side?' Tina said.

Gerard roared. 'We need to be ripped off to show we're normal! Is that it, Harry?'

'It's not how I'd characterise it exactly, no,' he said. 'It's more how stories work. The reader needs to relate, find something "human", is what I mean. Something which is surprising, individual to the person or persons they're reading about. In Second Summer Of Love, you - the Outsider - are what you are, Gerard. A big tough guy with an air of menace but-'

Tina, interrupting: 'Has a heart of gold.' She cocked an eye his way. 'Christ, Harry, you sound like a soppy romance book. Maybe that's what you should write. Or is that what you'll do in the future?'

Harry blanched, tried to laugh it off. 'I've never read one in my life - and listen, there's nothing wrong with romance, I-'

'Let's keep to the fucking point,' Temmy said.

'Point being,' said Harry, 'Gerard asks me, the author, for help with who ripped him off 1,000 Es, and suddenly he is displaying a different side, showing a new dimension to the stereotype of a Romany. What the stereotype might be.'

'This a social comment book now,' Tina said.

Harry baulked at Tina again: sarcasm laced with pinpoint observation. He got what Gerard saw in her.

He told her: 'You can frame it like that, sure. What I'm saying is, from the story point of view, it makes Gerard - the Outsider - even more fascinating. You know he has the humility, self-confidence to ask another outsider - an outsider to his world, the Romany world - for help.'

Temmy said, 'Frenchy, remind me why exactly you're in this fucking book.'

Gerard put a hand through his blond locks. 'Tina gets it, Thomas. I thought you did too. What's going on with acid house and the parties - this is a one-off, I know it is. A one-off means something like history, and we're part of that.' He kept rearranging his mullet. 'Harold's book could be read for years to come. If they ever want to know about Blackburn parties and acid house music, the whole thing - Harry's book will be part of it all. And there I'll be, you know - one of us, in H's fucking story about it all.'

Temmy snorted. 'Why put yourself, us, in danger? The pigs could get wind of who you are - from this fucking book, I mean.'

Gerard eyes twinkled. 'They know who we are anyway. You know that. It's cat-and-fucking-mouse 24/7. So why not enjoy the ride.'

Tina to Harry: 'As long as you don't misrepresent us.'

Harry, laughing: 'You sound like my lawyer. "Misrepresent". What did I just say? About Gerard, him asking me to keep ears and eyes out for who ripped the pills off? How it will show him in a different light, beyond the usual stereotype. If that's not showing the real Gerard, not "misrepresenting", then...' Harry took his time. Try and kill this, finally. 'One thing, are you able to say who supplies you?'

Knowing the response he'd get. The question a bluff, the answer immaterial.

A zero flicker from any of them. Temmy, predictable: 'Fuck off. How green are you?'

Harry played aggrieved. 'Pretty, I suppose. Stupid of me to ask.'

Gerard said, 'Tell you what: you hear who is doing this and I might tell you the full details of the set-up we've got going. The way we have to operate with the fucker we get the stuff off would surprise you, Harold.'

Harry nodded, smothered a grin at birth.

Doubtful. It would not surprise at all.

Chapter Thirty-Eight

Joey

The Carleton Club was cavernous. A cabaret hall with dimmed lights, darklit in low purple neon. A stage fronted a large dancefloor. To the left a DJ booth that had DJ Nancy Kools spinning acid house to Friday evening speed-snorters and pill-poppers. She did the early slot ahead of Ducky - Lancaster and Morecambe's established peerless No 1 record spinner. A whizz with vinyl and Technics.

Around the dancefloor - tables and chairs. Seated - goosed revellers and revellers heading for goosed. To the right the bar - long with a slight curve. Joey recalled a lad on a mushroom trip inside the joint about a year ago. The lad was spangled. Hung by the bar and told anyone who came near that they were actually in space while asking the same question over and over. What is time? What is time? WHAT IS TIME? Please, what is time..?

The lad was him. 'Two Brain' Joey Miller who was out of his two and copious other brains that night. He never did mushrooms again. Vowed never to take any narcotics again. Ever. It put him off magics, put him off pharmaceuticals. Until Sunday at Nancy's.

Tonight: Joey on his usual E-punting patch by the Ladies'. Girls the No 1 market; they bought pills and gave zilcho trouble. Didn't try and shyster a five spot off the price. Instead, this happened, at first: lads got wise to his operation, got in

197

Joey's face, tried to get reductions. Which was a hoot. Joey punted for Gerard Toces and no-one fucked with him. Once it got around Frenchy was Joey's boss then…

Until Frenchy, pills were a rumour. A myth, a folk story about a tablet only cockneys did. Even now E was a near novelty in Lancaster/Morecambe. Kids still could not quite believe what the magic dancing pill did to them. After the night at Nancy's, Joey understood the pill big-time. Precisely what the things did and why the kids couldn't compute it. Es were a lifetime of moments compressed into an unstoppable moment.

A girl wearing her hair in bunches coming at Joey now; he was half-tuned into Nancy's mix - it had the kids dancing, high on his supply taking star-rides to the moon and back, high on her tunes.

The girl: 'I'm told you sell E.'

Joey, the standard line: 'You the police?'

The girl giggled; she looked already gone. He told her, 'Pink New Yorkers - £25 each.'

'Three please.'

'Don't take them all at once.'

She tottered. 'You take them? You look - straight.'

'I just say no.' He palmed the three pills and counted £75 into his pocket. She tottered for the dancefloor.

The plan tonight - clear the whole supply but report to Gerard a sizeable number of pills went unsold. Tell him: a rare off night. Tell him: don't worry, the rest will be shifted at the warehouse. Gildersome ravers will clean them out once word travels about the rocket-fuel he punted.

Joey hadn't seen Gerard or Temmy in the place yet. Joey ruminated on his theory on the duo: Gerard would drop Temmy if he could but couldn't. Family, blood ties stopped this. Here he came now - dressed like he did all year long: purple shell suit, hooded top. Chains, a baseball cap, mullet glinting in the Carleton lights.

The peak of Frenchy's cap read "New Yorkers". Nice.

Joey ran through the patter he prepared for the Romany again.

Gerard with Tina. The girl always smiling like she wanted you to smile too. Joey did and clocked Tina's eyes: booted from E, whatever else she took. Gerard the same: the gear he did working up a sheen to rival the sheen of his shell-suit, eyes even more vivid like he could not believe what the current moment felt like. Revealing more of him than when straight.

Joey said, 'Those New Yorkers, eh?'

'You on one now you've seen the light?'

Tina laughed. 'Since you found love.'

'I don't mix business with pleasure,' he said. 'Tomorrow - at the warehouse, possibly.'

Gerard's eyes glittered. 'How's business?'

'Good.' Row it back as per your prepared patter. 'Actually, not the best night ever so far. A lot of regulars don't seem to be here - maybe because of tomorrow night. Keeping their powder dry.' Half-true - word had got around about Gildersome.

Gerard bought it. 'Can't blame them.' He pointed towards the DJ booth. 'But they're missing out - your girl's playing belters for sure.' He nabbed Joey's shades, put them on, twirled them a la Two-brain and grinned and put them back on Joey. 'Is it not too dark for these?'

He grabbed Tina and twirled her - once, twice. Tina's eyes fizzed and they hugged and broke and Tina planted a kiss on Joey's cheek, and a sweet aroma wafted and Gerard smiled a ten million dollars and led his wife to the dance-floor.

Joey felt a twinge: ripping Harry off meant ripping Frenchy off too. Then, the opposite emotion: what an unadulterated thrill. He was a film star. Nancy was a film star. Tomorrow - Saturday. The final scenes of their movie would make it a blockbuster.

Chapter Thirty-Nine

21st July

Midday, Saturday.

Joey and Nancy walking through Lancaster.

They passed the Slip Inn, roved by Horseshoe Corner. Shoppers, kids on pub crawls, kids smoking joints, a high sun hot and clear. The light sparkling; look at the way it twinkles. They hit Nicholas Arcade, crossed Thurnham Street, left Stonewall Post Office behind, glided right onto St Leonard's Gate, took the steps down to Sugarhouse Alley.

How they planned it - like this: casual, walk past the bin, drop in it the can of Coca-Cola Nancy swigged and her watch, too. Like the watch slipped off her wrist by accident and she had to retrieve it. Go digging, pull up the watch, and the bag with 1,000 Es they stashed in it.

Now, here - they reached the bin. Nancy held the watch in one hand, the can of cola in the other. Passerbys passed by; Nancy dropped the can in and let the watch drop after. 'Oh no,' she told Joey in a voice like it did slip off her wrist while she still held it hidden. 'My watch. One second, baby.'

'Sure.'

He watched her, tried not to look round, see if anyone watched them. He couldn't help it, did a quick glance, saw no-one. Watched Nancy as she stuck a hand in the bin, and rummaged and felt for the white carrier bag - there, at the bottom where they left it. She pulled the bag and palmed the

201

watch from her hand, as she retrieved this from the bottom of the bin. Put it on; held the bag casual, like she'd always had it with her, like she didn't just pull it out.

They kissed and walked to the bottom of Sugarhouse Alley, headed back to town. Job done. Simple.

Now.

Coming out of the Moon in the Stars - Harold Blue: he clocked the whole Nancy and Joey show. He knew now who ripped him off. It should have been obvious from the start. It was - now. Forget Tina, Gerard and Temmy.

He said, 'Jesus Christ', and walked the steps through the tunnel onto St Leonard's Gate towards the Bentley, the phone booth. Time to call Swaggert. Make sure the DI had it all arranged as agreed for the warehouse.

Access all areas.

With what he just saw he'd need it.

Watching the whole scene in a ginnel on the opposite side to the Moon and Stars: Gerard.

Harry didn't see him. Nancy and Joey didn't see him.

Now: Gerard understood who supplied him and who ripped off the 1,000 pills. He understood the whole thing. Frenchy headed for the white Sierra and started a low croon - one of his top Frankie Sinatra faves.

'That's life,' Gerard Toces crooned. 'That's what all the people say…'

This was, indeed, life.

Chapter Forty

The night was sweltering. The heat felt like the earth might burn. It felt good.

They were in Joey's Fiat 127. 'This is so romantic,' Nancy said. 'Driving to Blackburn in your loveable battered car. Like something out of a matinee.'

Joey pointed at the yellow bumper, the dirt-orange boot, rust-red doors and roof. 'You don't seem concerned that the tritone colour scheme might attract the police? Stopping because we're riding a death-trap.'

Nancy gave her smile. 'If they stop us, they stop us.'

'Okay,' said Joey. 'Right.' He stashed the 1,000 pills in the Fiat 127 wheel arch; survival sense kicked in. This was goodbye to their hometown. Their bags packed and in the boot. Packed for Ibiza, packed for adventure.

The sun flared yellows, reds. Before hitting the road for Blackburn, they drove the top of Lancaster via East Road onto Quernmore, by Williamson Park; Joey parked up.

The views across the bay to the Lakes. Dreamlike. Peaks and mountains - purple and brown-capped, colours glinted, colours danced. Joey said, 'Look at the sun.'

Streams of oranges coming off the great orb as if lava. A volcano in the sky. Nancy said, 'We are on a planet in space, we really are.'

Joey turned to her. 'We're earthlings and we're aliens.'

She pointed at the sun. 'Have you seen Blade Runner?'

He pointed where she pointed. 'I've seen pills ripped off like you wouldn't believe.'

Nancy laughed. 'If Gerard and Harry could hear you.'

'You are so right, Wonder Woman.' Joey laughed.

Nancy laughed. 'Look at the light compared to how dark it is in Blade Runner. Endless night. And rain.'

'I like night.'

'I like night with a sunset like this.'

'And I love rain.'

Nancy nodded.

'Rain is romance,' Joey said.

'Go on?'

'What's more romantic than a detective in the rain? That's Blade Runner.' Joey stroked Nancy's cheek. 'If you like the sun at night, read Raymond Chandler. LA in the thirties, forties, always drenched in vivid west coast light.'

'You've been to Los Angeles?'

'A million times in my dreams.'

'Why there?'

Joey shrugged and watched the sun flare in the dusk. 'Escape, fantasy.'

'Like Ibiza.'

'Except,' said Joey. 'That's actually going to happen.'

Nancy pulled her passport and waved it. 'Where's yours?'

Joey pulled it out.

'A one-way ticket to the White Isle,' Nancy said. 'Come on, let's go. The night is calling - romance here we are, romance here we come.'

Joey kicked the Fiat on, pointed the car for Blackburn; started the drive to hit the convoy that would take them to the warehouse party at Gildersome. He could've gone with Nancy direct to the warehouse. But the convoy to the party: it was goodbye to this, too.

Chapter Forty-One

They wound the windows down; the world rushed by. The left off Galgate roundabout, the left again onto the M6 slip-road south. For Blackburn; a thirty mile drive, west of the Pennines in the Ribble Valley, twenty miles from Manchester. Warehouse party central. Blackburn: stone houses and mills. Pill poppers and kids. The parties in their pomp: the town got flooded. Locals blinked and double-blinked and wondered what the hell went down. Every Saturday a thousand and more motors snaking through the streets; climbing the hill to Sett End on Shadsworth Road. There: the kids went inside and danced to acid house, and on lights went outside and the night took off. Horns beeping, vehicle lights blazing.

Waiting. For the convoy to start and move off and drive to Blackburn, Haslingden, Nelson, Accrington, Burnley, Darwen, Colne. The streets and cobbles blurred. Street-lamps flashed. The night a siren in the mind. A Las Vegas of the north. The music waiting. Pulsing and pounding.

Pulsing...

Anticipation buzzed. Joey and Nancy kept smiling at each other. They Fiat 127-ed by Forton Services, beyond Garstang; the M6 rolled on, the stash stayed stashed in the wheel well. 1,000 Pink New Yorkers. Their gold-plated ticket to the sun.

Joey tooled the motor by Preston, took the turning for Blackburn, on to the A677 up the hill, taking the right for Shadsworth Road, and seeing Sett End lit up in neon through the dark. Countless sleds already parked outside. The lights of Blackburn fluttered below. The valley imprinted in their memories. All that life down there, all the world up here and now.

Joey said, 'Sett End.'

'Or the Red Parrot.'

'Red Parrot?'

Nancy said, 'What Sett End's also called. Or was. Can't remember.'

Joey stared at her. 'I did not know that.'

'You do now.' Nancy pointed - by the door of Sett End, a longhaired dude in a Benny hat and granddad shirt. 'My lift to the party.' She leaned over, kissed Joey. 'Make sure you get there for the start. I'm on from midnight.'

'Cannot wait to see you kick it off. Good luck.'

Nancy pointed towards the wheelarch. 'Good luck to you - if this goes right, then–' She took Joey's hand. 'Remember baby, this is about us.' Another kiss; the night popped. 'See you on the other side.'

'Yes,' Joey said and raised and twirled his shades. 'Two-brain will see you there.'

He watched her get out the Fiat and walk and greet the dude in the Benny hat and they disappeared. He scoped his watch: gone 10.30pm. Nancy was due to kick the party off in ninety minutes. Joey kept his window down, listened to the kids, the buzz of the night. Watched more cars and vans and motorbikes and other vehicles pull in and wait. For the convoy to start. A group of girls walked past sharing a joint. He caught a snatch of conversation.

'Those lads are going down.'

'Where is it?'

'In Leeds somewhere, I've heard.'

'We'll know when the convoy starts.'

'No, we'll know when it finishes - where we end up at.'

Joey got a stab of guilt at what he and Nancy did to Harry. Ripping off the pills, pitting Harry against Gerard. And, Gerard: forget Harry. If Frenchy found out what he and Nancy did. WOW. But, then, his senses tingled; their movie rolled towards colour climax; final reel time.

A hand appeared, then Harry's face - leaning in through the driver's window. Joey jumped and saw a look Harry didn't show him before. 'We need to talk.'

'When?'

'Now.'

'Okay.'

Harry, pointing at the front passenger seat: 'I'm getting in.'

'Sure,' said Joey. 'Do it.'

Harry walked the Fiat and slid in next to him. Joey watched more motors arrive, join the convoy.

And waited. He got a queer feeling.

Chapter Forty-Two

Harry

Harry gave it ten seconds. Actually counted ten in his head like he saw dudes do in movies. Dudes far cooler than he would ever be. Dudes he admired, would like, no - love to be like. Cool, rolling with punches. The whole 900 yards.

Then picturing himself. Here, now: in the car sitting next to Joey. Doing what he was about to do. And seeing himself a different way. A nerd, sure. But: a cool(ish) nerd. Operating - not like the movie dudes did and didn't - kind of different; his way. Harold Blue Cool.

He got upset at what Nancy and Joey had done when he sussed. Post-seeing Nancy grab the bag from the bin outside the Sugarhouse. The two young kids. What were they doing? Who did they think they were: Bonnie and Clyde? He tried to look at it romantically; how Wagner might for a certain kind of symphony. Nancy and Joey were newly in love; believed they would always be. They were kids thinking that. Did anyone, ever, stay in love like they first fell in love? They acted like this summer could never end. Did they ever contemplate it could and would? And maybe badly, for them?

Who knew? Point remained this: business is business. The business of Harold Blue. He brainwaved instant what their plan must be: sell the Es at Gildersome and run away with the cash. So let them go through with it and collect the cash from them - after a warning.

The warning that was incoming right about now.

Harry reached ten, gave it eleven, then said, 'You ready for this?'

Joey looked at Harry. 'For the party?'

Harry chortled. 'What else?' Aloud: 'twelve, thirteen, fourteen, fifteen.'

He got a rise from Joey.

'What's the counting about?'

'I'm trying to be cool like you and Nancy are cool.'

'We're not cool.' Joey laughed. 'Well, maybe a bit. Nancy for sure.'

Harry chortled. 'This is why I like you, Joey - you talk the talk and walk the talk and even talk the walk. Ever since you were a kid. The self-same thing.'

'Is this for the book? Will you put this in?'

'Everything's for the book. Potentially.' A Harold Blue special grin. 'How art is art.' Another grin. 'The "development" I am here about is making a play for a lead walk-on part.'

"Development"?'

Harry nodded. 'I'm understating the situation.'

The kid waited, retaining his style.

'Ripping off 1,000 pills isn't cool though.'

Harry saw Joey stiffen. Harry watched revellers arrive. They quit their transport and buzzed around. Talking, smoking joints, wide-eyed from dropping E, acid. A grand parade of colour and vibrancy. Their clothes a riot of styles. Dungarees, flower power t-shirts. Smiley face neon-coloured acid house long sleeved tops, flared and bellbottomed jeans, beany hats, hippy-esque beads, sandals, Kickers, Adidas and Reebok trainers. The lads' hair grown and bobbed or tied back. Harry catalogued all in an instant. Kodak-ed the moment for his tome.

And he got it at last; something he had not been able to articulate and nail properly in Second Summer of Love.

What the kids possessed. A glow. The incandescence of youth. Light that shone as adventure surged. An irresistible force that flowed from Wilhelm Richard Wagner in Leipzig in the 1800s to a thousand and more kids hitting this night of July 1990 and living moments they could never realise were vanishing instant and forever and which were never to be lived again.

A mental note. Music. Everything started and ended with music. It always did and always would. Wagner was operas and emotion. Warehouse parties a symphony of acid and house music and feeling. The line clear from Richard W to what Harry watched from this beat-up Fiat.

Joey said, 'It isn't cool at all.'

Admitting he ripped the pills off just like this.

'Why you do it?'

Joey shrugged. 'Why not?' He looked at Harry. 'I thought it'd be fun.'

'Fun?'

'Yes.'

'You and Nancy did this for fun.'

'Leave her out, please.'

Harry flashed on Nancy in the Wonder Woman mask. Retrieving the carrier bag of pills from the bin by the Sugarhouse earlier today. 'She's not involved - that's what you're telling me I should believe?'

'Was my idea, for sure.'

'She is involved but it wasn't her idea.'

Joey smiled.

The kid grinning like he didn't care. 'You need to think about Gerard. Essentially, he owes for the 1,000. You understand what I'm saying? You don't return them and I inform him you ripped him off, then... the only reason I haven't already told him is because I like you.'

Joey looked at Harry.

'What I'm saying is, I won't like you if you don't put all the Es back where they should be so I can tell Gerard they've been located and he's off the hook.'

Joey nodded. 'You're being very reasonable, I have to-'

'I'm kind of relieved it's you and not someone difficult to deal with.'

'I can see that.'

'When will you do it?'

'As simple as this? I put them back, you forget about it?'

'I asked when you'd do it?'

'As soon as possible.'

'Go on?'

'When we get back from the party. I promise'

Harry found a hard tone. 'You haven't got the pills with you? In the car?'

Joey shook his head

'You know,' Harry continued, 'to sell tonight at the party? Seems an ideal ready-made market to me. If I was sitting on a thousand New Yorkers I ripped off and wanted to sell quickly. Where else than a warehouse full of partiers wanting to take E and dance all night? As Gerard says - are you with me?

'I've only got Gerard's pills to sell tonight.'

'Which are my pills, too.'

'You know what I mean. The Es he gives me to sell for him.'

Harry pulled a bottle of JR and swigged the blended whisky and offered it Joey. He took the whisky and bolted the firewater and returned the bottle, and the scene of the convoy outside Sett Ends bucked and flared. Harry said, 'You haven't answered my question - you have the thousand here in the car?'

'Though technically I do have some.'

Harry waited.

'Like you say, Gerard's stuff is yours.' Joey opened the dash compartment and showed him five bags of pills. '100 - if you want them? It's only a little of what I took.'

Harry closed the compartment. 'I'll search the car.'

Joey smiled. 'Of course.'

Harry drank more whisky and placed the bottle on the dash and saw how Joey ripped him off 1,000 pills and gave it the blithe act.

He started by reaching under his seat and got so far and needed to get out and crouch to achieve the purchase required. He did and banged his head and Joey laughed.

'You think it's funny I have to search your car for my pills you ripped off?'

Joey winked and Harry shook his head and felt under the seat and found nothing, pulled a pocket torch and shined it in Joey's face. The kid screwed his eyes up and turned away and Harry laughed. 'I thought it'd be funny,' he said. 'You know what I mean?'

Joey laughed and Harry pulled the front seat forward and pointed the torch in the back and got in there and searched.

Joey said, 'You can look as much as you like, you won't find the pills here.'

Harry shone the torch in his eyes again and Joey turned away. Harry said, 'I am confirming the veracity of your words.'

'I have to say I was surprised when I found out what you really do.'

Harry shrugged. 'What do people really ever do?'

'Why do you do it?'

Harry shrugged and squeezed away from the back seat and got out the Fiat. 'Time for the boot.' Saw Joey's face.

'Don't look so worried. You're telling me the pills aren't here. So I'm not about to find them.' He paused. 'In the boot. Am I?' He walked to the back of the car and Joey joined him and Harry pointed. 'Open?'

'You really don't need to.'

'Am I getting warm?'

Joey twirled his shades. 'We're getting a heatwave.'

'That's droll. Hilarious.'

Harry flipped the boot open, looked inside. 'You know I wouldn't be doing this if you and your girlfriend didn't rip me off.'

Joey looked up and down the road. 'I know and I'm sorry.'

'At last, he apologises.'

Harry scoped the boot, saw a pair of tan Timberland boots, a red puffer jacket. Asked Joey: 'Expecting snow?'

'Been in there since winter - Nelson's the last time I wore that coat.'

'When we talked about Nelson for the book you never mentioned being scared there.'

'I wasn't.'

'Other ravers I spoke to mentioned the moment of the raid, the police and their dogs, batons hitting them.' Harry felt the edges of the Fiat's boot - something he imagined the police did.

'That moment - it could've gone either way. You have to remember a lot inside were E-ing, on speed, trippin'. Having the time of their life and the next thing it's riot police and dogs like they're a lynch mob.'

'Fuck,' said Harry. 'What's this?'

'What?'

Harry heard Joey's voice crack and smiled. He indicated where his hand was - at the left wheel. Over the arch. He felt and pulled off a cover studded down in place to show an opening. 'What do we have here?'

Joey's features swarmed.

'You've gone a funny colour. I don't know what colour those who've tried to tell a story and know they're about to be exposed go but it looks like the colour you've gone.'

Joey kept quiet.

Harry pointed at the arch, at the opening, where he right this moment placed his hand inside. All the time eyeing Joey, seeing his fixed-on smile.

'You want to tell me something?'

Joey, instant: 'What are you talking about, Harry? It's the first time I've seen that cover - I had no clue that was there.'

Harry pulled his arm out the wheel arch recess and pointed at the right one. 'By the look on your face forget warm, I could be getting as hot as the heatwave that's incoming.'

Said this and winked as Joey did when he said the same line moments before.

He started taking the cover off the arch of the right weel. He kept on looking at Joey.

A loud and raucous and life affirming whoop went up from the throng, the parked-up motors.

In anticipation of what was incoming.

Chapter Forty-Three

Joey watched Harry lift the cover off the wheel arch and popped a sweat. Kept smiling. Harry winked again. Harry put the cover down and stuck his hand then arm in the recess. Two-brain tried to gauge how long Harry's arm was. He'd stuck the bags of Es in as far along as he could.

A flash on what might happen.

What if Harry found them? One answer: run; he'd have to take off. His heart pounded; he readied himself to run. It would be scary, it would be farcical, taking off, Harry starting to follow, unable to keep up maybe.

What a scene.

Harry's eyes gleamed and Joey braced himself, thinking he found the thousand pills.

That Harry was about to bring the carrier back out the wheel arch and give Joey no choice.

Braced himself to start running.

Blood and adrenalin mainlining.

Here, now, he's bringing his arm out-

Joey tensed - on his toes and-

Nothing. He stopped dead. Harry came up empty; nothing in his hand. Sweet beautiful nothing. A smile from Harold Blue.

Saying: 'How could I ever doubt you?'

Offering a hand.

They shook.

Harry gripped hard, eyeballed the kids still driving up in motors, getting out their sleds, hitting hot night air. The buzz tangible; it ran electric.

Harry said, 'See you.' Started walking off, turned. 'Joey – two things. No 1, drop the Es back off in the Sugarhouse bin tomorrow. Okay?'

Joey breathed hard. 'Sure.'

'No 2,' said Harry, 'is this – you know how to push it, for sure. I like that – kind of – you're young and, you and Nancy, you have something, and I like that, too. But do yourself a favour, Joey, don't mess me around again.'

'Of course,' said Joey. 'No problem. But leave Nancy out of it.'

Harry smiled. 'You love her, don't you?'

'Yes,' Joey said, 'I do.'

'Here's some advice then – don't do the "leave" her out of it thing. You may do it from some learned ideal of valour. You know, protecting your girl. I mean, I get it. It's chivalrous, in a way. But guess what? It's more chivalrous to treat Nancy as your equal, not a "girl who needs protecting".' Harry took a breath. 'The Russians do it, you know. Treat their women like this.'

Joey perked. 'Do they?'

Harry laughed. 'Not really, but I thought I'd throw it in there.'

Joey laughed. 'You make a good point.'

'This is all going in the book.' A beat. 'Names will be changed to protect the non-innocent. This is the saving grace of what you've done. It cannot be denied it adds to the story. Goes beneath happy ravers dancing and smiling all night from E. It's another layer – of what is also going on.' Harry shrugged. 'It's real life because it is real life.'

Joey wondered how Harry would feel about real life when he realised the Pink New Yorkers weren't going to be put back, and if the plan went right, he'd never see him and Nancy again.

Include that in your book.

He said, 'You are being great about this, so reasonable. Thank you.' A flush of confidence. 'And it is clever, I like it. I look forward to reading how you deal with the dude who is ripped off actually being you, the author. And the dude who ripped off the dude is me. Two-brain Joey Miller, one of Second Summer of Love's central characters. The author also supplying his Es to one of the other main characters - Mr Gerard Frenchy Toces.'

Harry shrugged. 'I can handle it. But you forgot one person.'

Joey blanked. Then, 'Sure - the other main protagonist being an equal and not protected by her boy.' He clicked fingers at Harry. 'In the pill rip-off - DJ Nancy Kools.'

Harry thought about it. 'The more this goes on, the more I got the apt title. So - time to say goodbye. Have a good time, you and Nancy. And make sure the thousand is returned.'

'Definitely.'

Joey watched Harry walk off, looking for his '87 Bentley in the endless cars parked up.

Phew! That was close. He was certain Harry would find the pills, blow their adventure apart. Kill their dream. But, no, the dream remains. The dream is ON.

He clocked Sett End and knew what he had to do.

The night began.

Chapter Forty-Four

Joey

Joey walked from the Fiat 127 to the Sett End entrance. Breathed in, a hit of nostalgia. Nights gone past - the rush of the place, house music pulsing, the bar packed out, everyone dancing, partying, young. Always young.

He walked inside. Since Nelson, the backside fell out of Saturdays here. Not tonight - the place fritzed, like the way it once was. Joey luxuriated in the vibe: Sett End: an old man's pub, a place from another time - the 1970s. Carpeted and scuzzy and low-slung and alive.

He made the bar, ordered a Red Stripe. The barman poured and Joey watched bubbles fizz into the pint glass, memories lighting the brain, senses. Exhilaration, exuberance. The DJ throwing out sounds, kids perspiring - sweat dripping off walls and faces. The place noise and excitement, buzzing off what was incoming.

Tonight: the same thing; the place bounced; sensation mainlined. The DJ played Young MC's Know How, the opening line a call to the floor to dance and forget everything apart from this.

'Some of the busiest rhymes ever made by man...'

Young MC rapped on; Joey bounced at the bar, rode the lyrics, words and notes strung together, making a magic, making him flutter. He swigged Red Stripe and felt his head rush at the night ahead, seeing the drive to Gildersome, a thousand sled convoy lighting the dark, beacons glowing from Lancashire to

219

the Pennines and on to the warehouse.

The moment you entered the still empty warehouse, lights swirling in dark. The venue becoming familiar through the hours and the beat going on and on until first light and dawn and morning. Nancy DJing: playing the next record and the next as the kids partied; wanting more and more and more.

He killed his Red Stripe and said a silent goodbye to Sett End for a last ever time. Blew the bar and the dancefloor a kiss and turned for the door. He might return here in thirty years to remember this then. But nostalgia was not for now. Nostalgia was the future. This moment was for what he did: walking back outside to hear a cheer go up followed by another and then noise. The sound of a thousand engines being fired on; renting the Blackburn air. Followed by more cheers. At the far end of Shadsworth Road vehicles started moving.

Cars and vans and pickups and Transits and VW Campers and scooters and motorbikes roared. Joey felt warm air and ran to the Fiat 127, got in the driver's seat, put the key to the ignition and turned it, fired the car on. Found first gear, released the clutch and rolled out and joined the convoy behind a green Fiesta packed out with girls garbed in dungarees, sleeveless T-shirts, beads; acid house blaring from the sound system.

Joey scoped the rear-view mirror. Behind: a battered light-red Transit van followed, Bob Marley piping; No Woman No Cry and the odour of cannabis. The driver was black and wore a Rasta hat, his two passengers white.

Chapter Forty-Five

The evening clear; a lit sky lighting the convoy as it reached the turning of Shadsworth Road, the lead cars heading left.

A thousand motors snaked down Haslingden Road, took the roundabout, onto the B6231. Horns blared, music sounded, and Joey thought: shit, the police will suss instant what's occurring. Then, this: they'd still have no clue where the convoy headed, where the party was.

Strange - zero sign of the fuzz. The convoy took another roundabout and headed south, staying on Haslingden Road. Joey clocked the rearview mirror and saw vehicles stretching endless, noise incessant. He let the Fiesta go ahead of him so a Robin Reliant could slip in, join the convoy. At the next stop sign a lad in a bucket hat hung out the Robin R window and blew kisses to drivers going the opposite way.

Haslingden Road passed Broadfield and became Roundhill, passing Roundhill Lane onto Hud Hey. Joey kept seeing Nancy - his girl setting up inside the warehouse, sorting her records, a beer on the go, eyes shining, ready to kick the party off.

The convoy took the A680 on to Hud Rake; Hud Rake became High Street, Rake Foot, Kirk Hill Road, Haslingden Old Road, Joey hitting play on a Nancy mix - called Tunes To Move Ya like she named all the mixes she mixed up at home.

This one started with Erasure, Ship of Fools; the song recast the world, Joey eyeballed passing houses, the people who lived there: what did they think of the convoy invading the streets?

The caravan hitting Rawtenstall and going on Newchurch

Road, Church Street and Turnpike and Booth - still no sign of the police - through Bacup village. The Erasure song played out; he wished Nancy was with him, seeing and feeling this.

He would be with her soon - Nancy and the beautiful light in her eyes. Up through Todmorden along the A646 for miles, and over the Lancashire border into West Yorkshire, New Bank, Godley and on along Leeds Road.

Joey started to flip - the venue was incoming; they'd soon be inside the warehouse, the A58 taking the convoy to Whitehall Road for another few miles, now Wakefield, now left up Street Lane, now a right down Town Street, underneath the sky, underneath the clear stars looking down.

The convoy did another right, and then:

Cars parking up, motors dumped, kids started running - Joey scanned for police, still saw none; he kept on driving - down to Gelderd Road, a half mile.

And, here.

Here it was.

Here it is.

Chapter Forty-Six

Joey went to the 127 boot, unclipped the wheel arch cover, felt for the carrier of Es, retrieved it. Glanced about - all clear - and looked for the backpack. There - behind their bags for the getaway tomorrow morning. From here to Manchester Airport and the noon flight to Ibiza on Escape Forever Airlines.

He put the pills in the backpack and slung this on a shoulder and closed the boot.

Grinned at the moon and started for the warehouse, walking with reveller throngs. Partiers in Chipie jeans, Gio-Goi T-shirts, Armani cut-offs, girls with perms and fringes and full-blown bobs. Boys with curtain cuts, pulled back in cornrows. Joey grooved on their style: the kids shopped at Afflecks Palace in Manchester, got kitted out in Wallabees, Kickers, Timberlands, Nike cross trainers, Marc O'Polo, Classic Noveau, C17. The look baggy and loose. Kids walked to the door. Kids ran to the door. Above, a sign - "PRINTWORKS" in black ink on crumbling brick. Joey made the place as an old newspaper/magazine printing press site.

He felt the thousand New Yorkers shift in the backpack and joined the queue, pulled out his ticket for the night the promoters called "Love Decade"; it was tri-coloured - showed a yellow twofaced head, a red, a green one. Beneath - the name and date of the warehouse. On the back of the flyer a "hotline" number to call - 0860 541493 - and info: "private party members only - £6". His came gratis, Nancy got the tickets comped.

Above the price a slogan: "feel the vibration/from the new generation/together as one/the earth's salvation".

Joey chortled; the ticket saying this too: "V.I.P. lounge for everyone"; informing those who couldn't make Love Decade that it would be "LIVE ON LOCAL FM RADIO".

Really?

He made the door. Mobbed out; Joey caught accents - Leeds, West Yorkshire, Blackburn, other disparate brogues. Visioned the kids of the northwest: Blackburn, Burnley, Nelson, Rishton, Darwen, Haslinden, Bacup, Accrington, Preston, Chorley, Oswaldtwistle, and Great Harwood. Lancaster, Morecambe, Galgate, Halton, and Heysham. As in the track, Hardcore Uproar: here were the hardcore uproar who had to be here. The kids of the Blackburn warehouses. The kids who were The Kids.

Joey waved his ticket and the girl on the door held up a hand telling him to wait, and fear flashed. Being gripped with a thousand pills was au revoir, Vienna - a ten-stretch for intent-to-supply class As.

The fear flashed and burned. The girl waved Joey through and he walked in. The warehouse started to fill; revellers were ready to dance and take E and dance more.

Windows allowed in light from the clear night; Joey saw broken panes, brickwork, a cracked floor - normal for an illegal shindig in a broken-and-entered joint. Joey saw copious faces he recognised, kids from previous warehouses, he saw Lancaster/Morecambe kids: DJ Hux, who was on later, Andy Stoddon, who was Ducky's acid house musicmaking pardner, MC Stuey Smudge, and the girl from two streets above his mum's house on Lily Grove: Melanie with two girlfriends, and-

What the? Melanie and her friends: they carried a bench. An actual bench. And he recognised it - from the kitchen from her house on Hope Street, on the second street above his mum's. He jawed for hours sat on it when dropping off pills for her and here it was being carried through the warehouse.

Joey walked over. They positioned the bench by a back wall. Melanie clocked him - a two-way hug. 'What,' said Joey, 'is going the fuck on?'

Melanie was bleached-haired, a few years older. She stood on the bench, got joined by her friends. 'Time to rave,' she said. "And this way we get to see everyone else raving, too."

Joey laughed and walked off and turned and took in the bench again and then turned back and clocked the crowd and considered strategy. Start with a few hand-to-hand sales. Get the word going around about the rocket fuel pills he packed

First, see Nancy. Joey clocked the DJ booth at the back, walked towards it, saw Nancy lit up by the rig. WOW: her freckles glittered - sun-dust and sparkles.

She saw him and Joey got flutters; what he felt the first night at her house - amazed in her presence. As the lights came on, swirling greens and reds across the venue, Nancy leaving the booth, her eyes in his, a look like this was about tonight, about nights gone before and the nights all to come.

'Hello Two Brain Joey Miller, how are you?'

She kissed him and sashayed back to the rig where she pulled a record and double-thumb-supped and placed a record on a deck and hit play on the first tune of the warehouse.

And:

Sound HIT.

The Gildersome warehouse was on. Love Decade kicked off.

The sound of Nancy's opening track, the sound of a siren like the police were incoming. An air-raid warning. Notes of persecution and alarm. Pulsing tremors hit Joey, he synapse-snapped and buzzed like never before. Everyone the same. A whoop and cheer that was animal and carnal and communal. Religious if religion is glee that electrifies. That bolted all. As fists clenched and arms haywired and they danced to mark they once got born.

Joey knew the tune Nancy spun, would never forget it, he heard it inside copious warehouses at other parties.

As the siren sounded on and snare drum started, beat bucked, the lyric spewed: 'IT'S MAGIC/IT'S MAGIC - NOW YOU'RE CAUGHT UP, SO WHAT'S UP???'

Joey reached across the decks to take Nancy's hand; she had a headphone to an ear, cueing the next track in and he blew her a kiss and pointed to the backpack.

Time for business.

The warehouse not yet packed out - Joey got a flash: fuck, if the police close this down sharpish there'll be no market, zero kids to shift pills to. The dream will be deader than dead. A scan around him - girls and boys by the DJ booth, fanning out from here towards the back, lights swirling, illuminating them a moment before they were thrown back into darkness, the wonder of the warehouse, adventure ratcheted up by not knowing where you danced, where you stumbled. Joey caught an idea - got Nancy's attention so she leaned over the decks. 'How about we save our E until you've finished, let's do it together.'

'Yes.' Nancy breathed into his ear. 'It will be really special then.'

He winked and let go her hand, moved towards a group dancing a few feet off, started dancing by them - performed an E-ed up, goof-ball jig. It worked straightaway. A girl in a lilac shirt walked over, chin wobbling - like she already did one.

'What have you had?'

Joey closed the sale instant. 'Pink New Yorkers. Fucking brillo.' Continuing the act. 'The rushes - wow.'

Lilac shirt girl: 'Who you get them from?'

'Can't say but I can get you some.'

'How much?'

'£25 a pop.'

'Give me a second.' She made her friends and Joey saw money being counted, handed to her. Here she came back. 'Ten please.'

Joey buzzed. '£250.' She palmed him the money and he told her to wait. Counted it as he walked towards the back through kids dancing to Nancy's latest tune, recognising it from her sets: T. N. T. - Piano Please. The eerie start, the girl's vocal

- 'OOOOOOH-YEAHHH, OOH OOH YEAH' - and the killer line, a dude simply saying: 'Piano please.'

Joey paused and heard the whole place singing and joined in: 'ARE YOU READY FOR THE MUSIC? YES, WE'RE READY WITH THE MUSIC!!!'

Everyone went bat-shit, Joey danced and twirled his shades, made revellers catch on - who's the lad in the sunglasses so obviously off it?

We HAVE to have what he's had. They did.

As Nancy mixed in Kamara - Back In The Time - kids came up to Joey. He did a blur of hand-to-hands. A world record salesman of the century act. 1/2/3/4/6/10/20/40/75/100 pills. He lost count: of the number sold, the money he stuffed in the backpack, Pink New Yorkers were the bomb, the throng around Joey hit E ecstasy nirvana, rode E-rockets to planets. Kamara and Back In The Time an anthem for this moment. An ode to being here, right now. Kids necked pills and jumped off mountains and bounced back up. They tiptoed on clouds, zoomed in and out of heaven. Became transformed. Existence, simply this: moment after moment after moment after the MOMENT of this moment.

It all went down in five minutes flat.

Joey quit the throng. He still had the girl in the lilac T-shirt's £250. He made the back of the warehouse and turned and danced, trying to see the girl through the crowd. Impossible. He pulled a twenty-bag of pills from the backpack and counted ten and palmed the £250 into the pocket of the bag and made back to find her.

There: with her friends in front of the DJ booth. He counted the ten pink tablets into her hand, fielded 'Thanks yous' and smiles of gratitude and walked off, catching Nancy's eye.

She saw what went down; he double thumbs-upped and pointed at the mass grooving to her tunes - time to execute more business.

Joey did. The stuff FLEW. The pills an H-bomb candy-caned rocket ship to fantasia world where minds were blown interstellar. The kids resided in Pink New Yorker-ville. It's magnificent and mystical. The roof's going off the place. Revellers went wide-eyed and hugged. They second-summer-of-loved. They could not believe how beautiful they were and could not believe they only realised now how beautiful they were.

Joey floated. Sold pills like he sold eternal life, the elixir of youth, like he discovered the start of the world and why the universe was endless. And, lost count: of the pills he punted, the money banked. There were twenty bags of fifty at the start; he checked the backpack and guessed half were gone already. That was 500 at £25 a-pop. That was 12.5K and the night remained young.

Time skated; Nancy waved to Joey as she brought her latest tune in, Joey waved back and punted another quadruple batch of pills to two lads in Stone Island sweaters, felt a tap on his shoulder and turned and saw Gerard.

With Temmy.

And Tina.

He drenched an instant sweat and his heart electric shocked. Gerard gave him the broad smile - the one that did something to Joey inside where anything that did anything did something to anyone. This time the feeling was regret: why did he rip Frenchy off? Gerard was always straight with Joey. Gerard had zero malevolence for anyone straight with him.

Joey said, 'Frenchy - how are you?' To Temmy: 'How are you, T?' Tina: 'Tina, how you doing?'

They nodded and smiled and Gerard said, 'How's business?'

Joey fronted it truth. 'Brilliant, to be honest, never been better - as good as we did at Nelson - the pills are flying - and this place is smaller and there's less in here at the moment.'

Gerard's smile broadened and Joey got prickles - like the Romany sent him a message. The message this: that he knew. Temmy moved in close, like he was delivering the news

Gerard's smile carried. 'We hope so. Remember we-'

Joey held a hand up to pause Temmy and finished the sentence. '-"Are watching you even when we're not".'

Temmy's features flickered. 'No, Joseph lad. I wasn't going to say that.' He laughed - at himself - a total one-off. Temmy Toces didn't know how to take the mickey out of Temmy Toces. 'I was going to say,' he said. 'That you should remember that we like you, so no funny business.' His features became a smile that was Gerard-esque warm.

Disconcerting.

Something wasn't right-

Gerard said, 'What Temmy's saying is that you need to know the police are outside - they've surrounded the place and you need to be careful. How many pills you got left?'

Joey sweated on the news: the fuzz - outside; he adlibbed to Gerard's question. 'Not many - maybe five or ten.' Sweating on this too, if they ask to see inside the bag-

Temmy held his hands up. 'Good news then. The way you're selling, who cares if the police get in. We've made our money.' He grinned, scar flashing in warehouse lights. 'Just make sure you do get rid of those last ones. For your own sake.' He looked at Gerard and Tina and chortled. Sarcastic: 'You can get in trouble having those on you.'

Joey said, 'They're going to close the warehouse down?'

Tina shrugged - her eyes glittered. 'Listen to us, Joey, you need to be careful - there's loads of filth out there. If they're not here to rush the place then why are they here?'

Gerard took Tina's hand. 'Don't worry him too much, Tina.' His eyes glittered like his wife's. 'Tell you what, Two-brain, see how many pink tabs you have left and let's split them - get rid of them.' The Romany put his hand through his mullet. 'Make sure you don't get gripped with any.'

Joey surged gratitude at Frenchy - looking out for him this way - and popped more sweat, felt them watching as he went through the act - opening the backpack. Not the side pocket that held the pills he and Nancy ripped off from Gerard and Harold. That also had the cash from selling them: bundles and bundles of notes.

No: Two-brain preternatural-ed for this moment; thinking he was bound to see Gerard inside tonight. He looked in the main compartment where he stashed two bags and pulled them - some Es were broken, others still whole. He palmed the bags low - like the police might be watching, told them: 'Looks about six left, if you include the bits.'

'Tell you what,' Temmy said. 'Why don't we take the four whole ones and you and your bird-' He pointed at Nancy who had a headphone to her ear. 'Can have what's left.' Temmy's grin razor-sharp. 'Is that fair?'

'Of course,' said Joey. 'Here.'

His hands - shaking, heart racing: the fuzz outside, the bag compartment packed with the ripped-off pills and cash, Gerard and Temmy and Tina watching. He was surrounded by kids E-ed on his supply - only some could be explained legit from Gerard's supply.

Joey pushed his fear away and palmed two pills to Gerard and Tina, palmed Temmy two.

'No,' said Gerard.

Joey shuddered.

Then, Gerard saying, 'Give Joey one back Temmy, with the broken bits he and his bird will have one and a-half each. Fair is fair, she's playing great tunes and they're lovebirds so-'

Gerard took Tina's hand and kissed it. 'Like me and my lady.'

He gave a goofy smile and Temmy said, 'For Christ's sake, Frenchy,' and palmed Joey the pill back and Joey flashed on the ripped-off pills and the ridiculousness of the situation and killed laughs at birth, tried to fix a serious face on.

'Thanks, Gerard,' Joey said. 'It's very kind of you.'

'No problem,' the Romany said and kissed Tina again and she said: 'Wait a minute - what about the money he's holding?

If Joey's shifted nearly all the 200 at £25s that's close to five grand he has to explain if the police do grip him.'

Gerard put his pill in Tina's mouth and Tina put her pill in Gerard's and they dry swallowed and Gerard said: 'That is young Joseph's problem.' Flashed his smile.

Joey took the cue. Gerrard Toces only went so far. 'I get it,' he said. 'Of course, I'll keep hold-'

Joey stopped because-

Nancy on the decks: she dipped the levels up and down on the next record, playing the crowd, as Joey started to recognise the track, as Gerard did too, as Temmy's always-mean grin got dropped, forgotten, as the Tina who was the essence of Tina shone through her sixteen years, as the four of them, this disparate and strange and connected-for–how-long-who-knew quartet hooked together into the sound DJ Nancy Kools gave the warehouse, the bass rumbling, the treble ratcheting, the vocal starting to arrive like the first days of summer beginning, and these first days ones that would and could and should never do anything else except never cease - the vocal announcing as if in unison with the earth and the planets and the stars and what else out there in the celestial canopy, and this vocal epic in this one moment:

'LET'S GET READY/IT'S MORNING TIME FROM THE OUTHOUSE'

A pause.

As Nancy held the crowd. As emerging through the faces, the swirling lights, came the orange seller girl from the very first Blackburn warehouses. As in a mirage. As in something made up. Not real. Joey didn't see her for a long time. He thought she'd stopped coming to parties. Here she was. Eyes like strobes, a smile containing endless smiles, the familiar red headband over curly locks, and the string of oranges draped around her shoulders. Vending oranges like all of our ancestors did vend wares or ideas or themselves or what else down along the atavistic ley lines.

She stopped. Held four of the fruit up. Like she knew each would take one. They did. Joey took the first orange and handed it Tina. He took a second and handed it Temmy. A third to Gerard. The fourth his.

Joey palmed the girl a £10 note and kissed her on each cheek careful, and she smiled and took a fifth orange and pointed at Nancy and blew them a kiss and moved off, away into the throng.

Wow.

Joey goofy smiled. Gerard, Tina and Temmy danced.

As Nancy took the record and back-spinned it, the vinyl rewinding to the very start. Kids whooped, the song started back in, thud-thud-thud!

As, this time, the build-up to the vocal went overloud, Nancy playing the decks like a choir of opera-voiced angels, as the piano - always the piano in house music - bounced the whole place into a group ecstasy that seemed like it could never end.

A gradual and amazing fade and then-

A window smashing nearby. It got followed by whoops. Kids cheered, let go shouts of, 'PIGS!', 'THE FILTH!', 'FUCK THEM WE'RE HERE TO DANCE!'

Gerard told Joey: 'We're getting out of here, you're not the only one holding.' Tina leaned into Joey and kissed his cheek. Her eyes were large - like the pill she did hit instant. Gerard's eyes were golf ball eyes. He grabbed Joey's throat and said, 'Temmy's right - we do like you, course we do or I wouldn't be letting you drive my car to all those warehouses - Nelson, New Year's Eve at Ewood, by the canal where the fucking roof nearly fell in, good times all of them were they not-'

Temmy grabbed him. 'Frenchy, not now.'

Gerard swayed - like the E he did was about to blow his head off. 'Point is-' Slurring his words like he was drunk, Joey stifling a giggle, seeing Tina do the same. 'Point is-' Gerard began again and stopped. He waved a finger in the air at no-one. 'Point is –' A third time; Joey couldn't keep it in; he let go a laugh and couldn't stop. It got Tina going, she started laughing. Gerard's eyes rolled and bent double from the force of the E he chomped.

He came up for air, his eyes blue orbs and stared android-like.

Temmy pointed and started laughing, stomach stitches at the state of his cousin. 'Jesus Christ, Gerard lad. If you can't handle your pills, don't do them, you know what I mean.'

Gerard smiled and opened his mouth slow and said, 'Thomas lad', and took Temmy by the throat and lifted him off his feet.

'You silly fucker you,' he told him.

Joey stopped laughing instant; Frenchy kept holding Temmy, his eyes far off. He looked at Joey and indicated his cousin with a finger. 'What can you do with a character like this, Joseph?' Temmy trembled. It looked ridiculous, Temmy looked ridiculous.

Gerard indicated Joey. 'You can laugh all you like - you know what I mean? Why: because you're you, Joey Miller, seventeen, a baby.' Slow, putting Temmy down, smiling as if never more benevolent. 'Thomas, you should know better.'

Temmy said, 'I'm sorry G-' and stopped dead as Gerard held a hand up that told him shut the fuck up now.

Tina took Frenchy's hand. 'Come on, Gerard, let's go. Temmy. The plod - they're coming.'

More sounds of windows smashing, shouts and jeers. Joey sensed a mood-shift - the kids started to think about what occurred - the spectre of Nelson haunted: was this going to be the same?

Gerard's chin juddered like he was gone again; his cheeks bulged.

But-

He snapped into a fresh clarity, saw all that was happening.

As: more noise sounding above them, from the roof. Joey flashed on the police being up there and his backpack - the cash and the pills - and knew he had a problem.

Tina said, 'Joey, be safe, if it gets too much dump whatever you have to.' She winked and she led Gerard off, Temmy following, and Joey watched and then lost them in the crowd.

Nancy waved and pointed at the decks - the last tune coming up. Motioned him: come here, let's stand together.

He moved towards and behind the 1200s and took Nancy in his arms and they hugged. As if children again. As if already old, their life behind them. All a memory of what was this eve.

As the moment went on. As revellers danced and those nearby saw them embrace and whooped and cheered. As the moment spread and the whole warehouse caught the mood. What was happening. The police outside and the kids inside partying.

Joey and Nancy broke their embrace to cheers, applause.

Broke to the sound of:

NOISE.

WINDOWS BREAKING AND CRACKING. SHOUTS AND SCREAMS. The police incoming. Emotion mainlined, revellers danced, fists got raised, arms went aloft - this is everything, here, what the whole thing is.

More sound; like the police would storm the party any moment, the sound urgent, cutting through the record-

No; not cutting through the tune - becoming the only noise as Nancy slowly, agonisingly, brought the record down, dialled volume low.

The place went bananas, the warehouse party hit delirium, energy rocketed, taking them all - as if the noise was them and they were the noise.

Nancy whispering in Joey's ear, 'The Night Writers - Let the Music Use You. What a beautiful record.'

Now, silence.

Then: THE SILENCE IS OVER.

Nancy dialled the volume on the record up halfway. Held it here, drawing the crowd in, closer. They forgot the fuzz and moved towards Nancy; DJ Kools raising the volume 1, 2, 3 notches and sending the place batshit ballistic.

The lyric euphoric, ethereal - a thousand lids singing: 'This song is from heart/hey hey can't you see/everyone dancing with me.'

Joey and Nancy locked arms and twirled, the place together, together.

Always.

Closing their eyes, goose-bumps and prickles, the moment exploding for a long happening.

Now: Nancy faded the song down slowly, let the silence occur again.

Long.

Shrieks and shouts. The place going CRAZZZZY.

As, agonizingly, Nancy brought in ANOTHER tune - a bonus track. The reaction as the crowd recognised bars of piano, knowing what was incoming.

Together - Hardcore Uproar.

Nancy said, 'This is what we are.' She pointed at kids out of their minds on hope, at Joey and herself. 'Them and us, you and I, DJ Nancy K and Two-brain Joey.'

He blinked a tear, two more. Nancy leaned in. 'Look at them.' She waved at kids and kids waved back. 'And you and I have not taken a bean, never mind a pink bean.'

'One delicious pink bean.'

'But they have taken one. Several.'

Hardcore Uproar started in Nancy zoomed volume up; the space-age synth soared, they all soared, the kids floating up together away from earth and through the stars and past the planets as Jupiter and Mars and Saturn and Mercury and Venus and Uranus and Neptune floated past, all orbs and the sun incoming in the dark and incandescent light of all.

A symphony - paean.

The vocal ridiculous, the vocal surely not true, the vocal like this tune, like all house tunes that got the soul of the kids, a magical occurrence that was the senses, that was life informing all, simply, to come-the-fuck-on-right-the-fuck-now:

HARDCORE UPROAR!!!

The vibe fritzed, the place stoked; walls shook, kids danced like this WAS their last dance.

AS: the police started raiding - on ladders at windows, from the roof, via verandas outside.

Nancy said, 'Come on, let's take one.'

Joey smiled. 'Let's fucking do it.'

'You do have a couple left?' said Nancy.

'Oh yes.'

He reached in the backpack and brought out two Pink New Yorkers.

'Shit,' said Nancy. 'Look.'

At the back of the warehouse a ripple of heads and bodies. Like something moved towards the kids who danced there and they flinched. Joey put one of the Es back in the bag and halved the other and handed Nancy hers.

'This is all we need,' he said and leaned forward and placed the half he held on her tongue. She placed the half she held on his tongue and they closed their eyes and kissed and took the half a pink new yorker from the other's tongue and swallowed and hugged.

A moment. Forever.

To the end of timelessness and beyond and back again.

They broke and started to dance and Nancy made her hands into a heart and Joey the same. He touched his to Nancy's and felt her fingers tremble and she said, 'How many you sell?'

'More than half - makes around 300 left I reckon.'

'Listen,' she said. 'Whatever happens between now and then - you and me. Always. Promise?'

It jolted him. 'What you mean? 'Now and then'?'

'The police are outside; we've still got a lot of pills left. Who knows what's going to happen?' She put a finger to his lips. 'Don't worry - I've got a plan.'

'A plan?'

She smiled slowly. 'It's simple and it's genius - that's the genius.'

Joey twirled his shades. 'I thought genius was my department.'

She giggled. 'Too-vain - quick, duck.' She bobbed down behind the decks, pulled him with her. 'Give me the bags of E.'

'What?'

'Time's ticking - come on.'

Joey opened the backpack, looked at Nancy. 'There's actually only four bags - that means 200 pills, means we cleared 800.'

Nancy gave him a kiss. 'Even better.'

'What's 800 times-'

Nancy's eyes gleamed. '800 times 20 is 20,000 by my maths. 20K - £20,000.'

'20,000 fat spondoolies. We did it,' said Joey. His eyes gleamed. 'The sun here we come. Ibiza here we go.'

'Not yet, we still have to get out of here. Now give me the bags.'

Joey palmed them Nancy and she tied her hair back into two thick plaits and winked at Joey and said: 'Watch this.' She pushed one bag into her left plait and Joey watched it disappear. 'Hey Presto!'

'Jesus,' he said. 'Hey fucking Presto.' Handed her the other bag and she hid this the same in her right plait and they clasped hands and stood back up and Nancy said, 'One last record - a last tune to move ya.' She pointed at the throng, dialled down Hardcore Uproar slow to shouts and shrieks and cries for more.

From the back - more windows breaking; a voice through the chaos, via a megaphone:

'THIS IS DCI DAVID STONE OF WEST YORKSHIRE

POLICE; WE HAVE YOU SURROUNDED.

PLEASE BE AWARE MY OFFICERS ARE ENTERING THE BUILDING AND WE ARE GOING TO ARREST EVERYONE INSIDE. WE WILL BE FILMING. PLEASE COME QUIETLY!'

The kids booed raucous and Joey said, 'Fuck - arrest everyone. You'll have to be quick, Nancy.' He popped a sweat, tried to keep his nerve. Nancy squeezed his hand and pulled a disc from her record bag.

A powder-blue colour, a sparkling 12-inch.

'This is the sound. Of us.'

She placed it on the left Technics 1200 and took Joey and led him out of the DJ rig.

More sounds of chaos, getting closer/louder. The police were incoming, fear pounded through Joey - they were about to be gripped; if they got searched and the pills fell out of Nancy's hair.

Joey, breathless: 'If we get caught, if they find the pills on you - in your hair, I'm saying I made you do it. Made you hide them there - I pulled a knife and gave you no choice.'

She put a finger to his lips. 'Ssssh.' Took hold of Joey's forefinger and placed it underneath hers and leaned over from the front of the DJ rig to the deck where the powder-blue record waited, and guided their fingers towards the play button.

Whispering: 'For always. Press.'

She kissed Joey - the world tilted and spun.

And they pressed the button.

Pressed play on the last tune of Gildersome, the last tune of the last ever warehouse party for the kids.

HIT.

Acid squelch, twelve seconds of cha-cha jive, Joey recognised the sound instant, one of the few house records he knew the name of.

A Joey Two-Brain and Too-Vain whoop and holler:

'DREAM 17 by Annette!!!'

And Nancy shouted back: 'FOR MY BOY!!!'

The bass was ridiculous - the place shuddered, kids forgot the fuzz breaking in, raiding; this was about them.

As, the vocal - what a vocal - told them, the world: 'You know I'd walk round this earth just to be a part of you, boy.'

Joey sang to Nancy. He changed 'boy' to 'girl'. As the bass pounded on - Nancy saying: 'Picture it, what we've done.'

The tune soared; the night soared.

'Now,' said Nancy. 'Come on, let's go. I know where.'

There - police, scores of them; a blue wave in the dark, lights swirling over their heads, the heads of the ravers, the kids.

'Where?' said Joey.

She pointed. 'Up. I saw when I got in here. Thought it might be handy. You know, for a moment precisely like this, when we need to skedaddle.' She took hold of his lips and kissed him and led him.

Joey saw a side wall, fire-escape steps. They moved towards them - the record played on. They weaved through revellers, hit the fire-escape, took stairs quick - the fuzz might see, they had to take the chance.

Two stairs at a-time, reaching halfway and hearing noise - loud, near. They looked behind and down. 'Come on,' said Nancy. 'Move.'

Here - a line of police moving slowly, methodically. They've got the place under control, in near-lockdown. Corralling kids; arresting them. Nancy and Joey kept moving, reached the top, hit a mezzanine platform - gridded - that gave a view to below.

They crouched and watched.

The police - in complete ascendancy. They set up cameras on tripods. They started leading kids past them to be filmed, documented. Dream 17 played on - it neared the end.

'Jesus,' said Joey.

'They mean business,' said Nancy. 'There's nothing that scares the people more than their morals scaring them. Look at the

239

cameras, recording everyone, like they're criminals rather than kids having a good time.'

'Scary,' said Joey.

Nancy smiled and shook her head. 'Don't be sucked into their panic. That's what Thatcher, the government want. What the police need. Fear feeds on fear. Take the fear away and fear goes hungry and dies. Remember Nelson when they stormed the place - I was dancing right at that moment and this policewoman dragged me out, and you know what I said? In this riot caused by them, the police, I said, 'What are you scared of?' She laughed and said: 'You're the one who's scared because you've taken God knows what and now, you're regretting it.'

'Joey - I told this policewoman: 'Look me in the eye and tell me you're not scared - of what's going on here - and I'll tell you why, and it's not because we're what Thatcher wants you to think, it's because you can't be more than twenty-years-old yourself and you're scared you're missing out.''

'What she say?'

Nancy shrugged and saw something - someone - below. 'Nothing. She kept dragging me out.' Nancy pointed. 'Look.'

Joey saw the fuzz in control, revellers laughing and walking out of the warehouse. 'What is it, baby?'

Nancy pointed to a camera-tripod set-up. Standing by it, two uniformed police and two men in suits. 'Wow. It is. Look - look who it is.'

Behind the uniforms and suits in the shadows.

'What, Nancy?'

'Not what - who.'

Where she pointed - Harry. Standing there watching kids get led out, arrested, filmed. Not being arrested or filmed himself. Standing with the police. Joey comprehended instant. Two-brained what went down: Harry did a deal with the fuzz - the two in suits; they had to be plain clothes, CID, almost definitely Lancaster fuzz. Did a deal - for his book.

Joey could hear Harold saying: 'I can get you info on this illegal rave happening on 21st July, near Leeds. I give you the info, let you make collars, get a big win in front of your bosses, and in exchange you let me come and get stuff for my book. The book is called Second Summer of Love and is going to document the evil and pernicious Acid House warehouse party scene.'

Harry couldn't grass him and Nancy up to the plod - too chancy, as they were in his book; he couldn't risk them being arrested before the party. Would kill a central swathe of the tome - their inside-Gildersome account of the swan-song, crash-and-burn of the Blackburn warehouse scene. Joey the 'raver' and Nancy 'the DJ'. But what Harry could do was word up Lancaster police for some quid pro quo.

Joey telling Nancy: 'Harry is smarter than we thought. How he got into his E dealing operation I'd love to ask but will probably never get the chance now. He's obviously done a deal with the fuzz to get in here, watching this.'

Nancy took Joey's face. 'I can feel my eyes.' They glittered. 'The half,' she said. 'It's coming up.' Her eyes pulsed like what she said direct affected them.

'Yes,' said Joey. 'Yes.' The half he did started to work. 'Wow.' He pointed at his temples and fluttered his hands in a thaaaat's showwwwbiz gesture and giggled. 'Mine, too. What a feeling.'

Nancy's eyes glittered on. 'I tell you what was comical - at the Brown Cow, when we dosed the women with those bits of E.'

Joey remembered Amber. 'Harry's wife enjoyed herself.'

'Like never before.'

'And Harry.'

Nancy smiled like a thousand volts synapse-snapped her. 'I am sure they "enjoyed" themselves when they got home.'

'Haha - I never thought of that.'

They kissed and Nancy said, 'Let's go. This is the bit when we escape.'

'To dreamland.'

'Exactly,' said Nancy.

Joey's eyes went on stalks. 'How?' The half an E made it feel like nothing mattered.

'The only way is up.'

'Sure is.'

'No, silly.' Nancy giggled. 'I mean it is up - up.' She pointed behind them - another fire escape, this one to the roof. 'Come on. I checked this out, too. Before.'

Joey's eyes went wider. 'Wow. You are amazing.'

Nancy smiled. 'This is the final reel.'

Joey got E-prickles; his limbs quivered. 'Where we run away - fly away, take a jet-plane to the sun.'

'This summer,' said Nancy. 'Never ending.'

They started moving, staying low to keep from being seen - by the police, by Harry. They reached the fire escape. Up there - the roof, outside.

The waiting world.

Chapter Forty-Seven

Harry

Five minutes earlier

Harry wore a full beamed up smile. This was great. The story went off like a bomb, the book was close to home-and-hosed. He was inside the warehouse. He watched, luxuriated at the sight - glorious if you were Harold Blue, penning a yarn called Second Summer of Love. Glorious if you knew there was going to be a raid on the party taking place in a warehouse at Gildersome, 21st July, 1990.

Glorious if you were playing both ends. The Nancy/Joey/Gerard end. AND the police end.

Standing next to the cameras filming kids being led out. Kids with large eyes and grins and an excitement the police did not share.

Harold B is excited. He played this as if a lost Mozart symphony named Rapture in Gildersome. Standing next to two "raver pals" in plain clothes. DI Walter Swaggert and DC Brian Ball of Lancaster Police. The quid pro quo for the snitch stuff on the warehouse party: details on the raid and a birds-eye-view of it. As now. Swaggert and Ball there at West Yorkshire Police's behest. A thank-you - a big one - for the red-hot info Swaggert and Ball furnished. There, also to observe which Lancaster and Morecambe miscreants attended.

Grafting for the party organisers.

Grafting selling E and speed, acid and dope.

Harry saying to Swaggert: 'What have you got?'

The DI in his usual ill-fit suit and black shoe combo. Swaggert said, 'Who, you mean. And the answer is - lots. Example.' He pointed at two lads in hooded T-shirts and Wallabees. 'Drew and Davey Burns run that cowboy promotion company - West End Productions. Well, they're nicked. Nicked and on camera.'

Harry ducked to the side; the brothers knew him from the Lancaster Guardian feature he wrote up on them.

Ball clocked the move. 'Friends of yours?'

Swaggert laughed. 'Everyone's a friend of Mr Blue.'

Harry watched the Burns bros walk out. 'I interviewed them last year for the Guardian - Drew's the younger one, the operator.'

'Why the Walter Mitty act?' said Ball.

Swaggert said, 'Walter Mitty?'

Harry told the DC: 'Walter Mitty, Brian? I think you mean the Scarlet Pimpernel.'

Ball smiled.

Harry watched the kids being led out. 'How many you think got in here before your West Yorkshire friends broke the party up?'

'5,600,' Swaggert said.

Harry scanned the lines of kids walking out. 'Looks more to me.'

Ball said, '900 is my guess.'

Walter nodded. 'You may be right.' A glance at Harry. 'Let's be honest - you usually are, Brian.'

Harry kept on looking at the kids being led out. For two specifically: Nancy and Joey. He watched it all, the party unfolding after getting in here early. Saw Nancy DJing, Joey selling pills. Selling pills that were of a number far beyond what he would legitimately have from Gerard. Pills Two-brain had to source elsewhere.

Which was, of course: the 1,000 Joey and Nancy stole from outside the Sugarhouse. Knowing this 100% because Harry felt them in Joey's Fiat when he put his arm in the wheel arch and knew then Joey lied when denying he had the pills with him.

Not lying - that was harsh. The kid was seventeen. He spun Harry a yarn because Harry was Harry. A nerd Joey didn't rate, felt no fear of. Harry saw it clear and it was a boon - to his self-knowledge, to the book. Second Summer of Love featured a main character who ripped off a thousand Es and when cornered by the dealer, the character lied.

Harry loved it; what a plot twist. He'd do some authorial sleight-of-hand, gild the lily. Shift who ripped the Pink New Yorkers off away from Joey - and Nancy - because Harry couldn't finger them in print. He'd make it the anonymous, Gerard Toces' character, the E-dealer, who would claim the 1,000 pills ripped off him but was the actual thief and so the actual liar.

Fabricated it happening - to try and get ahead: because that's what readers believed a character like him would do.

Also: he'd shift it away from Joey and Nancy because they were in love and he saw what they did as - yes - romantic. Was really why he let it pass when he felt the pills stashed in the wheel-arch.

Now: Harry looked for Joey and Nancy and couldn't see them. He scanned every corner, wall: nothing.

Then - he clocked a fire escape and he saw where the stairs went to the top and he saw a grilled mezzanine and two figures.

Shadows.

Disappearing as they took a second fire escape up.

To the roof. Scarpering. Nancy and Joey trying to elude the police because depending on how many pills they sold; they held the thick end of 20K in cash plus however many leftover pills. Unsold Pink New Yorkers that were Class A drugs and would get them ten years for possession with intent to supply.

Harry had a choice. Snitch them to the police, make Swaggert look even better to his bosses. Or he could say nothing. It was no choice at all. He told Swaggert: 'I'm going for a look around.'

'Knock yourself out.'

Harry nodded and headed for the fire escape and took the

stairs, slow, watching the scene below him start to ease. The lines of kids being led out past the cameras thinned. The lines of uniformed police followed, taking no notice of the middle-age man reaching the mezzanine.

Harry seeing Swaggert and Ball leaving too.

The second fire escape.

There - windows showed it was still dark outside. Harry walked to the stairs and looked up - at the top a door to the roof.

He took the fire escape and made the door and opened it. The roof, a half-moon giving light. A single cloud, stars in the sky. 'Mid-period Constable,' Harry whispered and laughed. He scanned the roof - in the middle a disused hut with broken windows, a kicked-in door. Beyond - an adjoining warehouse. Harry made the hut and looked inside: nothing.

He walked the front edge of the roof and peered over.

WOW.

Rows and rows of police cars and vans. There had to be hundreds. Harry saw straightaway that West Yorkshire Police was going to arrest every kid inside the warehouse and take them away. They began lining them up. Hundreds of lines of kids ten or fifteen deep.

A first light of morn coming through the inked night. Harry saw kids E-ed out of their heads. Eyes made large by the coming dawn. They laughed and they danced on the spot. The police meant nothing to them.

What he didn't see: the two lovebirds.

Where?

He walked to where the roof met the adjoining warehouse and jumped and walked on. This roof long and thin with a skylight window splitting it along the centre, a trapdoor going downstairs. He opened this - tried to. Locked. He walked the front edge of the roof and watched as police began leading the lines of kids to their cars and vans.

'Wow,' said Harold again and walked to the back of the roof.

Here: rust-coloured fire escape steps to the bottom. Nancy and Joey surely escaped this way.

He started down the steps.

The new dawn.

It came on more.

Chapter Forty-Eight

Nancy and Joey

The same time

Nancy and Joey stood on the hill and watched police put kids in cars and vans and drive them away. The dark still held, the dawn came through it. The kids looked blitzed. The scene made them feel something they never felt before.

Happiness and sadness.

The hill was above the warehouse, looking down on the Treefield Estate. 10,000 volts of MDMA surged through the kids. Many of them took their pill moments before the raid. Nancy and Joey were electrified too.

Kids kept being taken away. The lines that went, endless.

Nancy pointed. 'Look at the stars and light coming through them.'

'Beautiful,' Joey said.

'Oh no.'

'What?'

'There.' Nancy pointed at the warehouse next to the warehouse that got raided. Coming down the same fire escape steps they took: Harry.

'Jesus,' said Joey. 'Come on.'

'No,' said Nancy. 'Let's not go yet - I want to see how this ends because we both know this is it. It will never be repeated.'

'He'll see us.'

'Not from behind that tree - come on, while it's still dark.' She took his hand and led him to the tree and they ducked behind. 'Can you believe he's still nosing around?'

'Harry's not nosing around, Nancy. He's looking for you and me. He must've seen us before, when he was standing by the cameras with the police, and followed us.'

'You think he guessed what we did?'

'Forget guessed. He knows.'

'Knows?'

Joey clicked on how. 'When he searched the car outside Sett End. I think he found the pills, felt the bag when he searched the wheelarch. Felt them and said nothing. He is one operator.'

She said, 'Why did he let you go on then with the pills?'

Joey smiled. 'For the story, his book.'

Nancy watched Harry reach the bottom of the steps. 'You sound sure.'

'I am.'

'I think you're right.'

The dawn shifted; warm night air became warm morning air. 'What is he doing? I mean, in a general sense?'

Joey shrugged. 'What Harry does.'

Nancy smiled. 'The question is: why?'

Joey glowed from the half a pink new yorker he took. 'Same reason we want to go to Ibiza, flying away to the sun.'

'A risky way to go adventuring - flood Lancaster and Morecambe with Es, supply them to Gerard Toces.'

Joey shrugged. 'As dangerous as ripping them off.'

Nancy laughed. Her eyes fizzed. 'We're the same. He's a nerd in his suit, listening to classical music, while we-' She clasped Joey's hand. 'We are in love…'

Now: the first streaks of sun in the sky, rays turning the cobalt blue a warmer hue.

Joey said, 'Did you say we're in love?'

Nancy felt a warm E-surge. 'No doubt.'

'Not since the first time I saw you.'

Nancy giggled. 'That was years ago. When we were kids.'

Joey thought about it. 'I only realise it now.'

He stroked her hair and the light of the sun streamed between them and they looked at the other and held the look and then the moment broke.

The scene below: Harry disappeared. The last kids were being searched, put in cars and vans and driven off.

Finally, two - a girl and boy. They held hands and were led by uniforms to a van and taken away out of the carpark.

A silence.

Now - a straggler walking up Gelderd Road, past the parked-up cars left by kids who got arrested. The straggler stopped by a fawn Vauxhall Maestro and opened the driver's door and sat inside and wound the window down, started the motor and didn't drive off. He turned the motor back off and looked towards Joey and Nancy.

He couldn't see them - they were still behind the tree.

Now: music.

Music coming through the sunrise, through the orange rays lighting the vista of offices and derelict buildings and outhouses and garages and parked-up cars and vans and minibuses of this Sunday morning on the Treefield Estate.

The opening bars - Nancy squealed. 'I do not believe what is playing.' Her eyes grew and Joey felt his E go large and he felt prickles and goose-bumps.

'Strings of Life,' she said. 'Rhythim is Rhythim.'

The sun rose further and they kissed and felt the heat on them and here came the sweet piano riff of the opening to Strings of Life. The kid in the Vauxhall got out the motor, leaned on the bumper and lit a spliff and flamed it. A plume of blue smoke swirled in clear morning air. He swayed to the sound of piano and strings.

'Magic,' said Nancy.

They held hands and danced and the kid smoked and swayed. Joey and Nancy watched the kid and they came from behind the tree and jigged around this once and the birds chirped and the sky got lightened by a sun that turned golder in these moments. Nancy and Joey started skipping down the hill and they reached the warehouse and there were no more police or cars or vans or kids and as Strings of Life faded out in that silence of the new dawn, they slowed and they did a full circle of the warehouse building. When they reached again the front they looked inside through a set of broken windows and saw how this again was a disused building and nothing else.

They swapped looks and moved towards the Vauxhall.

The kid still smoked the spliff. The kid looked at them. The kid said, 'Where did you come from?'

Nancy pointed at the warehouse. 'In there.' She pointed up the hill. 'And there.'

The kid nodded and Joey saw how young he was. 'What about you?'

A sigh as if far older than his callow years. 'I got here last night, parked up for the party, and went to my girlfriend's round the corner as she was babysitting for her sister for a bit, but I fell asleep on the sofa and when I woke up and got back here the party was over.'

'You know what happened?'

'What?' The kid looked at Joey.

'The police raided it. Got inside about four, took everyone out, lined them up, arrested them all, put them in vans and cars and took them away.'

'Fucking hell,' said the kid. 'Everyone?'

'Fucking hell,' said Nancy.

Joey nodded. 'Mad when you think about it.'

The kid nodded and they shook and Nancy and Joey walked away to find the Fiat 127 Extra.

They didn't look back.

Chapter Forty-Nine

Gerard

One minute later

Gerard sat in the Sierra and watched Joey and Nancy get in the Fiat. Tina in the front passenger seat, Temmy the back. The Sierra parked ten cars down from Joey's sled on the other side of Gelderd Road, where it curved, where Joey and Nancy couldn't see it unless they kept on down the hill.

Joey fired the Fiat on and hit first gear and the gas and started driving him and Nancy away, and Gerard fired up the Sierra on and waited for the Fiat to pass.

Here. Sailing past the Sierra on Tina's side. Gerard's eyes booted; Tina and Temmy's eyes the same. Fizzing from the banquet of Pink New Yorkers and pre-cut cocaine. Frenchy like he tripped his own personal fantasia, saying: 'There he is.'

The Fiat reached the bottom of Gelderd Road and Gerard waited for it to turn and fired the Cosworth up and followed them.

'Now,' he said. 'Let's see.' He got eyes that whirled in response: two sets.

Chapter Fifty

Harry

The same time

Harry kicked back in the cream-coloured Bentley '87 Turbo. He looked at the light and the sun rays and the orange-yellow tinctured sky. He looked at the white-coloured Sierra Cosworth further down Gelderd Road and made out Gerard in the driver's seat, Tina next to him, Temmy in the back. He looked at the Fiat 127 in-between his sled and Gerard's, half-way down Gelderd Road, and made out Joey and Nancy.

He chuckled; Harry laughed harder and harder. He watched Gerard T who watched Joey and Nancy. This some kind of Russian doll set-up. Two-brain and his girl nested in Gerard T's set-up and Gerard nested in Harry's: 100% matryoshka dollie stuff.

Harry flipped open the dash compartment to show a row of three unopened half-bottles of Johnnie Red. They lay on their side. They waited to be cracked. He pulled one and cracked the seal and unscrewed the top and bolted a healthy nip.

The world flared and bucked. The buzz he got from the blended whisky buffed and sheened the whole deal. That's what it was for. That's what his classical music was for. Affect the senses preternatural.

Everything swelled up before Harold Blue. The night just gone. The book he penned. Second Summer of Love was gloriously near full cooked. The warehouse went off swell, the police raid,

Joey and Nancy ripping him off, Harry's liking of them doing so, the colour and backstory he accrued about the Nelson party, all the other warehouses since the scene started two years ago.

The whole acid house thing was a youth culture tsunami Harry sensed would keep on after-shocking endlessly.

Ahead - the white Sierra pulled out slow; ahead of Gerard's sled - the Fiat hit the end of Gelderd Road and hung right.

Harry fired on the Bentley '87, watched on and took one more slug of Johnnie R and felt the universe expand in waves eased ,his sled out behind Joey and Nancy in the tritone rusted-up Fiat, behind Gerard, Tina and Temmy in the white-coloured Sierra.

Show-time.

Chapter Fifty-One

Nancy and Joey

Joey pulled the passports. He pulled the flight tickets to Ibiza. He kept on steering the Fiat. He twizzed his shades and said, 'You know the way to Manchester Airport?'

'Erm, no,' said Nancy and giggled.

'Neither do I.'

'Not that it matters,' said Nancy.

'Which is funny,' said Joey. 'Because I agree.'

He balled the Fiat into Birstall and passed stone houses and shops, took a roundabout, passed a red phone box, a church, motoring through treelined lanes and hit the M621. The sun went higher, the heat shimmered. The 22nd of July 1990 was one more scorcher.

He drove two miles and hit the M62 and a thought flashed.

Lancaster.

The thought became a decision.

One big yes. A sweet moment of inspiration. Of doing the right thing at the right time. He knew what he - THEY - should do and knew Nancy would agree. And - like she got a sixth-sense she took his hand. 'You want to go back.'

Joey's eyes lit a brighter green. 'And I think you know why. So, together - come on. Let's say what we're going to do.'

Their eyes fizzed, their smiles could never end. They took a breath and raised fingers and counted '1, 2, 3'.

Then, louder: 'LET'S RETURN THE MONEY!'

A second, centrifuging. Everything that contained everything blasted through them and they laughed and Nancy said: 'Brilliant - we don't need the money.'

'This way,' Joey said. 'Gerard can pay Harry back and no-one need ever know and everything ends sweet. In light.'

'Because,' said Nancy, 'all we need is you and me.'

Joey grinned and saw the turn for the M60 and took Junction 15 towards the M61 and then onto the M6 for Preston. They'd hit junction 33 for Lancaster in twenty minutes. Then, the fun would begin.

Behind them, unseen: Gerard, Tina and Temmy did lines of coke in the Sierra as they followed. The bag passed between them all the way from Gildersome to Preston. They went through grams and grams; the motorway whizzed by and the day got hotter; the sun this hot Amarillo jewel that would never stop shining; they a threesome who could not stop laughing at Joey and Nancy.

Ahead: Joey tooled the Fiat 127 past Forton Services, reached Junction 33, took the turning, hit the curve for Galgate roundabout at speed. The Fiat's tritone colour flashed in the sun. He took right to the village. They headed past the Plough; Nancy pointed at the bin outside the pub and smiled. They headed under the bridge, where they parked their first night together. Where they pilfered the pills the first time, then returned them. Where Gerard and Temmy drove past and nearly saw them.

Now: they left Galgate, towards the university. The day kept on getting hotter.

Chapter Fifty-Two

Harry

Seconds later

Harry got a feeling he wanted to be correct. Surely, though, the feeling couldn't be true. Could it? He trailed Gerard trailing Joey. He had to be careful - his cream-coloured Bentley stuck out like Gerard's white Sierra. Heavy traffic gave cover, the blazing sun, the umpteenth hot July day brought out day-trippers.

He kept his eyes on Frenchy's sled and the Fiat. The feeling still remained there, went stronger - he pondered: is this wish-fulfilment? Can this be what is going to occur? He had Mozart's 10th on - it gave the sun, birds flitting from trees a symphonic sense. Like stuff was pre-created. All was here before it ever was. Call it god or godly.

He fixed on the eternal question: why life? And, what was life for? Could send him mad ruminating on this. Trying to imagine the beginning of time. Before the beginning of time. Was there anything? Was it only him who needed to know?

They'd motored from Gildersome to Galgate. Ahead - Joey and Nancy passed the Plough Inn, followed by Gerard, Tina and Temmy in the Sierra. Harry pushed the Bentley '87 past the Plough, eyed the bin-drop, ruminated on the Es he wholesaled to Gerard the last six months. The connection with Frederick Street the most - only - outlandish act he ever pulled; falling into a role when he met the Fredster in that Rhodes Town bar.

Like he was street-smart and somehow naïve; sensing Street would be intrigued, would buy the act as genuine. Harry had no clue why he did it. How this emanated from some part he had thus far be unaware of was inside him.

Now, passing the Plough and clicking this was where Joey found out what he did. Clicking on this, too. Becoming more certain: about where Joey and Nancy were driving, what they were doing.

If he was correct, what about Gerard? If he did not get to Joey and Nancy first, before they could do what Harry was sure they were about to do, this was going to turn out bad - for Joey and Nancy and for Harry.

They could spill who wholesaled Gerard the pills; who Harold Blue really was - before he could intervene.

Chapter Fifty-Three

Nancy and Joey

Joey balled the Fiat through Scotforth and Greaves and hit South Road and said to Nancy, 'Fancy a drive?'

She laughed. 'We're having one now.'

They passed the Lancaster Infirmary; hospital windows glinted in sun rays; parked ambulances gleamed. Time pulsed. Joey said, 'Let's do it, then.'

He pointed the Fiat towards the Grammar school, zipped through town, up the hill, took Wyresdale Road for six miles through Quernmore, through farmland/countryside, drove up, up, until they hit a tarmac strip and Jubilee Towers, the towers actually a single turret edifice that gave views over Lancaster, Morecambe, Heysham, the sea, the Lakes.

Joey pulled the Fiat up so it pointed at this vista. 'Lancaster Riviera in all its glory.'

Nancy said, 'How's your half an E?'

'Nice and mellow.'

'Same.' She pointed at the skies. 'I've never been up here at this time of day.'

'What time is it?'

Scanning her watch: 'Gone 8am.'

'What a morning.'

'Come on then, why we here?'

Joey shrugged. 'Thought it would be nice. I've never been up here at this time either. In fact, I've not been up here for a long time.'

'When was the last time?'

Joey shrugged. 'Good question.'

'With your mum ever?'

'My mum? She doesn't drive.'

Nancy said, 'How much do you think about your true dad?'

Joey took her hand. 'Maybe I should think about him more but I don't. I mean if I think about him, like now, then I do start to-' Leaving it there - not sure what to say: he didn't really ever think about a dad he never met.

'Start to..?'

Joey flashed on his mum - how she'd never speak about his dad. 'I start to wonder if he thinks about me. Got to be honest - how can anyone leave a kid behind, a baby, like I was?' Joey grinned. 'Could be worse. When I found out the idiot, Tony, wasn't my dad, Jesus, I was relieved.'

He thought about it. 'But, it did give me a weird feeling. Like - who am I really? You know what I mean, Nancy? And, also, if my mum, bless her, could lie to me about that, like I told you before, for so long, telling me that he, Tony, was my dad, then what else could she lie to me about? Not the best feeling ever.'

A tear pricked, stuck in his eye; Nancy brought her hand to the tear and kissed it. 'You've got me now. And one day, we'll have our own kids and you'll be the dad to them you never had.'

He looked at her. He never felt so good. 'Thanks,' Joey said and hugged her, then broke, fired up the Fiat, and turned it towards town.

'What about your family? If you go off to Ibiza like this, what will they say?'

Nancy smiled. 'We talked about this. And, I'm not fourteen anymore - I'll call them from the airport before we take off.'

Joey nodded, twirled his shades, hit the throttle, put the Fiat in first and started off. Towards the Lancaster/Morecambe border. Towards Gerard's place.

Chapter Fifty-Four

A minute later

Joey took the road down from Jubilee Towers, passing a turn to a farm, passing a dirt track where he and Nancy failed to see Frenchy in the parked-up Cosworth - with Tina and Temmy - watching as the Fiat headed for Wyresdale Road, and Lancaster.

They didn't see the car. Didn't see or hear Temmy, eyes wild from coke and E, screaming through the back window of the Cosworth. 'What the fuck we waiting for? Let's fucking follow that rust-bucket and grip them. Search the lovebirds, their shithouse car. We'll soon see if they ripped us off. Gerard - what you saying? This is serious.'

Joey and Nancy didn't see Gerard turn in the driver's seat, throw Temmy a look, telling his cousin calm down or he'd calm him down. Didn't see Gerard's eyes flash and the smile he permawore go thin, like a knife pared this back. Didn't see the Romany wait a few seconds, fire the Sierra up, ease it into first and point the motor after them. Didn't see the way he fixed on the road ahead and did more and more coke that Tina passed him on a key.

Chapter Fifty-Five

Harry

Three minutes later

Harry was deep in a bottle of Johnnie Red.

He had Schubert on the sound system. He watched the two-car caravan move along Wyresdale. He took a perch on the corner of Langthwaite and Little Fell behind a farmyard building, could see Joey's Fiat and Gerard's Sierra, but they couldn't see him.

Rewind to fifteen minutes ago: as soon as Harry clocked Joey point the Fiat past Williamson Park, he knew they headed for the Towers. It was young lovers stuff. Harry and Amber used to go there when they were kids. He smiled at the memory and watched two starlings flit across the horizon, turning in the sun before flitting off.

He laughed at the memory. Harry and Amber. Harold Blue and Amber Blue nee Cross. They met at a Bentham Hall dance; a disco put on by the local church. It was twee, it was sweet. Amber was a vicar's daughter; her father gave services at St John the Baptist Church, the place dated to the Domesday Book and further: once fresh love gave way to non-fresh love the joke between them was how they were always doomed.

Except. Harold got a new feeling about himself, them. Amber and Harry. This routine with the Es and running around Lancaster and Morecambe in secret, like a Columbian drug magnate. He got a moment of clarity, dialled up the Schubert and heard the music differently, saw himself differently. If self-realisation is what you search for then embrace it here and now. Understand who you are, what Lottie, your beautiful daughter, and Amber, your beautiful wife, mean to you.

Connecting with a part of himself he never knew existed. Like the streetwise/naive act with Frederick Street in the Rhodes Town bar. But in a different way.

The revelation about the thousand pills and Joey and Nancy ripping them off. Fooling Joey about not finding them in the wheel-arch outside Sett End and watching him sell them in the warehouse.

He didn't know why he did it at the time.

He thought he was ensuring fresh material for the book - imagine writing up Joey's E-stealing act, imagine how the reader would love to see how that went down.

But it ran deeper for him. He saw this - at last.

Saw it clearer than anything Harry ever saw before. By allowing Joey to go sell the pills; by allowing him and Nancy to do what they did, he worked karma his way. A good start on redressing the wrongs of what he did to Amber and Lottie, what he did to himself.

Let Joey and Nancy go and forget his E wholesaling biz and move on. Return himself to himself by concentrating on Amber and Lottie rather than concentrating on himself. He got a warm glow. The Johnnie Red helped, the warm morning helped, Schubert's strings helped. He nipped whiskey and mind-mapped more. The concern was Gerard - the Romany was a good man but he could not control what Gerard might do to Joey and Nancy. And: what Joey and Nancy might do to get from under Gerard.

Things like this were never over until a character like Gerard decided.

Harry started to get a plan of how he might get Gerard to decide it was over. Over in a good way for everyone.

Chapter Fifty-Six

Nancy

Nancy was unsure.

Returning the money to Gerard felt a sweet and beautiful idea. It still felt the same but she became concerned - if they drove right up there onto the site, Gerard's large and extended family, friends, the whole place would clock them doing so and she didn't think they could drop the cash made from selling the ripped-off Es, then swan out of there easy.

Joey broke her thoughts. 'Look - my old school.' He pointed at gates as Williamson Park became Douthwaite Fields - the Grammar school cricket ground shining in the sun - Joey saying, 'I'm out of there a year and it feels like yesterday and a lifetime ago.'

Nancy said, 'When is your birthday?'

'December.'

She smiled.

'21st.'

'A Christmas baby.'

They took Wyresdale to Moorgate, down the hill. 'Wait - you told me you were going to warehouses from, like, October. You were sixteen then.'

Joey pulled his shades up and Nancy got a flutter. Joey, in faux-cool voice: 'Baby, I did - I been driving to them pesky warehouses since October.'

She giggled. 'Driving.'

Another twirl of the shades. 'A true story.'

'When you were still sixteen.'

'For a couple of months, yeah.'

'How did you learn?'

'Where did I learn, you mean? Where we're going now - Gerard's. On the land on the site, all the Romani learn to drive on it from kids. One day I'm there, collecting some pot to knock out - what I'm doing before Es for Gerard and he asked if I fancied a go in his car.'

'The white one?'

'He had a different Ford then, a silver one. This is before I started making serious dosh selling Es.'

She said, 'You're telling me one time in a car and you could drive?'

'I'm telling you it took two, three times - this is last summer - and for a few hours each of those times, messing around.'

Nancy threw him a yeah-sure-buster look.

'Think about it,' Joey said. 'If a driving lesson is an hour and you do ten, twelve lessons before taking the test and passing, then doing two or three days, for 5/6 hours adds up. Especially for a lad with two brains.'

Nancy laughed. 'Wow - that is impressive.'

Joey steered the Fiat along Moorgate, then right across Brewery. 'Thing is,' he said. 'I loved it.' A look at Nancy - he needed her to understand this. 'I loved it because Gerard fascinated me. Gerard plus Temmy and Tina - the excitement of being them. Of being around them being them.'

Nancy got it - like she was thrilled by house music and DJing.

'But it wasn't only fascination,' said Joey. 'It was that Gerard trusted me. No, not trusted me, liked me, and didn't think twice about letting me drive his car, learn to drive in his car. Those days, when I learned to drive, I won't forget. At my age - our age - stuff goes in here-' Joey pointed to his heart. 'Deeper than when were older, I'm betting.'

Nancy took and kissed his hand and he went right along

Lodge Street, then Edward, took another right to St Leonard's Gate, left on Bulk Road over the River Lune to Greyhound Bridge, the water on Nancy's side.

She said, 'You mean experiences are more - what's the word - indelible?'

Joey cracked a grin. 'Exactly. It's because we're young they carry extra poignancy. And with Gerard, I think he kind of befriended me. He somehow knew about all the shit at home with my mum and that idiot Tony. I think, too, he sensed something about me - even if he couldn't and wouldn't describe it that way.' Joey thought. 'And, there was a kind of attraction on his part too.'

'Attraction?'

'Like I held a fascination for Gerard, believe it or not. Like I said, he wouldn't articulate it that way. He befriended me. And when home life is not great that means something.'

Nancy squeezed his hand. 'All this going on in your head.'

'Since I was a young kid. Always thinking, working stuff and people out. Myself.'

'What does it do?' she said. 'All the thinking.'

Joey shrugged. 'Keeps things interesting.' He pointed to the backpack at Nancy's feet, the money they made from selling the pills inside. 'Like last night - interesting. Like now.'

Nancy said, 'Who'd think giving thousands in hard earned cash back would be 'interesting.'?' She snuggled in close, taking his hand, and they shifted the gearstick into fourth in unison. 'But, you are right - it is.'

Nancy took her hand from his and watched him kick the Fiat forward; she looked through the windscreen as they bolted along Scale Hall, the relaxed pace of the drive gone, an edge to Joey's driving, vehicles zipping by the other way.

'Who you trying to overtake?'

He pointed in the rear-view mirror. 'Not overtake, get away from. Look.' The mirror showed cars behind, a No 12 bus with MORECAMBE COLLEGE on its front.

Nancy said, 'What?' She turned to catch a clear view and saw: a white Cosworth flashing in sunlight - Gerard's. Four cars back. 'No.'

Joey turned right off Morecambe Road along Scale Hall. 'Oh yes,' he said, and saw she only half comprehended the situation. He jerked a thumb over his shoulder and said, 'Look again. Past Gerard.'

She did, saw this:

The white-coloured Cosworth on Scale Hall Road in front of a blue Ford, a pickup and - coming into view - waiting to take the junction, a cream-coloured car that looked like-

A Bentley - a Bentley like Harry's Bentley; meaning it WAS Harold Blue's Bentley. Nancy said, 'It can't be, can it?'

'It is, baby. We are being followed by Gerard who is being followed by Harry.'

'Why?'

'Is a good question. I mean Gerard's following us because he's onto us, has to be the reason. But Harry, I'm not sure, I mean, if he's onto us too, then-'

'How long they been following?'

'I noticed as we came over Greyhound Bridge, saw Gerard's car in the mirror - I couldn't believe it, didn't want to, but when I checked again knew it was him. I'm thinking what the... then, I see that colour, the cream shade that makes Harry's motor individual round here, and...'

Nancy shook her head. 'Now what? This is bad.'

'Another good question. Don't turn around, don't let Gerard know we've seen him.'

Nancy eyeballed the rearview mirror. 'Looks like Tina and Temmy are with him.'

'Straight from the warehouse, they must've followed us all the way.' Joey smiled, rubbed her nose. 'We've been too E-ed up, loved up, to notice.'

'Wait - you think Gerard, Temmy and Tina know Harry's following?'

Joey shook his head. 'Not sure - they may be too battered to notice.'

Joey took a left at the end of Scale Hall, took a roundabout, hit Torrisholme Road, drove a half mile, eyeing the traffic, seeing sun still flash off the white Sierra.

He couldn't see Harry's sled. He knew it would be back there. A double-decker bus with BATTERY on its destination plate swung between them and Gerard's car and Joey saw their chance. 'Nancy, I'm going to get rid of both of them.'

She nodded and Joey swung the 127 into the carpark of Morecambe College, watching behind them.

No sign of the Cosworth or the Bentley. Joey remembered the layout - you could motor through the carpark and around the buildings and out the other side onto Morecambe Road, up from the turn-off for Asda and Gerard's place.

Which is what he did; took the driveway, and veered along by the college and grass fields, came out the other end. He scoped the mirror - no Cosworth or Bentley.

'Wow,' said Nancy. 'I think you've done it.'

'We've done it.'

She twisted around in the passenger seat to look behind.

'Though,' Joey said. 'I don't think it will be long until Gerard susses.'

Nancy faced frontways again. 'I still don't see either car.'

'Gerard is as smart as Harry. I had him down as smarter than your average operator, now I see I underestimated him.'

He headed to Asda roundabout, went right, going toward and then through the sunshine for Gerard's place on Mellishaw Lane.

Nancy got the same thought as before. 'How we going to drive up to his place and leave the cash and get away without anyone seeing us?

'I think I've worked it out,' said Joey. He twirled his shades - nervous. 'I've seen enough movies.'

Nancy: 'Go on.'

'We're going to be seen. That's the idea.'

'Seen?'

Joey nodded. 'What we are going to do is ride in up to Gerard's and park and get out with the bag of money in hand and walk up to his place, leave the bag outside it, by the front door. Then - walk away. Simple as that. Like it's expected and there is nothing to see here.'

Nancy thought about it; they drove past Asda, up Ovangle Road, took the mini-roundabout on Mellishaw and Joey hit gas. 'Just like that?' she said. 'Not giving a shit. I like it. Has style.'

She looked behind them - zero cars.

'Fuck,' said Joey. 'Look.'

They passed the copse he parked behind when seeing Harry drive into Gerard's the other day and Nancy saw what Joey saw: Harry's Bentley parked up, hidden behind trees apart from the bumper. Nancy: 'Can that really be his car?'

'Yeah,' said Joey and got it. Harry knew where they were going, knew they headed for Gerard's, so stopped following and took a shortcut and waited. 'Harry also sussed what we're up to,' he said. 'Has to be. What he's up to - I'm not sure.'

A moment later - solved. 'This has to be about the book, the fucking book - he's thinking what a yarn this is for Second Summer of Love.' Joey laughed. 'As Gerard would say - you with me?'

Nancy nodded; they pulled up outside Mellishaw Park, the fields burnt yellow from sun. Sky an ocean of blue.

Showtime.

They drove inside.

The time near 10am; the site looked like it always did when Joey visited: kids and dogs and horses scattered around, older Romani sat outside their chalets - doors and windows open. Barbecue wafts in the air, like it was fired up already - the all-day meat and booze session kicking in. Music warbled - old time crooning stuff Gerard liked - plus acid house playing from somewhere, too.

There: as they pulled across from Frenchy's the sounds going louder; a hundred yards up the chalet-row a group of lads and girls had the grill going. A smell of sizzling sausages hit, made Joey hungry for the first time in a long time. He said, 'I could murder a banger.'

Nancy laughed. 'Come on, let's do this. One question, though: what do we do if someone comes up and tells us Gerard's car isn't here, Gerard isn't in, no-one's at home.'

Joey's eyes fizzed. 'No problem. Remember, we're giving all the cash back, including - as our apology - the cut that would usually be mine for selling his pills. So if that happens, we still leave the bag outside, no-one's going to rip off Gerard.'

Joey felt a calm sensation; they got out the Fiat. He brought the backpack, felt eyes watching them. Clasping hands, they walked up to Gerard's chalet and Joey knocked on the door and Nancy whispered: 'What happens if they arrive now?'

It was possible. They'd have to play that if/when it happened, like they played everything this way.

Like, now - Joey saying aloud, for show: 'Nancy, I don't think they're in. I don't think Gerard or Tina or Temmy are about.'

Nancy smiled, widened eyes in faux-surprise. Over-loud: 'I think you're correct, Joey.' She tapped the bag, like she wanted to keep their business between them. 'What should we do?'

'Well,' said Joey, catching Nancy's tone. 'That is a good question. I'm thinking since we're in a hurry, we could just leave the bag here.' Louder: 'No-one, I'm sure, will take it.'

Nancy, quiet: 'You know what, I'm not sure about this - what happens if we leave all this money on his doorstep and it does get taken? If that happens, all of this is for nothing.'

Joey took a step back and did a slow circle, taking in the row of chalets: they gleamed in sunlight - a row of white doors. Kids played by them. Beyond the chalets, meat smoke and heat shimmered.

He said, 'Whatever happens we have each other. This is never for nothing. This is for everything.' He handed her the bag and said: 'Do this and we go start the rest of our lives.'

Nancy took the backpack and his hand so they both held a strap and they put it down, rested £20K of cash on the step of Gerard's chalet and turned around and walked to the Fiat, and Joey opened the boot and pulled a bottle of red wine and unscrewed the top and handed the bottle to Nancy.

'For now, the future.'

She got a look like they should be driving off and a look like she didn't care, too.

The bottle sparkled in the sun. Joey watched Nancy shake her head and decide let's drink. She unscrewed the top and lifted the bottle to her lips and drank and closed her eyes and opened them and handed the bottle to Joey and he took the bottle and sat down on the grass.

Nancy: 'What you doing? Let's leave while we can - now. As in yesterday.'

He knew she was scared - why she was. He felt the same. Except, no. He should be scared but wasn't. It was the half a pink new yorker; it gave a sensation of invincibility, of everything being in the right place.

Nancy, again: 'What are you doing?' She bent and stroked his face. 'Not here, Joey. Our final scene is not being caught by Gerard and Temmy - who knows what they'll do to us. Harry, too. Come on, please.'

Shit. What was he doing? 'You're right, sorry.' He stood up. 'I felt like nothing could touch us, ever.'

Nancy took his hand and looked around - still no sign of Gerard's car. 'I know,' she said. 'And, listen - you don't have to apologise, ever to me.' They kissed - a smooch; the barbecue throng whooped and they raised each other's arm and whooped back.

Then, hit the Fiat; Nancy taking the driver's side and holding out a hand. 'Keys, come on. I want to drive.' He laughed and palmed them her and she searched through Joey's cassettes, found the tape she wanted - TUNES TO MOVE YA AT THE CARLETON, DJ NANCY K - and slid this in the sound system, hit play. Turned the key in the ignition, fired the Fiat up, placed the motor in first and did a U-turn, eased them out of Mellishaw Park: past trees, fields, past where Harry parked the Bentley '87 - except his sled wasn't there anymore.

They didn't care.

'Come on,' said Nancy. 'To the motorway, to our plane to Ibiza.' She pointed to the stereo and whooped. 'Richie Rich - Salsa House.'

Nancy slowed the Fiat at the roundabout - a car pulled up: they didn't see it turn, until too late; turn and block them in.

Seeing the car now. Seeing it's a white Sierra - Gerard's white Sierra. Gerard, Temmy and Tina all getting out, bowling towards them, smiles all round.

Smiles Nancy and Joey didn't like. Smiles they were smiling because they saw Nancy and Joey were not smiling.

Chapter Fifty-Seven

Gerard reached the Fiat first, made Joey's side, leaned on the door, his head through the window. The Romany's eyes like he was happy about something. Temmy went to Nancy's side and bobbed his head in/out her window, eyes pinned from pills and powder. Tina stood next to Gerard with a calm look - she saw this all before.

Gerard: 'Going somewhere, lovebirds?'

Joey laughed. 'Just a drive, Gerard.' Winked. 'You know how it is, after a night out, the back end of a killer half-a-pill still working its magic.'

Temmy, through Nancy's window: 'Don't be a dickhead all the time, Joey.'

Nancy moved her head back - Temmy got too close - and Gerard grinned at Joey.

'That was a laugh wasn't it, Mr Two-brain, the warehouse party, how the police got in, arrested every kid in there for a good time. Apart, of course, from present company, who I do have to say I'm proud of - not being arrested, escaping the plod, shows none of us are dickheads, to use my cousin's word. You know - not being gripped by those dickheads.'

Joey said, 'Agreed, Gerard.'

Nancy, catching his attitude: 'Me, too.' She laughed and Gerard blanked and Temmy and Tina stayed straight-faced and Joey laughed now.

Both thinking: laughing in Gerard Toces's face: far from smart.

The big man nodded - slow. Like he calculated what went on.

Joey quivered - you cross Frenchy Toces and he finds out-

'I tell you what, lovebirds, how about this? Temmy gets in your motor, in fact drives your motor, and follows me and Tina back to our place for a chat.'

Joey and Nancy looked at each other: a synched-flash on sun, beach, cocktails, warm Ibiza nights. There and not there. Tantalising, scary: like it all might be taken away from them. They just dropped off the money made from stealing Gerard's Es. Gave it back.

But now - no escape.

Gerard got a mean look; Nancy tried to play cool. 'Why go to yours for a chat?'

Temmy laughed and Tina said, 'I think you and your boyfriend know, I think we all know what Gerard's saying, why we're here right now.'

Nancy shrugged - calm as always. 'Sorry, I don't know and I don't think Joey does either.'

He nodded. 'I haven't a clue, to be honest.'

Temmy leaned in on Nancy through the window and she flinched. 'Haven't a clue? Have you heard this, Frenchy? All of a sudden 10,000 brains and his girl are in the dark - funny that.' He rubbed his scar, pulled his head back out. 'You lovebirds will soon have a clue. A big one. Don't worry about that.'

Tina said, 'How about this as a starter - the other night we were ripped off and we think you know something about. A thousand pills were stolen which means we owe our man for them. That means we owe whoever ripped us off.'

Joey, trying to control tremors: 'I'm still not-'

Gerard shook his head, stopping Joey dead. 'Nancy, get in the back. Let Temmy drive. Do it.'

Nancy looked at Joey and he nodded and she got out the driver's seat and sat in the back. Temmy took the keys and Gerard said, 'See you in a moment.'

He made the Cosworth, Tina following; Joey threw Temmy a

Hollywood smile and got a flash on all of them when they were old: what would they remember of this, what would they forget?

Gerard and Tina drove away. Another flash: would they still be together then - in old age? Gerard and Tina were like him and Nancy. Still young. But that would change.

Temmy started the Fiat after the Cosworth along Mellishaw Lane. Nancy touched Joey's shoulder. 'You alright?' He turned and mouthed 'yes' and they looked at each other.

Temmy said, 'Yes love, he's good, never been better. Why would he not be? That's right isn't it, Joseph lad?'

'Yes, Thomas, I'm good.'

Temmy said, 'I'm not sure you've got one brain between you, the way you two have been carrying on. I thought the one thing you lovebirds, me, Tina, every fucker around here knows about is Gerard.' He whistled - the sound of concern, turned his stare on Nancy, pointed at Joey. 'You sure about this one? You sure he's as clever as he's supposed to be? Thinks he is.'

He steered the Fiat towards Gerard's place. 'You just got together with him. Now you find yourself in this mess. Listen - I'm the ugly one with the scar and the mouth, sure, but my cousin-' Another whistle. 'I have never ever seen him lose his temper; you know what I'm saying? Frenchy Toces. Think about that a fucking second. Not once. You know why? Because no-one dares make him lose it. I'm talking about from when he's a tot to now.'

Temmy pulled the Fiat in behind Gerard's sled. 'And you know how we can be.' He waved at the row of chalets. 'We don't mind the odd scrap.' Temmy laughed, stopped dead.

They followed his eye-line; what he looked at.

What-

Harry. And Gerard. With his hand on Harry - holding Harry by the neck.

Jesus.

* * *

Tina sitting at the table outside their chalet. Around them, the regular scene. Horses, ponies chomped grass. Kids playing by chalets. Teenagers boozing at the barbecue in the sun. Older folk at tables drinking cider and wine and beer. All of Mellishaw Park rubbernecking the Gerard Toces-Harold Blue show.

There - Harry's Bentley stationed by Gerard's front door. Joey got what went down: they passed him hiding behind the copse when coming in the park to drop the cash for Gerard. When they drove back by the copse - no Bentley. He must have moved, parked elsewhere for a view of the park, waited for them to leave, then hit the site, Gerard's joint.

Why?

Gerard let go of Harry's shirt, waved them over. The genial smile with the cooled blue eyes. Frenchy took a chair by Tina, pointed Harry to sit the other side, Nancy and Joey take a seat, Temmy joining.

Gerard to Joey/Nancy: 'Good to see you - again.' A wild crocodile grin. The rubberneckers lost interest, went back to their drinks and sun. The barbecue re-sizzled - fresh meat got loaded - aromas wafted.

Gerard indicated Harry. 'Look who I found as I drove up, after seeing you down the road.'

Harry wore a vacant look: blank - non-concerned? Temmy - a queer expression. He eyed Harry, could not stop looking at him. Tina: 'You know what he was doing, T?'

Temmy's expression shifted. Like it started to light-bulb why Frenchy gripped him. 'The fucking book I told Gerard never to get involved in.'

Gerard shook his head. 'No, Thomas. Jesus.'

Harry, speaking at last: 'Temmy's correct-'

Gerard shot him a look. 'How's that then, Harry? How have me and Tina drove up and seen with this-'

He pulled Joey's bag. Put it on the table. 'You were here for your book, were you?' His eyes gleamed. He indicated Tina. 'It's all material - you told us from the start. But you're not here for this-' Gerard indicated the bag.

'You ripped off the pills from us.'

Temmy's eyes bulged - shithead Harry.

Gerard: 'Found out about them being dropped for us. Where. Ripped them off and had them sold. A thousand of our pills.' His voice ice and eyes showing he knew more about Harry than Harry would ever know. 'Then, you bottled it, thought, what the fuck am I doing? Harry Blue, messing with big bad Frenchy Toces.' His eyes glittered bluer. 'Frenchy's a Romany, one of them: what will he do to me when he finds out the thief I am?'

Gerard's voice found an interesting tone - call it sorrow. Like he sensed what drove Harry to this 100% mug move. 'You thought you could come back, drop the money off, scarper, and all would be fine.'

Harry's expression: what? You really think this?

Nancy and Joey swapped looks: Gerard thinks Harry ripped him off? JESUS. Joey tried to tell her: this is going to be okay. Nancy's look deepened: Harry's going to get hurt. This isn't our sunset ending. Or his.

Joey said, 'Thing is Gerard, I-'

Frenchy raised a fist, slow. Threw Joey and Nancy a faux-grimace. Removed his shell suit top to show a white vest with cheesecloth holes, muscles. Joey making Gerard nineteen going on fifty.

Joey, again: 'Harry don't - I'm going to-'

Gerard gave Joey a look that shut him up instant. Shook his head. 'This joker has involved you in his snide act. Why do you think we followed you? We clocked you in the warehouse, serving up countless Es. A grin. 'I was surprised. You've got balls.' Gerard indicated Harry. 'We find him here with the bag in his hand you had at the warehouse. A bag stuffed with cash.'

He pulled out a handful of notes - let £5s, £10s, £20s flutter onto the table. 'Plus leftover pills. Looks like all but 50, 100 gone. Then I see what really happened. Harry rips me off, gets you to sell the pills for him.'

He shrugged. 'I'm surprised, I'm not surprised. I know what you're like, Harry. When you told me about the book, you say you're ambitious. Had enough of your wife. I get it: you use the book to hide your plan to rip me off and make a big score from getting Joey to sell the pills for you. Then you're going to do a runner with the money?'

Harry nodded hard - like he was happy for Gerard to think this. The Romany's smile went craftier. 'But, of course. It's not all I know. About you. These two.'

Pointing at Nancy and Joey. Joey's eyes on Nancy, trying to tell her maybe Harry is more in control than it looks; difficult to decipher: what's Harry's game? Why is he happy for Gerard to think what he did, that he ripped Gerard off, got Joey to punt the pills.

Harry smiled. Joey eyeballed his suit - Joey didn't notice last night, outside Sett End, this dark blue number. High-end, expensive. Padded shoulders - loose - and the suit near-baggy, like you could get another Harry inside it. A departure - he usually sported modest numbers. And the shirt - open-necked. Joey got a jolt. The upgrade in threads; the first time Harry went tie-less.

He wondered why he noticed.

Clicked.

A clue to what Harry really did. Like he dressed up for this. He's ready for business. Chess-played for what went down, dressed in costume to get in character, take Frenchy on.

Temmy started whistling; the sound familiar and unidentifiable, then becoming That's Life, the song Harry played at the Brown Cow in-between acts, as Amber introduced the next night creature.

Harry smiled at the sound - like he understood Temmy taunted him; the sly intent behind it, Temmy showing again he's not as simple as the Frenchy-underling act he portrayed.

Harry said, 'Nice song. I'm sure Gerard agrees - as a fan of Frank.' Gerard smiled.

Temmy kept whistling - the song melodic. Mingling with summer air, sun, barbecue aromas. The way this was going...

Harry kept smiling; Joey got a new thought; Harry isn't going to drop them in the shit. He's going to take it all himself, try and say Gerard got this part wrong - that Joey and Nancy were not in with him on the pill stealing caper.

The same Q: Why??

Here, answer - incoming. Harry: 'Gerard you're correct in what you say - kind of. I brought the money back, and the Es being ripped off was me. But these two.' Indicating Nancy and Joey. 'You have this wrong, there is no way-'

Gerard leaned in on him and Harry flinched and Gerard drew back and ran hands through his mullet. Threw a wide grin, followed with a head-shake.

Temmy tensed; Tina's face showed shades of Gerard - disappointment at this whole scene.

Nancy felt for a first time how young she clocked Tina. She was no more than eighteen. But her expression was ages-old-weary. Like she couldn't believe what Harry did, this nice man supposed to be respectable because he wore nerdy clothes and wrote a book he asked her husband to be in.

'It's all on you, is it Harry? Really?' said Gerard. A grimace. He said, 'Temmy, do me a favour, get the stereo.'

Temmy made inside the chalet. From the barbecue a radio blared: Nessun Dorma, Pavrotti sang the Italia '90 World Cup anthem. Joey rewound two weeks to England's semi-final penalty defeat to West Germany in Turin, the heat of summer, watching the game on a red-hot night at the Waterwitch boozer by the canal.

Pavarotti finished crooning, a new song came on, the radio tuned to Radio One. The DJ: 'This is Bruno Brookes, and this is one of the sounds of this hot, hot summer - Adamski and Killer.'

The opening bars started;

Temmy came back out the chalet with a blaster, two cassettes. He held the tapes up. 'Tunes to Move Ya - The Carleton. And Tunes to Move Ya - Nelson.' He gave Nancy a leering smile. 'Has to be Nelson - that was a warehouse party until the plod got interested.'

Temmy put the tape in the blaster pressed play and listened. Said, 'What's the tune?'

Nancy said, 'Everybody Wants To Rule The World - Ain't Dead mix.'

Gerard's tone shifted. 'Now we're all listening to the wonderful DJ Nancy Kools, back to business.' Blue eyes glittering; he might be gazing at the sun dipping into Morecambe Bay. 'Harry - why?' He slammed a fist on the table and Harry flushed and reflexed arms like he got punched in the head. Gerard motioned Temmy and his cousin gripped Harry and Gerard went in and out the chalet double-quick, returning with a blade with a serrated edge.

Pulling his chair close to Harry's. 'You do this to me. You pay.'

Harry went a hue Nancy and Joey never saw before. Gerard: 'You think this is funny - some artistic fucking thing for your book, plus a way of making a load of cash off of me? The problem with artistic types is their art is usually always boring. You see what I can't quite get to, what I'm having trouble here with, is why you did this. That's bothering me. For myself, sure. But more for you. You're frustrated, sure. But this? You know what people think about me - there's no need to give Frenchy Toces a wide berth as long as you don't need to give Frenchy Toces a wide fucking berth.' Harry hued paler. Stuttering. 'Of c-c-c-course.' Harry - finally losing it, his own particular brand of swagger housed in the suits and nerdy image that was part PR, part truth.

Gerard switched eyes to Nancy and Joey; a synched thought hit them: this is spinning out of control. The pink new yorker cocktailed with fear giving a terrible falling sensation. If Harry told Gerard what really occurred. To save his own backside. Who really ripped the 1,000 pills off, then–

'Tina, can you get us a beer from the fridge – for this gentleman too, please.' Gerard took the knife from Harry's face, showed him the blade, serrated edge silvery in sun. Tina came back out the chalet with cans of Red Stripes, put them on the table.

Gerard indicated all take one.

Red Stripes got cracked, cold beer drunk, sun and booze re-upped the half a new yorker inside Nancy and Joey. Light sparked and sparkled; senses floated. This is surreal. The world shifted, Gerard cradling the serrated blade Nancy noted was a Bowie. Recognising it from the encyclopaedias Paolo still had from the old country, from childhood – her dad a child fascinated by the world beyond Calabria.

Gerard placed his Red Stripe on the table. 'You see, Harry, what is going on here is another symptom of the shit I've had all my life. Because… this is me, Gerard Toces. Hello!' He knocked-knocked close to Harry's temple – anyone home? 'You think you're better because you've got an education – a type of education, let's say, I don't have – you with me?'

Harry regained a little colour; the Red Stripe started working. 'You really want a discussion, I'll say I do carry a sense of being better than you, Nancy, Joey, Tina, Temmy.' A pause. 'Or, rather, different from you. And, that you, Gerard, have the same feeling: that you're different, apart, from Tina, Temmy Joey, Nancy. And, that Tina has the same sense, and Temmy, too, plus–'

'Shut up with your deep shit,' Gerard told him. 'It's not even fucking deep. Truth is truth.'

'It's "deep shit" now is it,' said Harry. Quietly. Everyone double-took on Harry. What is he saying? 'I – I get into this with you and you don't like it. Interesting. Wh-what I'm saying is we all think we're different to each other – call it better if you like. I do have an education you don't have, and you have one I don't.'

Gerard snorted. 'School of life bollocks time is it, now?'

'I mean your experience; outlook is one I don't have and never will.'

Gerard flipped the Bowie through the air, caught it. 'You ripped me off.' He moved towards Harry, and Harry still tried to front this out.

Telling him: 'Wait a moment - please.'

Gerard stopped and Harry drained his Red Stripe, mashed the can, pulled a half-bottle of Johnnie Red from his jacket and slugged a bolt. Offered it round. Joey did a slug, Nancy the same.

The world - the same thing again; colour and sound whisky-shifted, everything grew large, expanded. The bottle reached Gerard last. He grinned and looked the double of Temmy for a moment, cousin-to-cousin; he bolted scotch and placed the bottle on the table, raised the bowie knife. Like a cartoon crook. All the realer for being genial mannered Romany Gerard 'Frenchy' Toces.

'You've had a moment, Harold Blue. Now, this is a moment for me to tell you all a tale.' Chip-blue eyes glinting sun off Gerard's teeth - whiter than white. Saying: 'This is funny. With a capital F like there's a capital F for Frenchy, as in Frenchy Toces. You get me?'

Saying this to Harry, saying this to Joey and Nancy.

'No. You see, you all think you know. Know who I am. But you don't. Frenchy. You want to know why I'm called this?'

They waited.

'Concerns what happened about four years ago - when I was a bairn, fifteen. Haha. Right, T?'

She nodded.

To Harry/Joey/Nancy: 'You know Devil's Bridge?'

'Up near Kendal,' Joey said.

Harry: 'Kirby Lonsdale.'

'Yes, Harold.' Gerard smirking. 'Devil's Bridge is by Kirby Lonsdale. The bridge that's a giggle to jump off into the Lune on a hot day like this. Now, bonus point for anyone who can name the next bridge along, you go further up the river?'

Joey and Nancy shook their heads; Harry: 'Frenchman's Bridge.'

'Harold Blue is a regular local trivia fucking expert.'

'Well, I mean it's not that- I mean I grew up around there - Hornby-'

'Shut up, Harold. And I mean, like yesterday.'

Harry quivered.

Gerard said, 'I'm fifteen, had to go up to Kirby Lonsdale on business, was asked a question I had a few answers for-'

'Gerard, these don't need to know the full story.'

He flashed Tina a smile. 'No-one is going to hear the full story, T. Rather, what these people need to know that what took me there was a question of loyalty - a fucking characteristic, these, especially Harry and Joey, have zero fucking idea about.'

Harry's hands: shaking; Joey nodded, starting to see where this headed.

'Loyalty. This is what I am talking about. You see, the reason I'm respected is because of what happened up in Kirby Lonsdale.' A thin smile. To himself. 'This was about Tina and about this dickhead who decided Romani were "gyppos".' Gerard's eyes flickered blue. 'When I get there, I'm told to go to the river, and there he is - this lad who thinks it's okay to badmouth Tina for not doing what he wants her to do - talking all this shit when he's forty-three, and she's twelve. You know what I am saying. She's underage, and he's a pervert.'

He moved to Tina, stroked her cheek. 'A lovely day that day - made me think about being younger, when I was six or seven, the kind of age you don't realise you're alive, I suppose. And I realise something that is mad for me to realise.

'This: I've never really been a kid. A kid like other kids are. I say this to this pervert and you know what he says?'

Joey regretted the bottle of wine, insisting on drinking it here; if he did not then he and Nancy would have escaped, be on the way to Manchester Airport right now.

Gerard: 'He says, "I know what you mean - I miss my mum

holding me when I was a baby".' A smile. 'I'm having a serious thought - how I've never been a young boy in my head and this pervert, who's all scared and knows what's about to happen to him, comes out with this shit. Last thing he said to me, of course. But I've never forgotten it.'

Gerard roared laughs. It's the funniest thing ever.

'Fucking hell, Gerard, lad,' Temmy said. 'You never told us this before-'

'So,' Gerard said. 'This is what I hear every time I hear "Frenchy", A grimace. 'After what happened at Frenchman's fucking bridge with the pervert.'

Another pause. The day shrunk, convulsed; Harry got the worst feeling he ever felt. Joey's hand soaked wet in sweat in Nancy's.

Harry's eyes jumped to Joey; he started to say something and Gerard gave him the hand. 'Guess what,' said the Romany. 'Loyalty: I'm big on it, hooked. Fuck Es and coke and phet. It's family and friends. Loyal.' Pointing at Harry and Joey. 'You two - you've never learned what it is. Ever.'

A hard tone. 'I'd laugh. I mean it is funny except for everything. Everything I've done for you. How I feel about you. Both of you.'

A sigh.

Then: 'So - here we go.' He indicated the bag. 'The pills and the cash - let's have a chat about this.' The grin going from thin to broad - warm and lit up. 'You see, Harold. I know you didn't rip off the 1,000 pills and get Joey to sell them last night.'

Joey and Nancy froze.

Lowering his face to Joey's. 'You.' Jabbing a finger close to Joey's eyes. 'Great work, Two-brain. Finding out where we collect them, then stealing them. Our pills. Wow - taking your girl along, too. Going the Plough Inn and stealing them from the bin outside.'

'Joey didn't make me go,' said Nancy.

A Gerard shrug. 'We saw you at the Plough, then going to your car where you parked it before the bridge. We drive up and park up by the Plough, then you blaze past us in your rust bucket, going towards Dolphinholme. I'm surprised you didn't see us there.' He tossed his hair. 'Puzzled us for a while, that night - why were the pills still in the bin when we looked in it? Why didn't you take them then?' Another shrug. 'But then Thursday, the Sugarhouse, her in the stupid fucking Wonder Woman mask-'

A look that chilled Nancy. A look that had Harry's eyes hitting the ground. 'Stealing the pills then - that made what happened outside the Plough look like we disturbed you or it's a dry run, maybe.'

Gerard's broad smile a smile that incriminated them all, incriminated the world. 'Doesn't matter, because here we are...'

Nancy felt a plunging feeling; Joey nauseous. Flashing on stuff, events he should have noted. 'Fucking hell.' A glance at Nancy, those brave eyes coming back

Saying: 'Fuck's sake.' Mind-whirring back to the night, Frenchy's Sierra Cosworth driving past as they walked to the Fiat; the Cosworth parking up across the road, headlights beamed direct at the bin.

Temmy lunged for Joey and Gerard got in the way, ordered his cousin to sit-the-fuck-down.

To Joey: 'I will deal with you. And I'll deal with Harry.'

He walked away from the table, walked back. Clicked a finger at Nancy. 'Wonder Woman. Nice touch.'

Harry's eyes popped, his face slackened - then, quick, his eyes hit the deck, realising he gave himself away-

'Yes,' said Gerard. 'Wonder Woman. I believe you had first-hand experience of Wonder Woman, Harry. And why? Because, drum roll, big finish incoming, Frank at Carnegie Hall: 'You. You're the Mr Crime Baron around here. You are my pill dealer. Are you not?'

Harry gasped, went an off-white pallor.

Joey sucked in breaths. Nancy nodded - she saw the whole thing. Gerard shook his head. 'Before you ask, it's a small town and I own it: that's the answer. You're seen with the lad from London and his dickhead mates and I when I hear that - well… put this this way - Frederick Street, you think I might not know he is? How he might have come to me with a similar deal you took him up on. How I might have declined for reasons none of your business.'

Harry, speechless.

Joey: 'Fucking hell.'

'Scrap Two-brain or Zero-brain Joey Miller, say hello to Fucking-hell-brain Joey Miller.' Temmy and Tina cracked up; Gerard nodded. 'They can laugh. But you two - no way. Bottom line is this - you, now, with me.'

He pointed at the Sierra, any semblance of humour gone.

Joey and Harry shit bricks. The world stopped dead.

Gerard: 'We're going for a drive. Temmy - come on.'

'With pleasure.'

'No,' said Nancy. 'Don't do this.'

Gerard shrugged and light flashed out of his eyes. 'They give me no choice - your boyfriend and Harry. Now, Tweedle-dum and Tweedle-dummer - let's go.'

Nancy gripped Joey's hand, not wanting to let go. He took her face in his hands and kissed, lingered, broke away. Felt the world collapse. Walked on for the white Sierra. For - what?

Harry, quivering: 'Please, Gerard, please no.'

The Romany's eyes flashed again; he jerked a finger at his sled. 'Do it.'

Harry scanned the site - surrounded. No way out. Woods all around. Gerard's people everywhere. No friendly witnesses to help.

No choice.

Still looking - like he looked for something.

He slumped and started walking towards the Sierra.

Chapter Fifty-Eight

Temmy took the driver's seat - Gerard opened the back passenger door, waved his hand at Harry, welcoming him in. A grim expression - it's come to this.

Harry shook, hesitated - no choice - he bent his head and got in the back passenger.

Gerard waved at Joey - follow, come on. He told him: 'No time like the present.'

Joey raised a smile - difficult; he trembled like Harry, didn't show it like Harry did, got in the back passenger door quick, sat alongside him.

Gerard closed it, hit the front passenger seat.

Closed his door, turned, gave them a slow look. Turned to Temmy. 'Thomas, go - and you know where.'

'NO!' said Harry.

Joey: 'Gerard, I really think tha-'

There, now-

A car racing towards them, leading two black-and-whites to the chalet; the car parking up by Joey's Fiat, by Gerard's Sierra. One black-and-white going behind the motors, the other taking the chalet side.

Out of the car: two men moving quick; Joey recognised the pair, couldn't place them. They came towards the Sierra with badges, with that look that was like they aped it from TV cop shows.

Looking in the sled; looking at each other. The detectives nodded - this is where we should be. Gerard inscrutable; Temmy rubbed his scar, Tina kept looking at Harry sat in the backseat: like she knew the dude grassed them; that he was even dumber than he already showed for doing so.

Two uniforms - coming out the black-and-whites, following the detectives. Each of the detectives in stiffy suits, one in black patent leather shoes, the other brown Hush Puppy numbers. Nancy clocked Hush Puppy as senior; Joey did the opposite - made patent leathers the head honcho.

Here they are, smiling in the sun. Hush Puppy held back a fraction and Joey knew he was right: look at the body language, look at those brogues.

The detective in black patents grinned, peered through the Sierra windscreen.

'Gentlemen, what a lovely scene. How pleasing. So very cosy and what's more the sun is shining like it has been doing all this fine July. Very affirming. This is what it is all about.'

To Nancy, Tina: 'Ladies, I do hope you are well, too.'

His partner moved towards the front passenger seat, keeping eyes on Gerard. Jerked a finger at him and said, 'Out of the car, please. And your friends.'

Gerard did it - in near slow-motion, like he quit the Sierra in instalments. Temmy followed, grinning; Joey and Harry got out the back - looked at each other, then pointed eyes at the ground.

The barbecue throng - rubbernecking; drinkers sitting by chalets eyeballed the scene, kids playing in grass stopped. Horses, ponies, dogs sniffed air - got a definite/certain sense: something's afoot.

Harry, recovering poise: 'Walter, how are you? Brian, how are you?' To the others: 'Meet DI Walter Swaggert and DS Brian Ball - two of our esteemed local constabulary.'

Gerard clocked Swaggert, Ball, the uniforms stood waiting for instruction. He laughed. 'You seem to know these fine police well, Harold.'

Another Gerard laugh. He said, 'I mean, I do too, but that's to be expected, given I'm a "gyppo" and Swaggert and Ball think we "need watching".'

Swaggert and Ball sarcastic-grinned. Joey clocked the same thing Gerard clocked: Harry was breathing easier, calmer.

'I met Walter when he kindly did a piece with me for the Lancaster Guardian all about policing techniques,' Harry said. 'How CID use-'

Swaggert pulled a sheet of paper, put a finger to mouth. 'Enough of the small talk. This,' he pointed at the sheet, 'is a warrant to search the premises of No 12 Larn Lane, which is the home of you two-' A point at the chalet/them. 'Gerard and Tina Toces, I believe.'

Gerard grimaced - like you don't know who I am.

Swaggert: 'The reason for the warrant being this: that I, Detective Inspector Walter Swaggert of Lancaster and Morecambe Police Force, as lead investigator, have reason to believe you may have controlled Class A substances on the premises. Can you confirm now, please, that this is your home.'

Gerard fixed eyes on Harry; Tina smiled. 'Enjoy yourself.'

Swaggert smiled back. 'It is your home then?'

'You know it is,' said Gerard, eyes still on Harry.

Swaggert scanned him, moved towards the chalet, nodded to the uniforms who followed him inside; they started tossing the place.

Harry to Ball: 'Take a seat, Brian.'

Joey knew he wouldn't.

'No thanks.' Ball looked at Gerard and said, 'You're looking happy considering the pickle you're in, Mr Toces.'

"Pickle?' Nice.'

Ball smiled. Joey's eyes went to the bag: FUCK: 20K of hot cash inside plus the leftover Es. When the fuzz noticed it, searched, found the loot: Gerard was done trying to explain that away - he stared at serious time for dealing copious Class As.

Nancy looked at him - her eyes saying: stay brave.

Gerard said, 'Do tell us more, Harry, about this story you and police detective Swaggert did together?'

Subtext: Frenchy told Harry it was obvious what Harry did

- grass him to Swaggert.

Harry, puffed up - the old Harold Blue. 'I said, did I not? The story was about policing, detective techniques in the local area-'

Fast: Swaggert came back out the chalet followed by the uniforms. The uniforms went back to the black-and-whites. Swaggert took a seat, face puce, eyes raging: nothing in the chalet.

Then, a slow take. In front of him the bag. A bag that looked prime for a search.

A second take.

Now -

Smiling, Swaggert: 'Your bag, Gerard?'

Gerard eyeballed Harry, said nothing.

'I'll take that as a yes.'

Joey and Nancy killed gasps; Harry wore a thin smile that went thinner - like he miscalculated again, a different way.

Swaggert unzipped the bag - in a split-second he'd find 20K, leftover pills, bits of pills, powder: a live crime scene.

He put his hands in, started looking.

Then-

A gasp - Swaggert now: hands coming out the bag holding-

Nothing. Holding thin air. No cash bundles, no Class A Es. Nothing.

Meaning zilcho on Gerard.

Joey took a second. Nancy took a second. Harry looked like he could triple heart-attack. What the-

Before: Gerard pulled money from the bag: £5s/10s/20s - holding them up, letting them drop on the table.

Now, nothing.

Then, Joey saw Gerard - saw him still locked on Harry but eyes lit like he knew how this was about to go down.

Joey shuddered: why did he ever think he was smarter than Gerard Toces?

Swaggert had a furious look. He scanned them all, came back to Harry. 'What the fuck-'

Now, like it wasn't happening but was: Ball to his boss. Pointing: 'What about the side, Walter? There's a side pocket. Look.'

Joey, finally realising. Nancy sussing it too. Harry following a nanosecond later.

Gerard had hidden the 20K, the leftover pills BEFORE.

Before Gerard, Temmy and Tina chased Joey and Nancy down - after they dropped the bag at the chalet door. Before Harry arrived.

Which meant the money Gerard pulled before was from the side pocket. Where he'd looked inside and said there were-

Unsold pills still. 50-100 Pink New Yorkers ecstasy tablets.

Meaning they were about to be found, meaning Gerard was, now, about to be done for dealing copious Class As.

The side pocket had Swaggert smiling again. 'Brian,' he said. 'What a good idea. I have always warmed to you and your detective skills and this is precisely why. I will, indeed, do that. Take a look.'

He reached inside.

Shit-

Swaggert's hands coming out with cash - £5/10/20 notes - and: pills.

Ten pills.

Ten?

ONLY TEN???

And the notes - it looked a couple of hundred, nothing more.

Swaggert still with a smile fixed to maximum wattage. He held the bag up - pink pills glistening in the sun. 'Gerard, oh Gerard, with your record already, your sheet of shame that has to be longer than your fucking mullet, this is prison for you, no doubt. A nice stretch.'

Gerard's eyes - ice-blue.

Swaggert looked at Ball, then back at Gerard. 'Okay, play it silent. Won't help.' A smile - broad. 'Gerard Toces, I am arresting you for-'

Joey got an idea - of what he should do - he looked at Nancy.

She was already looking right at him.

Their eyes met, everything said with nothing being said, words not needed.

Nancy - nodding at Joey, yes, you are right:

DO IT.

A moment - an agonising pause; the past few days flashed/ strobed through him. Joey and Nancy. What they hoped for, what they dreamed about. Gone. If you do this now. And, slow, Two-brain Joey Miller did.

Starting to speak - hearing his voice. Hearing his voice say:

'No.' To Swaggert. And again. 'Now. Tha-that's my backpack and those are my pills. They are nothing to do with Gerard. Nothing.'

Harry double-took; Nancy went to Joey and got hold of his hand. Temmy got a look like he saw Joey for a first time. Tina smiled. Gerard's eyes - icier-blue. He poker-faced.

Swaggert - staring at Joey.

And he felt it - plunging - everything is falling - collapsing; it's all FINISHED.

'Is that right?' said Swaggert. He took a moment, studied Joey. 'Really? Okay then. Your full name, please?'

'Joseph Miller.'

'Address?'

Joey told him. The world started moving again; he got led to a black-and-white, blew kisses to Nancy, was put inside.

Seeing Harry stare after him.

Seeing Gerard looking - for the first time - now - finally a grin, a genuine, bona-fide Frenchy Toces grin.

Seeing Nancy - tears in her eyes - coming towards him to kiss him through the back passenger seat window as he got handcuffs placed on wrists, as he put his face up to the window to kiss back.

Summer.

Summer was over.

Chapter Fifty-Nine

Mid-August - four weeks later

Harry waited for Amber outside the Brown Cow. He took a table in the sun. Harry thought about stuff - lots of it. His life, where it had been, and where it went. The farce, the wonder of it. He thought about his family, about Amber. How he neglected his wife; writing Amber off as inferior. He loved Lottie like he should so why not his wife? Second Summer of Love was done. His tome accepted by a local publisher - Blue Tiger. He'd written it as a non-fiction novel. A page-turner. It came together sweetly - flowed out of him.

As did other stuff, realisations. The narrator of Second Summer of Love was unnamed and had the same plot-line Harry did. Well, not the same exactly. Sure, he wholesaled Es anonymously; then had 1,000 Pink New Yorkers ripped off. But: the anonymous narrator tried to work out who did it to him. Found out, fronted Joey about it - fronted him in the book - searched the Fiat outside Sett End like Harry actually did in real life. Then: the story moved to Gildersome, the warehouse, catching Two-brain's stolen-pill-punting act, followed him and Nancy back to Lancaster, the whole thing.

The other tweak, this: Joey and Nancy were not called Joey and Nancy. Of course they were not. They now went un-named; just like Gerard Toces. Who was after him now- in real life. Gerard thought he - Harry - grassed him to Swaggert and Ball. Was the reason why they rolled up, hit Gerard's place, hoping to bust him for copious Class As, put him away for a long time.

BUT: he never. NO way. He wasn't stupid. And he was no grass either.

Not that Gerard would believe Harry and Harry had to admit this: it played crystal clear as if it WAS him. Who else could it actually be? Whichever way you sliced and diced Swaggert and his goons arriving, Harry seemed the OBVIOUS and ONLY prime suspect for it. Harry still tried to see who it was, who DID grass Gerard to Swaggert: Harry had a feeling he knew who it was - kept nearly getting it, sussing it out...

Point remained, though. Glaring unavoidable FACT: Gerard was after him.

But, Harry had an idea how Frenchy could be handled, a fine idea he reckoned was bombproof. Offer him 20K to match the 20K Gerard nearly lost to show he was truly sorry for what went down - whether he believed or not it wasn't Harry who grassed Gerard to Swaggert. And, tell him this: that Harry was getting out of the E-trade pronto and he was handing all his business over to Gerard.

Now - here came Amber, walking towards him. She held a sheaf of papers - the final draft of Second Summer of Love.

She leaned forward, kissed his lips. And smiled a dazzler that went through him electric.

Electric bolt.

Of inspiration.

YES.

EUREKA moment.

As, now, Amber waved the final draft of Second Summer of Love before his eyes. Saying: 'This reads like a thriller, Harry. A real page-turner. Maybe you should consider that novel after all. A whole new line of work for you.'

He got it; he knew.

AMBER.

SHE told the police about Gerard. She must have found out

about Harry - what he did, all his creeping about, the night at the Brown Cow and after, back at the house, Harry pulling an E out for them to do. Then somehow found out about Gerard - it's a small town after all. Amber, yes. She did it for him - to get him out of the life he got sucked into; the E-dealing. Did it because the truth was plain and simple: Harry had been lost; Harry lacked the balls to get out himself. So, Amber; beautiful and caring Amber Blue did it for him.

All of this flashing through Harry.

'No,' said Harry. He smiled his own dazzler. 'No need now. No need at all for me to be penning novels.'

Chapter Sixty

Mid-September – Four weeks later

An early autumn sun - morning.

Joey walked out of Lancaster Magistrates Court on George Street holding hands with Nancy.

'You're free.'

'A £1,000 fine and six months suspended sentence - first offence - basically like the lawyer told us it would go down.'

Nancy smiled. 'I can go to £500 but I'm not sure-'

Coming towards them - Gerard, alone. No Temmy or Tina.

'Fuck,' said Nancy. 'Look.'

'I see him.'

Gerard reached them. Smiled. 'How you doing?'

'Good thanks,' said Nancy.

'Good,' Joey said. 'Listen Gerard, I am so sorry about-'

The Romany raised his hand. 'Quiet - please. Here.'

He handed them a backpack - a backpack like the one from Gildersome, the one that had held the boosted pills, the 20K.

From two months ago - a lifetime ago.

Gerard, smiling: 'Look inside.'

Nancy laughed. Joey told her: 'Open it, baby.'

She did.

Saw:

Two rolls of cash, showed these Joey. 'Jesus - Gerard - there has to be, what, a grand here.'

'Two,' he said. 'Enough to pay your fine and go somewhere nice.'

'But-'

The hand again. 'Forget the speech, Joey.' Gerard gave them a thumbs-up, turned and walked off towards town.

Joey and Nancy watched Frenchy Toces disappear.

'Wow,' said Joey.

'Wow indeed.' Nancy took his arm. 'I know where we're going. Time for the final scene of our movie.'

'Where?'

She pointed across Thurnham Street. 'Thomas Cook. I hear the closing parties are amazing and start about this time next week.'

'Closing parties?'

'Space, Amnesia, Pacha. Ku.'

'Eh?'

Nancy stopped, kissed Joey's nose. 'Ibiza. The closing parties on a white isle named Ibiza.'

Joey's eyes gleamed. Nancy's eyes gleamed.

They crossed Thurnham Street, headed for the Thomas Cook.

Balearic sun in their hearts.

Pounding through their dreams.

Always pounding.

Always dreaming.

Acknowledgements

Massive thank you to Matthew Brook for pure love and reading everything from the very start and Scott Fletcher, the same, the Poynton years onwards XXX. To Sean Stockdale for looking after me from he knows when; everyone else who has shown the pure love of friendship - Paul Hirst from whirl of hackery, particularly. Finally: to all the novelists I've ever read and the bookstores of the world, and the stars and the skies and the suns and the summer of Ibiza '91 XXX

NORTHODOX PRESS

FIND US ON SOCIAL MEDIA

www.northodox.co.uk

@northodoxpress

@northodoxpressofficial

@northodoxpress

@northodoxpress

@northodoxpress.bsky.social

www.northodox.co.uk

NORTHODOX PRESS

SUBMISSIONS

CONTEMPORARY
CRIME & THRILLER
FANTASY
LGBTQ+
ROMANCE
YOUNG ADULT
SCI-FI & HORROR
HISTORICAL
LITERARY

SUBMISSIONS@NORTHODOX.CO.UK

NORTHODOX PRESS

SUBMISSIONS

CALLING ALL NORTHERN AUTHORS!

DO YOU LIVE IN OR COME FROM NORTHERN ENGLAND?

DO YOU HAVE AN INTERESTING STORY TO TELL?

Email *submissions@northodox.co.uk*

- ☐ The first 3 chapters OR 5,000 words
- ☐ *1 page synopsis*
- ☐ *Author bio (tell us where you're based)*

* No non-fiction, poetry, or memoirs

SUBMISSIONS@NORTHODOX.CO.UK

A
DROWNING
MAN

A Manchester Noir

JOHN STOREY

JACK BYRNE

UNDER THE
BRIDGE

BOOK ONE IN THE LIVERPOOL MYSTERIES SERIES

JACK BYRNE

ACROSS THE
WATER

BOOK TWO IN THE LIVERPOOL MYSTERIES SERIES

JACK BYRNE

BEFORE THE
STORM

BOOK THREE IN THE LIVERPOOL MYSTERIES SERIES